SCARS OF THE PAST

A DCI MCNEILL NOVEL

JACQUELINE NEW

www.jacquelinenew.com

SCARS OF THE PAST
DCI MCNEILL Book 1

Cover design: The Cover Collection
Interior Formatting: Jesse Gordon

Visit the website **www.jacquelinenew.com** to sign up to the no-spam NEW CRIME CLUB. You'll get news, updates and more.

Never miss a new release.

For Karen Macleod, with thanks.

Dear Reader,

I'm thrilled to introduce a brand new series character and genre to you: DCI McNeill, head of the Edinburgh Serious Crimes Unit with Police Scotland. Having written twenty mysteries under a pen name, all with strong female leads, I wanted to write a book with a male at the helm.

'Mac,' turned up almost fully formed during lockdown and with a name like McNeill, he couldn't be anything other than Scottish. Therefore, setting it in one of my favourite cities was an obvious choice.

Over the following months, I fleshed out his background and experiences along with a tragic backstory which will be explored more in subsequent books. Once all that was in place, the rest of the team and the plot came together remarkably quickly.

The result is book 1 of what I hope will be a long running series: 'Scars of the Past,' which I enjoyed writing immensely. I hope you enjoy reading it just as much.

Jacqueline New

PROLOGUE

———————

THUNDEROUS EXPLOSIONS ECHO from the depths below as waves assault the rocks with relentless force. The wind, a merciless thief, steals warmth from flesh, carrying with it shards of freezing sleet from the Atlantic's icy heart. Callum's face is a mask of numbness, the brutal chill having claimed feeling hours ago. He stands in the frozen rain, a solitary figure hidden in the shadow of the old bus stop, the sting against his skin a fleeting distraction. The other pain, the one buried deep within, refuses to be washed away. Each icy shard that hits his face is a cold reminder of life's harsh, unforgiving reality.

Callum stirs.

A man approaches. Hunched over with hands in pockets. A slightly swaying gait. There's a pub down the road and he's been there all night. Had he been to that same pub the night he killed Iona? The night he raped and murdered her? Did it matter? No. Nothing matters anymore except this.

The man, Mark, draws level with the decrepit shelter. It's a square structure of brick, big enough for two people to sit inside, if the wooden bench hadn't long ago rotted to nothing.

He doesn't see Callum. Doesn't see him take the empty plastic sack that used to hold chicken feed from his pocket and quietly leave the shadows as he passes. Mark senses something as the bag is lifted, starts to turn. Too late. The bag is over his head and he can't see his assailant. Can't see anything. Mark is thin, the kind of thin you look at and know wasn't achieved through Slimming World. The kind of thin you only get by constantly abusing your body. Mark's a master at it.

A blow is landed into his side, doubling him over. Then one to the back of the head. Another one. Another. Callum drags Mark off the single track road leading into Portree. Batters Mark the way the waves are battering at the Isle of Skye. Through long grass and weeds. Mark's feet are dragging. He's barely conscious but the blows keep coming. Then they're behind the bus shelter and the dark consumes them both.

Tears fill Callum's eyes as he lets go of his victim. Mark slumps against the brick, sliding down in a broken heap. Limbs numb. The ability to defend himself torn away. Callum is kicking now, as well as hammering with sore fists. A car goes by, but the headlights can't penetrate the shadows. No-one sees the vengeance taking place. No-one knows how close Mark Souter is to death. Finally, Callum picks up a piece of brick, mossy and half buried. He raises it over his head and stops.

This is wrong.

The huddled shape at his feet could be anyone. That isn't the point. Callum has to see his face. Has to know that in the end, Mark Souter knew his killer. Knew why he was about to die. Once he saw Callum's face, he would understand. He would deny his guilt, beg and plead if he still had enough of his senses left to do it. Callum wanted him to suffer. Fear was far worse than pain.

Teeth gritted and breath hissing, Callum reaches down and snatches away the bag, tearing a clump of hair from Mark's head. He raises the brick, ready to smash the rapist's brains out. He stops again. The man is huddled, covering his head with his arms. There's a growing stain at the crotch of his trousers and he's whimpering, saying something over and over. Callum tries to shut it out, but he can't. The words reach him over the wind and the waves and the blood pounding in his ears.

Mark Souter is begging for his mum.

Then the brick comes down. Both hands drive it and before it slams home with bone crunching finality, Mark looks at him. Right at him.

CHAPTER ONE

MAC CLAWED HIS WAY back to consciousness. The bed sheets were on the floor, kicked away as he grappled with a murderer in his sleep. He wore boxers and nothing else, his usual night attire. Black hair was slick with sweat. The pillow damp. He stares at the bedroom ceiling, seeing a pair of wide, terrified eyes. Hearing a voice pleading for his mother. Mac's heart was racing, his mouth dry. There were variations of the dream, a few different endings, but they all had the same effect on him. Dragging him out of sleep, soaked in sweat, heart pounding and muscles cramping. And in all of them Mark Souter died, horribly.

Reaching out blindly, his hand slapped against a phone, feeling the cracks in the display at one corner. Fumbling fingers caught the oblong piece of plastic before knocking it to the hardwood floor. He brought it up before his eyes, blinking away the stiffness of sleep to focus on the display. Just after three a.m.

With a groan, he levered himself up, putting his bare feet down on the cold floor. Opposite was a window with curtains open and the black metal railings of a balcony visible. Sodium orange light spilling in from the streetlight opposite. No point closing them, nothing opposite his flat's bedroom window except Leith Links Golf Course. An occasional dogger might get a glimpse of DCI Callum McNeill, Mac to his friends, getting up in the night for a slash, but that's about it. Besides, he always hated dark bedrooms.

The bed was the only furniture in the room besides the flat pack side table whose drawers held an assortment of neatly tied USB cables from various phones and stacked notebooks, a perfectly sharpened pencil attached to one of them with an elastic band. Another drawer contained five unopened boxes of fresh pencils.

Sleep wouldn't come back. He knew that from experience. His brain was too scared to put him under again after The Dream. He stripped off his sweat soaked shorts and dropped them into a hamper of laundry in the bathroom, then took a shower. A cold shower. The icy water sluiced away the images burned into his brain. Rinsing off the ache he always felt. Was it regret that he hadn't actually finished the job that night on Skye? Or that he had almost made himself a murderer in the name of vengeance? Or was it just the pain of knowing he could have saved his sister's life?

Out of the shower. Body spray. Toothbrush. Towel used once and dropped into the hamper. He closed the door of the en-suite bathroom as he left. Dressed in a black t-shirt and sweatpants. Made sure the door of the bedroom was closed behind him before walking to the open plan living room /

kitchen. Living room door closed behind him and a lamp switched on. Never the big light overhead. The lamp created an oasis of clean, white light in one corner, the shadows gradually reclaiming the room at the kitchen end.

After making an instant, black coffee, Mac sat on a stool at the island, which separated living and dining spaces in his flat. He opened his laptop and input his password by muscle memory alone. The Police Scotland logo disappeared from the logon screen and he opened Outlook, skimming emails. They'd been accruing in his inbox for twenty-four hours, a rape case his team member Melissa Barland was Senior Investigating Officer on, taking up all of his time.

An email update from Barland; Procurator Fiscal were happy the evidential threshold had been passed, confident they could get a conviction providing the witness remained credible. McNeill knew all of this. Another in more personal language; did he want her to step down as DI? Transfer to another area? He had been breathing down her neck the whole time, had taken over an interview with the suspect. She wasn't happy.

Mac frowned, scanning the email a second time for nuances he probably wouldn't pick up, no matter how long he spent on it. They'd got the case over the line. What did it matter? He ran a hand over a jaw already peppered with dark stubble and shut the lid of the laptop with a snap. It left a sour taste. It would take some talking to Melissa to smooth ruffled feathers, the kind of interaction he didn't like and wasn't good at.

Turning away from the laptop, he looked around the room for a moment, lost. It was minimalist. Wood floor, white walls. TV mounted on one of them. Hi-fi on a table below it. A shelving unit to the side of the hi-fi held LP's, cassettes and CDs, with the tapes taking up the lion's share of the space. This time three months ago, Siobhan would have been there when The Dream started him awake. Her long legs and flowing dark hair which always smelled so good. Her body which seemed to mold itself to his so well in the middle of the night.

Now he was alone in an empty, echoing flat. Still haunted. The pang he felt at that moment could have been a longing for sex, for Siobhan, for alcohol, or something stronger. It might have been nicotine. Something. Anything. His heart was as minimalist as his flat. Empty, echoing. Cold. With a burst of irritation, he turned back to the laptop, opened it and dashed in the password. He began an email to Melissa rebuking her for challenging his right to lead on a case. Who exactly was the DCI and who was the DI? Who owed her job on the Serious Crimes Unit to who?

The rant was interrupted by his phone lighting up. Probably a good thing. The number belonged to DS Nari Yun, a member of his team and on call tonight. If she was reaching out to him at 3am, it meant something bad had happened to someone somewhere. He welcomed it and closed the lid on his pain and his anger.

"Nari, talk," he snapped into the phone.

CHAPTER TWO

CRAIGMILLAR AT THREE IN THE MORNING. To Google, it was just an address, could have been anywhere. To Mac, a resident of Edinburgh since the age of eighteen, it was a lot more. Anonymous square boxes of flats. Not like the spacious Leith apartment Mac had just moved into. These were cramped and owned by a housing association. They looked soulless during the bright light of day, stripping the area of any individuality or identity. At three in the morning, though, they became bastions for those who didn't want their actions observed.

He turned the Audi into Castlebrae Court. A dead end in every sense. Red brick squares loomed around him and he could feel the eyes looking out. He didn't need sat nav from this point on. The strobing blue lights and police tape told him in which building the body had been discovered. A timer was running in his head. Had begun the moment Nari had given her answers to Mac's clipped, aggressive questions.

People always thought of him as aggressive because he

didn't waste time with small talk. He wore a simple dark gray suit, slim fitting, but not so much that he couldn't break into a sprint after a suspect if needed. Black shirt. One of a dozen identical shirts in his wardrobe. No tie and open collar. A plain, digital watch was on his wrist with a white strap. It was the kind a child could afford with their pocket money.

Clock is ticking. Once the police circus arrived, the locals would start gathering. Turning a corner, he could see a crowd of young men, faces masked and heads hooded. They loitered just outside the cordon, close enough to strut in front of the uniforms maintaining the perimeter, but not close enough to justify being moved on. A few men and women in dressing gowns, smoking and chatting loudly. A bit of drama to gossip about.

A uniform approached the car, and Mac silently showed his warrant card. The uniform signalled to his colleague and the tape was lifted. Mac caught the sour whiff of weed being smoked somewhere nearby. He pulled in behind a van bearing the SOCO logo, a scene of crime team already on site. A sign proclaiming Bute Tower was emblazoned on the side of the building in question. In front of the tall red brick box Detective Constable Kai Stuart stood yawning, when he wasn't talking to his Sergeant, Nari Yun. There was puppy dog devotion in his eyes. Or maybe just naked lust. He looked tired. She looked excited. But not by him.

Both wore forensics suits though, with hoods down and masks off.

"What's the story?" Mac asked, thrusting his hands into the pockets of his trousers.

Kai was standing in a patch of dirt, leaning on a wall leading to the building's communal entrance. It was supposed to be a raised flower bed, but the soil was scattered with cigarette ends and bottles of Bucky. Anything that grew through that wouldn't be pleasant to look at. A level glance from Mac straightened him up.

"Body found in a flat on the fourth floor," Nari said with a Glasgow accent. "Neighbours had been complaining of the smell from and then tonight it flooded into the one beneath. Housing Association duty officer was called, and he used a master key to enter the property with a plumber. Found what we believe is the tenant, Richard McCullough."

"Believe?" McNeill said, sharply.

"Body was in a state of decomposition and had been mutilated," Nari said as though reading the weather. "Housing association officer provided a picture of the tenant, but we couldn't be sure it was the same man."

"It's a real mess, guv," DC Kai Stuart put in.

"SOCO are in there now," Nari finished.

"When was 999 called?" Mac asked, looking through the double doors into the communal entry hall of the building. He could see a couple of residents milling about in there and gritted his teeth. Nari should have locked the place down.

"Call was placed at two fifteen. Local uniform attended from Niddrie Mains Road station at two thirty and called Clyde HQ for a SCU officer at two forty-seven. The call got routed to me and I was here by three fifteen."

Mac glanced at his plastic digital watch. Three forty-two.

"Locals have had an hour and a half to destroy any evidence in the communal areas. And our size 12s will have helped destroy the rest. Get it locked down. Everyone back into their flats until we tell them to come out. Then get SOCO to prioritise the communal areas so we can let people get to their work in the morning," Mac said.

Nari blanched, nodded curtly. Kai shuffled his feet and snorted at the mention of people here going to their work, but Mac would not be distracted correcting the younger man's prejudices. Time was critical. Mutilation didn't necessarily mean murder, but it was likely. The more time that passed, the more evidence was lost and the less likely the case would be solved. There was a tension rising in him, a level of stress that served as fuel.

A folding table had been set up on a patch of scrubby grass at the side of a cracked paved path leading to the building's entrance. It held boxes of sterile latex gloves and paper forensics suits with matching shoes. Mac snatched up a set and began to put them on. Before anything else, he would need to see the crime scene. A uniform opened the door from the inside and Mac went in, avoiding contact with the door and noting the uniform's lack of gloves or protective clothing with irritation.

"Nari, get these men properly dressed and get SOCO in here. Now." Mac shouted back through the door. "Kai, with me."

He would have preferred his DS, but wanted to make sure the building was properly locked down. After being caught out once, Nari would go overboard. Mac wanted that ferocious thoroughness. Ahead of him was a row of mailboxes on one wall and another door at the far end of the lobby. An officer stood before it. Two civilians stood between, one of them in a polo shirt and cargo trousers, a tool bag at his feet and an anxious look on his square face. The other was a tired-looking man in a t-shirt, jeans, and scruffy trainers. He had a lanyard around his neck and an ID badge.

A uniform was talking to each man, bulky in their stab vests and with two inches extra height from the thick-soled boots that made every police officer look like a giant.

"Kai, get those two civilians into a secure area. Maintenance room, broom cupboard, I don't care. Just get them out so SOCO can do their job. Catch me up."

He headed for a door marked *Staircase* as Kai jogged over to the two uniforms. Just before the door to the staircase banged shut behind him, he heard Nari entering the building, snapping orders to the SOCOs she had rounded up. Kai would know the names of the two men he was ordering around. Nari would expect everyone to jump because she outranked them. Mac began to ascend, keeping his hands away from the banister and the walls. The stairwell was dark, a light was out. And it smelled of piss and weed. Unfortunate combination.

It made him want to hurry, but he restrained himself, pushing the ticking clock to the back of his mind. No reason the assailant took the lift. Rushing because the place was unpleasant was a good way of missing evidence. There was graffiti at the first stairwell, red and incomprehensible. A bell rang in recognition at the back of his mind. Maybe a sectarian tag from one of the ultra-crews supporting Hibs or Hearts. He couldn't remember which, but did remember seeing it elsewhere.

More red graffiti at the next stairwell, circular shapes with lines intersecting at precise angles. It had taken time to paint, which made Mac stop and take a picture. Probably nothing.

Record it. File it. Move on. He was breathing hard by the time he reached the fourth floor. Mac was slim but no gym addict. His face was naturally angular, high cheeks, sharp jaw. It helped him look thinner and fitter than he was. Exercise was not his friend and the mileage of forty-four years had taken its toll.

He waited two full minutes before stepping through the door, not wanting anyone to see his exertion. Not if it made them question why he didn't take the lift. That tiny metal crate on a wire that would judder and shake as it rose high enough to squash him to paste if it fell. Which it would. The second he got high enough. He pushed aside the extraneous thoughts as he pushed open the door. Narrow hallway, stark lighting, cheap carpet.

Another uniform standing in front of an open door, SOCO inside. Mac took the paper mask from his pocket and attached it to his ears, covering his nose and mouth. Ten yards away, the lift pinged and Kai got out. Mac waited for his DC and then went to the door of the flat. The stench of death was overpowering.

CHAPTER THREE

MAC WAS ABOUT TO WALK IN when he glanced at the uniform's face. He stopped, frowning. The man looked at him, noticing his scrutiny. He had a scar on his right cheek, an inch long and the look of grizzled experience. Rough skin, hard face, lidded eyes.

"I know you," Mac said, faces flashing through his mind like shuffled playing cards. "You used to be based in Gorgie, right?"

Flicker of surprise. "Yes, sir. St Nick's Place station."

"So was I. You got that scar from one of Allen's men breaking up a fight in a club. Broken pool cue. I can't remember your name, but I'll have it soon."

"Hunter, sir. Chris Hunter," the man replied. "I remember you, but didn't think you'd remember me."

Mac nodded, unsmiling. "I remember you," he said, entering the flat.

Hunter had been one of many officers in the pay of Hance

Allen, head of the local crime organisation controlling the drug trade in Edinburgh and the east. Never proved. Mac wouldn't have remembered Hunter if he hadn't believed he'd been on the take.

Once through the door, his focus sharpened. Tight hallway with blood spatter. Two doors leading off on the left and one on the right. Ahead Mac could see a sofa, a black electric guitar lying across it, plugged into an amp as though it had only just been put down. He could see the red light on the front of the amp that said it was still on.

The door to the right led to a bathroom. It was open and the stench it emitted told Mac everything he needed to know. It permeated the entire flat but was strongest there. An enshrouded figure came towards him, pulled the mask down to reveal Derek Stringer, a forensic pathologist. He had a ruddy face with watery blue eyes and thinning hair, though this was hidden by the hood of the forensics suit. His stomach strained at the material, and Mac wondered if it would just rip through the paper if he was called out after a hefty meal.

He beckoned to Mac without uttering a word and spoke to two other men working in the bathroom, moving them out. Mac stepped in. White, plastic, suite. No side on the bath, revealing bare floorboards beneath, fully saturated. It was overflowing with pink water; the floor was covered in it. The body lay in the bath. Naked. Lacerated. Everywhere. From head to foot there was evidence of cuts. On the torso, there were several long wounds intersected by smaller cuts, many of which were curved or even circular.

"Cause of death, I would say is that particular fella there," Stringer said, pointing to a wound just under the left pectoral muscle. His accent dripped with the string of letters that came after his name in contrast to the unmistakable Lothian in Mac's.

"I would say they inflicted a cluster of thirteen wounds with a long, wide-bladed weapon which I have not seen here. Notice the skin is torn, and the wound is wider than the others. The knife was twisted more than once in that one. The other large wounds were delivered in short, sharp blows."

"A frenzy. Then a twist after delivering the coup de grâce," Mac said, picturing the scene.

Stringer glanced at him, then nodded. "Yes. A reasonable hypothesis. Blood in the hallway and living room suggests where the killing took place. Not in here," Stringer went on.

"What about these smaller wounds? They're everywhere," Kai asked.

"Performed post mortem and would have taken quite some time to inflict over such a large area of the body. And done with single-minded precision," Stringer said.

Mac had already deduced as much.

"Taps were running when the body was found," he stated.

"I didn't ask. They weren't on when I arrived," Stringer replied.

"Flat downstairs had flooded," Kai told him. "Resident was in custody at the time, so didn't notice until he got home in the wee hours tonight."

"I need a minute," Mac said to Stringer, who nodded.

Many forensics guys would object to removing their teams in the middle of their work, but Stringer knew Mac's methods and had seen them work often enough. As the SOCO's left the flat, Kai hovered. Mac wanted to send him out too, but stopped himself. He had promise or he wouldn't be on Mac's team. Kai needed experience.

"Stay. Follow me and don't talk. Just note."

He took out a fresh notebook from where he had put it in the pocket of the forensics suit and removed the pencil and elastic band. Kai took out his phone.

"Dinnae think I've written anything down on paper since I left school," he said, the mask shifting as he grinned.

"It's a good habit to get into," Mac said, turning away.

He'd absorbed every minute detail of the body in the bath. Marked in such a comprehensive way, it had to be significant. Hate? Revenge? Punishment for something? No sign of clothes in the bathroom, just a toilet, none too clean and a sink, same state. Mac moved to one of the other doors in the hallway, finding a bedroom and a room holding a dining table with a computer on it. Three more guitars stood along the wall with a bunch of other electrical equipment sprouting cables and wires.

A musician lived here. Guitar player. Posters on the wall told him the guy was a metal head. Mac recognised flyers from a range of local underground acts. He had many of their demos, though he had attended none of the gigs those flyers commemorated. Too many people. A box sat on the desk bearing promo leaflets for a gig dated more than a year earlier, all for the same band. Omega.

"I know these guys," Mac said, taken by surprise at the co-incidences of the universe.

"You're into this stuff, eh?" Kai replied, peering over Mac's shoulder.

"I am. This is raw, DIY black metal. As raw as it gets. They're not bad."

"You recognise the guy?" Kai said.

"His mother wouldn't recognise him in that state. The name doesn't ring a bell. They all use nicknames anyway. I think Omega comprised Stygian, Void, and I can't remember the names of the others. It's all theatre." Mac replied.

He went into the other room, the bedroom, and found a wardrobe lacking a door. Clothes were piled in a heap at the bottom, few hanging up as the rail was only attached at one end. The curtains were drawn and there was a musty smell in the room underlying the pervasive stink of decomposing flesh.

"His mother should have taught him how to clean his room," Kai said with disgust.

"You see any clothes in here with blood stains or slashes?" Mac said, carefully sifting through the clothes in the wardrobe.

A moment's search.

"Over here!" Kai called from a corner of the room.

Using his phone as a torch, he revealed a pile of t-shirt, jeans, pants and socks. All were drenched in blood, crusty with it. Holding up the t-shirt using his pen revealed the slashes made by the knife.

"Undressed post mortem," Mac said.

"Is that significant then, eh?" Kai asked.

"It confirms what the state of the body told me. The smaller wounds made post mortem were done to be seen. He was stripped and put in a bath, which washed the blood away. Made those designs all over him stand out more. They would have been hard to see under all that blood and dried gore.

Leave the taps running so that there's no chance of him being undiscovered for weeks. The flooding will bring someone up here in a few days. Which it did. This is all a tableau."

Kai frowned, and Mac resisted the urge to roll his eyes.

"In other words, it's all for show, right?"

CHAPTER FOUR

MAC LEFT KAI AND NARI to canvas the building while the re-directed SOCO teams secured the public areas that a likely killer might have passed through. The hallway outside the flat was hopelessly contaminated, but he had noticed CCTV covering the porch and the lobby, as well as the car park. Whether it worked or was simply there for show was another question. Kai would track it down through the housing association and their factors.

When he left the building, there was a sizable group of local press beyond the perimeter cordon and an even larger crowd of irate residents being denied ingress or egress to Bute Tower. Mac drove out of the estate as the sun was lightening the sky. The press would need to be handled, but the Serious Crime Unit press team would deal with it. They would arrange a press conference and he would likely be tapped to spout some noncommittal non-sentences before being allowed to go back to doing his job.

And they would insist on dredging up The Angel Killer. He drove west, heading for Niddrie Mains Road and a greasy spoon café he knew in Newcraighall, just off the A1. As he drove, he hit DI Melissa Barland's number on speed dial, watching bookies, pawnbrokers and tanning salons slip past. The sky was leaden; the grey appearing to seep into the very architecture.

"Yeah, guv?" Melissa's voice was loaded with sleep.

Mac looked at the time. Just after five. Sorry, Melissa, time to drag you away from your wife.

"We've got a homicide in Craigmillar. I'm going to brief Kenny, but I'll need you to liaise with the press team. We've got a hi-rise under lockdown until forensics have done their thing and...it's potentially messy."

"A building under lock down? I'll say it's messy." Melissa had come awake in the space of seconds, it seemed.

"The killing itself. There's something to it. They're going to be bringing up The Angel Killer again, I think. Just to give you a heads up. Kai and Nari are on scene they can fill you in. Keep the media off me, eh?"

There was a murmur of protest in the background and the sound of bedclothes shifting, then the closing of a bedroom door. Melissa spoke up.

"No problems, guv. I'll call Nari right now and see what the deal is. Anything else you want me to do?"

"Yeah, keep on forensics. Get them turned around fast and get the team some data to work with. We should have preliminary statements from the location by the time we convene at..." he glanced at the time on his phone, "...let's say eight. Oh, and we'll need some office space at Niddrie Mains Road

Station, so get onto the office manager for their CID team. Office, phones, computers, you know the drill."

"And what will you be doing?" Melissa said wryly.

Mac could hear a cat purring and the sound of a kettle coming to the boil.

"You mean apart from disrupting your domestic bliss? I've got some research to do over a coffee. I'll see you at Niddrie Mains in three hours."

"Sure," Melissa said, yawning into the phone.

"Mel…" Mac hesitated, thinking about the pissed off email she'd sent, looking for the right words, "I…"

She didn't help. Silence greeted him while she waited for him to speak. Screw it.

"Don't be late," he said and hung up.

He watched the immaculate greenery of a golf course pass by on the left and a public park on the right. There was a stark contrast between the play park with its municipal signage and ugly graffiti and the spotless sylvan paradise of the golf club. He was reaching for his phone again to call Detective Chief Superintendent Kenny Reid when the blues and twos started up behind him. He checked the mirror.

A marked police car had come up behind him and they weren't looking to get past. He pulled off, crossing two lanes without indicating to slip into the entrance of a retail park, stopping in the nearest parking space, opposite a Screwfix. The traffic cop followed him. Then his phone began to ring. It was Kenny Reid.

"Marvellous," he whispered, winding down the window and switching off the engine. A uniform walked up to the door and stooped, fixing him with a look that he was sure would have a civilian quaking in their boots.

"I'm on the job," Mac said, reaching into his suit jacket.

"Excuse me, sir?" the uniform said, looking back towards his partner.

"DCI McNeill, SCU. And that's my DCS on the phone now. Kenny Reid. One of the old school. A right one. Understand? So, shall we dispense with the usual lecture and you asking if I know why you've stopped me? Give me a penalty notice and let's both get on with our day."

"That's OK, sir. I didn't know you were on the force. This isn't registered as a police vehicle."

"It isn't and no, it's not OK. I could have killed someone. Or myself. I've broken the law and if you try and let me off, you might just find yourself back directing traffic," Mac said in an even tone that was hard as diamond.

He never looked away from the officer, pinning him with a black-eyed stare. Again, the officer looked back at his partner. Mac wouldn't let him off the hook.

"OK, I'll give you a penalty notice. You'll have 30 days to pay this or it will double. Alternatively..."

"I can take a course and avoid the penalty and the points. I'll be paying it I think. Now, I'm engaged on a murder case so let's move it, eh?" Mac talked across him, stare still pinning the officer in place. "Thank you, officer."

As the man walked away, shrugging and shaking his head, Mac picked up the call that had been ringing incessantly since he had pulled over and parked up.

"Boss," Mac answered.

"Mac, what the hell do you think you're doing leaving me hanging on for half an hour waiting for you to pick up?"

"I was being stopped by a traffic cop. There'll be a red notice on its way from Anti-Corruption sometime soon, driving while talking on a mobile phone," Mac replied, scrolling through his emails as he spoke.

They were lighting up. Some contacts in the press had got wind of the case and were looking for an inside track on the story. His team were mobilising, sending through progress updates on various actions. His focus came back to his boss, who had been swearing at him.

"You were about to call me about this Craigmillar thing," Reid said.

"I was actually. You beat me to the punch," Mac said.

"Word is already out there that Police Scotland has seized a block of flats with a population of over a hundred people and locked it down. Headlines are already being written talking about some black ops deep state operation, claiming we're going after investigative journalists who've been on this Commissioner Black story. Then there are the leaks that a body has been found minus all kinds of appendages. I've even heard the word Satanism mentioned. So, brief me, please."

"A member of an extreme metal band was stabbed to death and cut to ribbons for fun by a killer who wanted the body found," Mac said, summarising the case as succinctly as he knew how and glancing at the time.

Reid was silent for a moment, as though expecting more. Mac didn't give it. He was scanning SMS messages and saw Siobhan's name. A thrill ran through him like an electric shock.

"And the press?" Reid prompted. "I have to brief the Police Crime Commissioner and the city mayor so they don't get blindsided. How are the press on this already?"

"Because someone in Bute Tower decided to make a quid selling the story of a police lockdown to the local rags. And threw in that the poor kid was into Satanism for good measure."

"And was he?"

"How the f..." Mac began, realising that the message from Siobhan was an old one, "...hell should I know...sir. He was a musician playing up the symbolism for shock value. Probably not serious about any of it. But someone else might have taken it seriously. That's how the press were there almost at the same time we were. I've got Mel Barland across it."

The key to dealing with Reid was to attack. Deference to rank would get your throat ripped out. Nerves or anxiety the same. Mac and him had a long history. Reid had given him the post of DI in the SCU and recommended his promotion to DCI. Both bore the scars of their many run-ins.

"I see. Look, Mac, there's something else I should appraise you of." Reid's tone was suddenly, oddly conciliatory. The tone a senior officer was taught to assume when breaking news of death to family members. Mac didn't have anyone left to hear that kind of news about.

"I've heard a whisper that there may be an AC investigation in the offing."

Mac froze, staring into the rear-view mirror at a prostitute passing the car with the attitude of one who has had a long night. She observed the car with interest and then checked her phone before walking towards the driver's side. Mac didn't return her gaze, just held up his warrant card to the window. Next time he looked, she was nowhere to be seen.

"Hello?"

"I heard, sir. Me or you?"

Silence. Then, "I don't know. Just a rumour at this point. Just be on your toes, right?"

Hostility dialled back up to eleven. Defensive. Mac wondered what Anti-Corruption could have on Kenny Reid, one of their own and fantastically successful at that?

"Understood. I'll keep you briefed."

He hung up. His mind was racing. Images of the Craigmillar flat and the bizarrely marked body. Siobhan stirring languidly between the sheets, a heavy sleeper after pulling a double shift at the hospital. Kenny Reid, the Glasgow Pit Bull, under investigation. Or maybe Callum McNeill. His thoughts returned to the dream and the man he had left for dead outside Portree in the middle of an Atlantic storm. Mark Souter hadn't died that night. Maybe he'd drunk himself to death since. Or overdosed.

Or perhaps he'd made a complaint to the Police Complaints Commission and now AC were looking at potential connections to organised crime. He shook his head angrily, feeling an almost overwhelming urge to smoke. He didn't look back as he gunned the engine and swung out of the parking space in reverse, cutting up another early morning driver as he pulled out onto the Newcraighall Road, heading towards the intersection with the A1.

Screw it.

CHAPTER FIVE

NIDDRIE MAINS ROAD police station looked like a barracks. Windows were small and one way, showing a mirrored opacity to the world. It was squat and brooding, identifiable by its blue and white checked sign only. Mac found his way to a first floor open plan office from which local CID had been evicted. Mel was setting up a board at one end of the room with enlarged print outs of the crime scene pictures recently uploaded to the system by the SOCO team.

She was middle-aged, with mousy brown hair tied back in a bun and a compassionate, open face. Nari was on the phone and Kai was hunched over his laptop, oblivious to everything. Mel looked round at his entrance, giving him a smile to show there were no hard feelings. She was far too nice to be a cop. She should be a primary school teacher. Or a nurse. Nari made eye contact while continuing to talk. Kai didn't seem to notice he'd arrived.

"That's you," Mel pointed to a glass-walled office set apart from the main room. "DI's office. He's on holiday until next week. His team wasn't best pleased, but I eventually made them see reason."

"Hope you didn't do too much damage swinging your weight around," Mac said drily.

"I don't get to do it that often. Leave me these brief pleasures, Mac." Mel replied, smiling sweetly.

Mac barked a laugh. "No bother. I hope Cazzy has forgiven me for waking her up."

"No, but we're about to start another round of IVF and it's exhausting," Mel said. "So she wouldn't forgive the Pope."

Mac suppressed a wince, feeling that it might not be the best response but uncomfortable with the personal disclosure.

"Where are we up to?" he asked, opening the door to his office.

"Holding statement gone out to the press. Kai is working the CCTV footage through some whizzy software only he understands and Nari is tracking down someone to identify the body."

Mac nodded, looking past her to the crime scene photographs. "Good, good," he said distractedly.

Mel followed his gaze but knew enough about her boss's thought process not to question. She just waited. Mac was looking over the colour photographs of the body. The blow ups of the wounds and the blood spatter in the living room and hallway. The spray had reached up over the worn upholstery of a grey, faux leather sofa and then across a canvas that had been hanging on the wall above it.

His attention went back to the body again, trying to pin

down what his subconscious had just told him he'd seen. But he couldn't consciously see it.

"Nothing," he said, without being asked. "Alright, first presentation is witness statements in five."

Mel nodded, heading for the other two team members as Mac closed the glass door behind him and took his seat at the desk, which took up most space in the cubicle masquerading as an office. The room's previous incumbent had left out several documents relating to overtime requests from his team and a case file for a series of burglaries. The bin was overflowing with plastic bottles and crisp packets. He could barely bring himself to touch the desk but swept the papers into an open drawer, then found a space in the filing cabinet for the bin.

Sitting at the newly cleared desk, he contemplated his phone, seeing the old message from Siobhan. She would be getting ready for work about now. Her mum would have collected Áine to take her to school. Subconsciously, he rubbed at the strap of the cheap watch. He could just send Siobhan a message. Things had ended so badly between them it couldn't hurt to clear the air. Talking things over with her had always brought him clarity of mind. Things felt muddled now. He brought up a blank message but hovered over the virtual keyboard.

Finally, he put the phone down, discarding the draft blank message. What had been the reason for letting her go in the first place? She wanted kids. She already had one, a twelve-year-old daughter. But she wanted a kid with him. Wanted marriage. Screw it. He had no time for it. His hand went to the fresh pack of cigarettes he had bought after being pulled over. Taking them out, he looked at the sleek, shiny packet for a long moment, savouring the crushing craving that still afflicted him after nearly ten years' abstinence. Then he tossed the pack into the bottom of the filing cabinet and strode out of the room.

"Ok, what have we got? Tell me something we didn't know about this case three hours ago."

He sat himself in a vacant seat at one of the room's six desks, put his feet up and crossed his hands behind his head. Nari began.

"Neither the plumber nor the housing association duty officer saw anyone leaving the flat or the building when they arrived. The resident that called them was a Chaz Pollock, lived on the third floor and was just out of Low Moss, two years for possession with intent. He came home to find water dripping through the ceiling. Red water was what he said. Running down the walls and a foul stench in his flat. Wanted to kick the door in upstairs but he's on probation and is being a good boy."

Kai snorted. "Someone is telling him to behave, but it's not the Probationary Service, eh? Is that how he's got a flat waiting for him when he comes out?"

Mac nodded. It was an astute observation. There was one man in this part of Scotland who ran most of the county lines and estate drug dealing. That was Hance Allen. Advice from him had the power of a command from god in certain circles. In most circles. If Pollock worked for the Allen Company, then he wouldn't want to risk being recalled to prison and messing with Allen's distribution network more than he already had. In turn, Allen would make sure that one of his people had an easy ride when he got out of prison, legit job lined up and a place to live.

"We think this is something to do with drugs?" Mac asked.

"No," Kai replied quickly. "The mutilation doesn't fit."

"I agree. Too ritualistic," Nari said, looking at the close-up pictures.

Mac saw something that he hadn't been consciously aware of before. The mutilation wasn't random. It was hard to see at first glance, but several of the symbols on the chest and torso were arranged in a circular pattern. Marks on one thigh consisted of interlocking circles, Mac thought. The same shape was seen repeatedly, three circles arranged in a triangular shape and linked at the centre. There was also a series of vertical lines, with smaller horizontal or diagonal lines intersecting them.

"What kind of ritual?" Mac asked, thinking aloud but also throwing out sparks for his team to ignite over.

"Pagan?" Kai suggested. "I once dated a girl who had these tribal tattoos. They were kind of like those circular shapes. They're supposed to be Celtic or Viking or something."

Mac nodded thoughtfully.

"Some kind of occult thing?" Mel suggested.

"Too obvious," Mac said, waving his hand dismissively. "This is a second-rate musician jumping on a genre band wagon."

"You speak from experience?" Mel asked with an amused smile.

"I sometimes switch off Classic FM and kick back to some Brainbath or Rotting Christ," Mac said, deadpan.

"Rotting...? Charming." Mel said weakly.

"Next?" Mac put in, steepling his fingers.

"We haven't finished canvassing the residents yet, but we've got a list. More than half the residents are unemployed, so Kai and I will try and get round them all today," Nari said.

"Interrupt their Jeremy Kyle," Kai put in.

"Anything from the CCTV, Kai?" Mac said, jumping on his flippancy.

"Not yet. Housing Association gave me the name of the security firm that maintains their cameras. I'm chasing them down for the footage. Hoping it's digital. Then I can scrub it through the new software. One camera in the lobby works, apparently. It's pointed at the mailboxes, but someone going up via the stairs would cross its field of view. Others are either dummies or vandalised."

So CCTV was a slim hope then. Potentially useful only if the killer had chosen the stairs and not the lift. If the footage could be got and the software could clean up the images sufficiently. Still, better than nothing. Mac's eyes went to the pictures once more. He stood, striding towards the boards, and stopped inches away, hands thrust deep into trouser pockets.

"Well, get the rest of those statements and flag up anyone who might have a motive," he said without looking around.

He felt as though he were stalking a wild thought through the trackless forest of his mind. The elusive prey kept getting away from him, but he would pin it down, shoot it and mount it on the wall. But he had to figure out what it looked like first.

"Do we have any way of identifying the body yet?" he asked.

"Assuming this is the same man that's on the tenancy agreement, he's Richard McCullough with no next of kin listed or guarantors. He has a social worker, but she takes Mondays off..." Nari began.

"Then go to her home," Mac said, astonished. "Mondays off? Are you kidding me?"

"No, guv. That's what her office told me."

"Then tell them either we get their entire case history for Richard McCullough and someone who can identify him or I'll start pinning child abuse cases against anyone over there who I think could pass for a nonce," he barked.

Nari nodded, swallowing. She needed to toughen up. There was no-one more career focused than DI Yun, but she got discouraged too easily when Mac got frustrated and lost his temper. He turned back to the board with a barely suppressed sigh. But the interpersonal issues were distracting him.

"Mel, you take it. Get me an ID," he ordered.

"I can do it, guv," Nari protested.

"I want you with me," he said, thinking that it would placate her, make her feel better. "Kai is our IT expert, and Mel is the coordinator. I need someone in the field with me, eh?"

She smiled until she remembered she was supposed to be a tough, elite detective and steeled her features once more. Mac didn't need to try and hide his emotions. They were buried deep in permafrost.

"So, where will you be, guv?" Mel asked.

"We'll be heading back to Bute Tower to nail down Chaz Pollock. Sadly, only metaphorically," Mac said wryly.

CHAPTER SIX

"MUM? WHY DO WE STILL have a landline? I mean, in this day and age?" Maia asked, flopping down on top of her mother's bed, and shoving a slim, black cordless handset towards the sleeping woman.

Clio Wray was barely aware of her twelve-year-old daughter's words. She reached out and took the phone, eyes still closed and short, brown hair plastered to the pillow. She murmured into it.

"Hello?"

A man answered, "Doctor Cliodna Wray?"

He pronounced it fully, the way an English person would. Or an American. Certainly not anyone familiar with Gaelic or Gallic. Her blue eyes opened and met those of her daughter, who was already falling back to sleep. Clio pulled the duvet from underneath Maia and draped it around her shoulders. She snuggled into her mother's embrace and Clio smiled, settling herself against her pillow, staring at the ceiling as she tried to collect her thoughts.

"Well no. It's not Clee-*Odd*-Nah. It's Clee-nah. You see? Gallic."

"Oh, well I'm sorry about that. It's an unusual name. But that is you?"

"Are you delivering summonses or something?" Clio replied, digging a finger into the corner of her eye, and yawning prodigiously.

"Um, no. No. I'm a freelance journalist. I wondered if I could run something past you. I got your name from Doctor Karen Martins."

"Did you?" the name brought Clio to a more complete state of waking.

"She said that a project I'd brought to her would be better examined by you."

"Really? Usually it's the other way around," puzzlement at the other end of the line. "Does this relate to my fiction work or my academic work?"

"Definitely your academic work, I believe. Look, can I meet you for coffee, perhaps?"

"Coffee?" Clio was baffled. "What is this about? I don't even know your name."

"Ramsey Jones. Look me up. You'll see my blogs and my occasional columns for the Guardian and the Independent. I can give you some editors if you want a reference. I have some...inscriptions that I believe you can translate for me."

"What kind of inscriptions?" Clio asked, pushing herself up in bed.

Around her was a comfortable mess. Clothes piled behind

the door were dirty and prevented the door from opening completely. Clothes in bags around the wardrobe were clean and waiting to be put away. Assorted piles of books, journals, and paper completed the picture of a full and busy room.

She rubbed a hand through her short hair, rubbed eyes that were bright sapphire when fully awake. She wore a t-shirt over shorts for bed.

"Is this for a book?" she asked.

"For a story. I have some pictures and I need an expert on Celtic mythology and symbology to look at them."

"And you know that Karen Martins is one of the country's foremost authorities on this subject? I don't think I am more qualified or knowledgeable than she is," Clio pointed out, confused.

"She said she was intrigued, but had reasons of her own for saying no. She wouldn't elaborate further. Something to do with her son?"

Clio could have slapped herself across the face. Hard. Of course it was to do with Alex. What an absolute horror show that had been. How could she have forgotten that much?

"I'll pay for your time. Whatever you think is fair."

Clio looked down at the sleeping Maia. So like Clio's mother and so like Matt, too. Same nose, same mouth. She wondered if Maia's father was still living in Joppa. Still revelling in the image of the beach combing folk singer, playing acoustic sets at local pubs and impromptu gigs in woodland settings at full moon. She couldn't believe there had been a time she had seen it all as romantic. Now it just looked tacky. Still, it was Maia's thirteenth birthday next month and some extra cash around then was always welcome.

"OK, I can fit you in this morning, I think. Are you local?"

"I'm based in Edinburgh. I can meet wherever suits you."

"OK, there's a McDonalds at Cramond Bridge, just off the Queensferry Road. I usually stop there for breakfast after dropping my daughter at school. I can meet you there..."

"School? You know it's eight forty-five now?"

For a moment, Clio just stared at her disheveled reflection in the mirror propped against the top of her dressing table on the other side of the room. It took a moment for those words to sink in.

"I'll meet you there," she said and hung up.

Moments later, both Wray girls were in a whirlwind of activity. Clio was pulling a brush through her daughter's hair while shoving a piece of toast in her mouth. Maia was texting or DMing on Insta or watching TikTok or many other things to do with her phone that Clio did not understand as well as her child. It made Clio feel guilty, aware that she should be better able to protect her daughter from all the evils lurking out on the internet. But, it joined a long list of guilts.

Like not being organised enough. Like not finding a suitable partner to help raise Maia after her husband had run out on them both. Like being with him in the first place. Narcissistic snake that he was. Maia seemed to think the entire escapade immensely funny as Clio piled her into the Mini and hit the road too fast. Thankfully, they encountered no police and no speed traps for which Clio fervently thanked the universe.

Fifteen minutes after dropping her daughter at the school gates, she was pulling into the car park of the McDonalds that supplied her usual breakfast of a McMuffin and black coffee. She went in and took a seat in the window, looking around at the handful of patrons. Most appeared to be delivery drivers. A couple of mums with children. A man in a suit, checking his watch and then his phone as he sipped his coffee.

Ramsey Jones spotted her first. She had dismissed him when he walked in, the young man seemed very young. His face was fresh, with round cheeks and a smooth brow. His eyes were green and wide, giving him an earnest expression.

"Doctor Wray?" he asked in a Lancashire accent.

"Yes." She got up and shook his hand, invited him to sit next to her.

He unslung a leather satchel from his shoulder and placed it on the table in front of him. There was a seriousness about him that only the young could muster. As though his project, whatever it was, truly was the most important thing in the world at that moment.

"So, you want a translation of an inscription you believe is Celtic?" Clio said, deciding to cut to the chase.

She had a ton of marking to do and her own research to continue for the next book. Her publisher was turning the thumb screws as the deadline neared. Then there was her own deadline for the latest in her Viking romance series. And Maia's problems at school...

Ramsey slipped a laptop from the bag and opened it. He looked around at the restaurant and then turned it to face Clio.

"As I said, I will pay for your time. I can send money over now via PayPal or bank transfer. Before I do, you should now that what I'm about to show you are pictures of a fairly gruesome nature."

Clio knew then that she should just walk away. This was the kind of thing that would not end well. But it was the kind of stuff that she could not resist. It wasn't that she was un-happy with her life. It was more that she had always been drawn to mystery and making decisions on impulse. She suspected there was some neurodiversity going on in her makeup somewhere.

"What kind of gruesome?" she asked.

"A dead body. Symbols found at the scene of a suicide," Ramsey said.

He looked so utterly earnest, zealous almost, that Clio edged away slightly. She could see why Karen had turned the man down. Too close to what had happened to Alex. Far too close.

"Fifty, yeah?" Clio said in a whisper, though she didn't know why she was whispering.

"Fine," Ramsey said, "how do you want it?"

"Bank transfer. Let me get my details."

Clio fumbled with her handbag and then with her phone, logging into her mobile banking app, she found her details. Ramsey typed for a few seconds, and then Clio saw a notification of payment received. He leaned over, hovering his hand over the track pad.

"Ready?"

Clio nodded. Ramsey clicked, and the first image appeared on the screen. A circular symbol with a complex array of lines through it.

It was daubed in some kind of dark liquid, obviously blood. Clio wasn't squeamish, so what she was looking at didn't unduly disturb her. But she observed the images with an analytical mind, not an emotional one, concentrating on the symbology rather than the medium. The pictures went on and Clio became more and more absorbed, asking to go back through them to be sure of what she was seeing. Ramsey seemed impressed as she moved her face closer to the screen or asked him to zoom in. When the slideshow was over, she sat back and looked at Ramsey with obvious displeasure on her face.

"You showed these pictures to Karen?"

Ramsey looked confused. "Karen Martins? No. She refused to look at anything even before I mentioned the nature of the pictures. I know she lost her son a while ago, but..."

"Her son took his own life," Clio said. "Look, Karen Martins is my friend so I shouldn't be taking your money but...I need it so..."

"I don't understand. Why does being her friend present you with a problem?"

"Because those pictures you've just shown me are of Alex Martins. Her dead son."

CHAPTER SEVEN

CASTLEBRAE COURT looked even less attractive in the cold light of day. The sky was heavy and unrelenting. An easterly wind brought a chill to shave on. Mac kept an overcoat folded in the boot of the car, but he didn't bother with it now. Nari got out of the Audi's passenger door. She might have been a young exec. Her suit was sharp and professional, her black hair tied back to remove any hint of personality. By contrast, Mac knew there was stubble on his chin and his shirt was creased. Ironing was something he had little patience for. He thrust his hands into his trouser pockets and looked up at the blank and disinterested face of Bute Tower for a moment.

"Let me do the talking, yeah?"

Nari nodded. It wouldn't have been said had he brought along Mel. She was experienced enough to know the ropes and how Mac liked to work. Nari was learning and Mac had to remind himself that no-one was born knowing how to live the part of the detective. He had learned the hard way. So had

Mel, and so would Nari and Kai. With all the bruised egos and sleepless nights that went along with it. There was no room for a soft detective.

"Sure, guv," Nari replied, looking excited despite herself.

Mac led the way into the building, past the uniforms still on sentry duty. Forensics had been through with a sense of urgency and the common areas were opened up again. Mac hoped it had been done before any evidence had been destroyed. It was getting on for nine and footfall would get heavier. For those that had somewhere to go.

"I hate places like this," Nari said as she followed him in.

"You used to something better?" Mac asked, heading for the door to the stairwell.

"East Kilbride, then Airdrie. Ordinary enough. Just not in a tower block. They're so depressing."

"They are," Mac agreed, pushing open the fire door to the stairwell.

"Never heard you talk about where you're from, guv," Nari said.

"Edinburgh," Mac said, only partially truthful.

Edinburgh had been his home from the age of eighteen. A black hole that he had fallen into as he ran from the nightmare that was his previous life.

"I think Mel once said something about you being from the west?" Nari persisted.

Mac looked back over his shoulder at her as they climbed the stairs.

"A long time ago," he said, before resuming the climb.

"Sorry," Nari muttered.

Mac realised he'd made his reply sound like he was snapping, shutting his colleague down. His lips twitched in a brief grimace and he turned to look back over his shoulder, giving Nari a lop-sided grin.

"I sometimes think my ideal job is lighthouse keeper. I'm not great with people. Small talk, eh? You'll find that out. What's that saying about bark and bite?"

"Put a muzzle on it?" Nari said, a slightly cheeky smile dimpling her cheeks.

Mac laughed, the sudden sound bouncing around the walls of the concrete coffin they were ascending.

"I know a few journalists who'd agree. And could show you the bite marks to prove it," Mac said.

"Yeah, but who cares about journalists, anyway?" Nari replied.

"Not me."

They passed the graffiti again, the light in the concrete coffin no better at daytime than it had been at night. Mac's eyes registered the odd circles and intersecting lines at the same time as Nari spoke up.

"That looks familiar, guv."

"It does. You got some of those SOCO pictures on your phone?"

Of course she did. She brought up an image, zoomed in, and held the phone up against the wall.

"Not identical, but stylistically the same," Nari commented.

"And in a sequence," Mac said, pointing to the leftmost part of the daubing where a shape made up of what looked like two intersecting X's seemed to be repeated a few characters along, then again.

"Language? A code?" Nari wondered.

"Depends on the motive. Killed over drugs or money, seems elaborate. Killed to send a message...maybe. Have SOCO been in here?"

"Yes, I told them to cover every shared space, including the lifts and the stairs. These should be documented."

Mac resumed his long climb, trying to breathe through his mouth. At the third floor, he stepped out onto a hallway that was a carbon copy of the one above, minus the police presence. He knew that Chaz Pollock lived in 23 and found it three doors from the lift. The thin carpet outside the flat was damp, squishing under foot. Mac ignored it as he rapped sharply on the door.

The man who answered it was not who Mac had been expecting. He was tall and white-haired, cobwebs swept back from the temples and held there, defying gravity. He had a prominent nose which emphasised how deep set his eyes were. Nonexistent lips. He wore a dark gray, three-piece suit which screamed solicitor. In case that wasn't clear enough, he looked carefully at both Mac and Nari's warrant cards when they were offered.

"DCI McNeill, Serious Crime Unit. This is DS Yun. We're here to talk to Mr. Charles Pollock about the body he found."

"Michael Grainger, Grainger & Kisk Solicitors," the solicitor replied with a nasal Edinburgh accent. "And to be precise, he didn't find the body. He didn't attempt to enter the flat above, merely phoned the duty Housing Association officer to report the water damage to his flat. As the terms of his tenancy demand."

Mac didn't like mob solicitors, and Grainger was clearly

just that. He looked and sounded too expensive for a low level street dealer, which is what Pollock was.

"I just need to talk to Mr. Pollock about what he saw and what he found," Mac said.

"As long as there's no suggestion that my client has done anything wrong," Grainger said.

"No, but if you keep us standing out here much longer, I'll be tempted to run you in for obstruction," Mac growled.

Grainger didn't smile, merely nodded, and looked down from the height of his nose.

"I'll check that this is an appropriate time for Mr. Pollock," he said.

"Let them in!" Came a voice from inside the flat.

Grainger's cheek twitched, and his eyes darted to the left. Then he was looking back at Mac.

"Mr. Pollock is available. Come in, Inspector. Mr. Allen sends his regards, by the way. He's glad that you are the one assigned to this case."

Mac strolled into the flat and suppressed the urge to take a swing at the old crow. He could practically feel Nari's ears twitching at the link between himself and Edinburgh's most infamous gangster. Most infamous and most un-caught. Nothing stuck to him because of lawyers like Grainger. The flat was laid out exactly like the one above. The carpet was wet, bubbles appearing with every step. A pink stain covered the walls to either side of the hallway, and the ceiling plaster had caved in at several points.

The air stank of damp and the acrid tang of cigarettes. Chaz Pollock sat in the living room, an ashtray on the arm of the sofa. He wore a trackie, all gray with expensive looking trainers. He was long and skinny and had the insouciant atti-tude of one who knows he is under divine protection.

"Alright, mate," he drawled through a blue haze of smoke as Mac entered.

Mac looked around the room, sniffed and caught the sickly sweet odor of weed under the regular tobacco. He idly wondered if there would be enough of the stuff in the flat to run Pollock in for possession. But he wouldn't be that stupid. Besides, by the time a search warrant was obtained, the flat would be clean. Legally, if not literally.

"Nice place," Mac said.

Pollock sat on a layer of blankets and towels. The rest of the fabric sofa looked wet. Mac decided to stand. The lawyer moved into position behind Pollock, placing his phone on the back of the sofa conspicuously.

"I take it no-one objects to a record being kept of this con-versation?"

Mac didn't bother answering.

"No, we'll record too. You'll be glad to know," Nari said.

"So, Probation Service handing out flats now, eh?" Mac asked.

"My uncle leased it for me," Pollock said.

"Uncle Hance?"

"Don't remember."

"You don't remember your own uncle?" Nari asked.

"Big family, love," Pollock said, showing a yellow-toothed grin.

"Is this relevant?" Grainger inquired.

"Might be," Mac said. He moved to the room's only window, which looked out over a car park. "You told the Housing Association that your flat was flooded from the flat upstairs. What did you see when you went up there?"

"Who says he went anywhere?" Grainger replied.

"Because he was sitting in a flat filling up with someone else's bloody bathwater," Mac said, not looking away from Pollock.

"Aye, I went up. Couldn't stay in here, could I? Wouldn't be here now if it weren't for you. I saw the guy from the Housing Association go in with the plumber and then come out, like, really fast. White as a sheet, eh?" Pollock said, re-lighting his self-rolled cigarette.

"You knew him though," Mac said.

"That should be a question, surely?" Grainger was quick to reply.

"He wasn't a customer, then?" Mac asked.

"I'm unemployed at the moment. So, I don't know how he'd be a customer," Pollock said, flicking ash onto the wet floor.

"If we find your DNA in that flat, we're going to want to know how it got there. If we find drugs in that flat, we're going to know what you were doing there, eh?" Mac said, leaning forward slightly.

Then he raised his voice and spoke toward the phone on the back of the sofa.

"But you wouldn't be that stupid, would you, Hance? Not with one of your boys on the door last night."

Pollock froze with his roll-up halfway to his mouth. Grainger glanced down at the phone, which, moments later, lit up. He swiped at the screen, then picked it up and put it to his ear. He nodded a few times and then held the phone out to Mac, who stepped back with his hands raised.

"Just put him on speaker," he said. "We're all friends here."

Grainger put the phone back to his ear and then nodded again before putting the phone to speaker and placing it back on the sofa.

"DCI McNeill! How are you, my man?" Hance Allen said.

CHAPTER EIGHT

MAC GLANCED AT NARI, who held her phone towards the conversation, as she had since she began recording. He didn't want to tell her to stop, but didn't know what Allen might say. The rumor of an AC investigation was at the forefront of his mind. She looked back at him and he could read the question in her mind. Mac turned away.

"How's things, Hance?" he said.

"Aye, good, son. Good. And how's you, big yin?" Allen replied.

His accent was pure Glasgow, despite his business empire being focused on the east. Allen had been driven off his home turf long ago, though he had since staged a bloody come back that had required an enormous financial sacrifice to make senior police officers look away.

"I'm wondering if I'm seeing an elaborate punishment killing here," Mac said.

"Callum, Callum, how could that possibly have anything

to do with me? I'm a businessman, that's all. Now, I wanted to make sure that no suspicion fell on my friend Chaz here because of his previous record."

"A record of violence," Mac said.

"Yes, but the young lad has turned a corner. With my help, of course. And now he's flying straight. No need for you to be looking at him."

"He's a witness," Mac said.

"He saw nothing," Allen replied, an edge creeping into his voice.

"I'm wondering why a low level street pusher needs a personal intervention from a...businessman," Mac said. "I'm also wondering what forensics might find in that flat. Your man's DNA?"

"He's not my man," Allen said with the snap of a mousetrap. "I'm looking out for him as a favour to his mother,"

"Aye," Mac said flatly. "I forgot about his mother,"

"Now look. You and I are old friends. When I heard that a terrible murder had been committed in Chaz's building, the first thing I thought of was making sure that he wouldn't be the center of a nasty stitch up by the polis. My family has personal experience of that."

"I remember," Mac said.

"So do I. I will never forget that you were the one who cleared John-Boy's name. It hasn't been easy for you since, has it? Even with my help..."

"Hance, let's cut to the chase," Mac interrupted. He could feel Nari's eyes boring into the back of his head.

"Well, you were the one that wanted this little chat to be public, son," Hance replied. "Let's just say that I had nothing to do with this awful crime and have no knowledge of the victim. Chaz Pollock is a young man from an unfortunate background who has made some bad choices, and I am helping him get back on the straight and narrow. It would displease me immensely to see the polis decide to fit him up."

"I don't fit people up, Hance. And I will take this investigation where it needs to go. If that's to your door, then I'll go there. Now, if you've quite finished, you're interrupting my interview."

"Give my regards to Superintendent Dawlish," Allen said and hung up.

For a moment, Mac stared at the phone. Jo Dawlish was a Chief Superintendent of the AC division. It was an uncomfortable surprise that Allen seemed to know about the rumour of an investigation into the SCU. He glanced at Nari, who frowned back, confusion on her face, but she was too smart not to be speculating. Grainger and Pollock looked smug. Mac gritted his teeth behind a tight smile.

"I think we have everything we need. If we find anything linking you to that flat, we'll be coming for you in the early hours and drag you to the cells in your scants, eh?"

He turned away as Grainger fumbled with the recording app and his client sniggered. He walked out of the flat and headed for the stairs.

"You really think this is drugs related?" Nari asked.

"No chance. But when one of your witnesses just happens to work for Hance Allen, you can't disregard it. So, we account for all the DNA and cross check it against what we've got on file for Pollock. But something is telling me we won't find anything. It's all just a bit too elaborate."

Nari was making notes on her phone, holding it in both hands, thumbs dancing. They re-entered the stairwell, beginning to climb to the fourth floor. Mac went over the phone call in his mind. Allen was trying to intimidate, and he wondered why. The mention of an Anti-Corruption officer by name suggested a number of things. Or it could have been simple undermining him in front of one of his team. Either way, Allen was interfering, and Mac couldn't think of a reason for that unless the crime touched his business somehow.

"Check the CCTV footage for any interaction between the guy upstairs and Pollock. Anything on the estate or in the building. Then hit up some snouts, find out if our victim was a user and where he went to score if he was."

They reached the fourth floor and Mac had already pushed Hance Allen to the back of his mind. Whatever the motivation for his interference, the strategy for Mac was the same. Run down the evidence. Chris Hunter was still on sentry duty at the door of the flat. Mac ignored him as he walked in, heard Nari politely acknowledging the man. Was he Allen's mole? Seemed likely. Once inside, Mac went straight to the living room. It was well documented, but there was no substitute for physically seeing the place. SOCO had finished their job, and the body had been removed.

Fast work despite the sloppy beginning. He hoped it signified efficiency rather than corner cutting, accidental or deliberate. A glance back towards the door caught Hunter looking back at him. The officer turned away as Mac caught his eye.

"I've been thinking about what Kai said, about these

symbols looking tribal, Celtic. There could be something in that, look..." Nari said.

She held up her phone and Mac found himself looking at an array of images, from drawings to carved inscriptions to tattoos. All bore a marked resemblance in style to the marks made on the body of Richard McCullough, if that's who this proved to be. Not quite the same, but similar.

"And what do they mean?" Mac asked.

"All kinds of things. They're symbolic. Some represent health, some truth, some love. All the usual hippy stuff."

They were in the living room and Mac was looking at the blood spray pattern that ran up the couch. A hook in the wall showed where a picture had removed. He remembered the SOCO photograph of it. Blood sprayed across it thickly. That was to be expected. The attack had been frenzied, blood would spatter over everything. So what was it that was bothering him about this one picture?

"Nari, bring up the SOCO image of the picture that was hanging here," he ordered, staring at the wall.

No fading of the wallpaper, no sign other than the hook that something had been hanging here. He looked towards the window. The curtains were drawn, as they had been since the night before. Striding across the room, he flung them back. Pale daylight reached the length of the room, in-cluding the spot in question.

"I've got it," Nari said, turning her phone around to show the image. "Can't have been up for very long. The wallpaper is all the same colour still," she observed.

Mac smiled tightly, giving a sharp nod. He'd already reached the same conclusion. A recent addition then. He walked back for a closer look at the image on the phone, then zoomed in to an area just below the canvas. He went to the sofa, tracing the arc of the blood spray.

"Wait a minute. That isn't an actual picture that got sprayed with blood, guv; it's a blank canvas that got sprayed. Look, there's no image or drawing or anything beneath, just the blood spatter," Nari said.

Mac stared at the image on the phone.

"Who would hang up a blank canvas?" Nari wondered aloud.

Mac considered the problem. The answer was simple. No one. You didn't take a blank canvas and hang it on your wall. The image of a famous abstract action painting came to the forefront of his mind, the paint thrown at the canvas.

"Someone deliberately hung that canvas up. The blood is the picture," Mac said.

Nari looked from phone to wall and back again. "Why? A trophy? No, that wouldn't make sense or they'd have taken it with them. A message then?"

But Mac's mind was already a step ahead. He had discarded the question of the canvas itself and was considering the means by which it had been covered in blood. His eyes went up the sofa cushion, seeing the arterial arc of the spray, following its progress. Then he saw it.

"The blood goes up the back of the sofa and across the wall," Mac said, finally realising what had looked so odd to him when he'd studied the crime scene photos tacked to the board back at the station. He mentally kicked himself for being so slow. Especially because now he looked closer the spray's direction, when comparing the wall and the canvas, didn't quite match. But it was their first clue. He turned to his DS.

He saw the same sudden gleam in Nari's eye that he knew was in his.

"The canvas was about twelve inches above the top of the sofa," she said. "But the blood goes above those twelve inches, right across where the picture would have hung. So..."

"It's not McCullough's blood on the canvas," Mac finished. "If it sprayed across the sofa and the canvas, there wouldn't be blood behind it. It was hung after the murder."

"Meaning the blood was already on there," Nari said. "Either from elsewhere or maybe daubed with McCullough's blood after he was dead."

Mac shook his head. "It wasn't daubed on that canvas. You can see the force of the arterial spray. If it was done after McCullough was killed, there wouldn't have been enough blood pressure left. I think that blood belongs to someone else. It was placed there already bloodied, but not from this crime scene," Mac finished. "It is a message."

Nari was suddenly stabbing at her phone. Mac waited.

"This is DS Yun, SCU. I need to know if the blood on a piece of evidence from the Craigmillar crime scene has been tested yet and specifically if it matches the victim."

Mac grinned savagely. Nari was young and she could still make mistakes, but her mind was probably the sharpest in his team. He felt a surge of pride that she had reached the conclusion at the same time as he had, seen the same clues and made the same deductive leap. To his mind, it was the right leap, too. Nari gave the evidence reference number for the picture and listened. Her face fell.

"Alright, DCI McNeill needs it as a priority, OK?"

She hung up and looked at McNeill.

"They haven't got to the canvas yet," she said, crestfallen.

"Don't worry about it. I'd rather they were slow but thorough. But stay on them."

Nari nodded, making quick notes on her phone. "I'm across it."

CHAPTER NINE

———————

MAC TRIED TO FORGET about cigarettes. It was a win, a trail that led to another person. That brought about a craving as his heart pumped and adrenaline spiked.

"But we don't know who the blood might belong to, guv. It could be another victim or..."

"Or possibly nothing relevant to the case. But it's a trail that takes us out of this flat. Whoever did this came from the outside. Any evidence that leads us out is potentially pointing to them," Mac said.

Nari nodded, eyes bright, lips parted. She was pretty, very pretty. Mac would have to be made of stone not to see it. The thought made him think of Siobhan. Hit him like a bus, slamming his mood down and filling him with guilt. He grimaced, looking around the room.

"We'll have to wait for any DNA found to be traced to someone currently on the database. But, I want to keep up the momentum. We've got Mel scaring up a social worker to identify McCullough. We know of at least three other people who knew him. His band. They were a four piece, I think. Wait a second, there's an app..."

He swiped through his phone for a moment until he found the app in question, an encyclopedia of bands, specifically metal.

"An app?"

"Yeah, I use it all the time. Lists of bands, big and small, discographies, members, reviews. You see a new band no-one's heard of; you go on and log it. Back in the day, you'd just be trading tapes or CD-Rs. These days it's all digital."

"Still can't believe someone like you is into all that dark stuff," Nari said.

Mac glanced at her. "Maybe I'm darker than you think, eh?"

Nari laughed and there was something in her eyes, something he almost convinced himself was just in his imagination. Her dark eyes seemed to hold his for just a moment too long. *Shit! He'd need to stop that PDQ.*

"Damn it!" Mac snarled, going back to his phone. "The entry's been removed. Omega's not listed."

"Was it ever?"

"Definitely. I've looked them up, or I'd not have known about them. This is the bible. Bloody black metal nerds! I can remember the nicknames but...."

The real names were gone. Richard McCullough was completely unfamiliar, no hint of memory. The rest of them could have been anyone, Jock Stein, and Bonnie Prince Charlie for all he knew.

"So, we do it the old-fashioned way. Trawl his possessions, his phone, address book...." Nari suggested.

"Phone should be with digital forensics getting unlocked," Mac said. "Kai can chase them up."

DF was a career path Kai Stuart probably should consider. Mac had spotted the young DC's affinity for tech and exploited it to the full. Kai had a good rapport with the tech guys and got good results out of them.

"The analog stuff will be in storage until it's all been catalogued and examined. Job for you, Nari. Get down to forensics and start looking."

"You don't want me along with you, guv?" Nari asked.

"No, too much to do. I need names from McCullough's possessions. Let Mel handle ID'ing the body and tracking down any family there might be."

"And what are you going to do, guv?" Nari asked.

"I'm going to focus on this...writing, if that's what it is. See if I can find someone who can translate it for us."

Nari left, making more notes on her phone. Mac went into the bedroom and took a seat at the desk where the computer had sat. Forensics had removed it, leaving a square of clean space amid the dust and detritus of an untidy mind. He resisted the urge to swipe it all aside and take a wet cloth and a bottle of bleach to the surface. Instead, he took out his phone and started a search for academics with an interest in Celtic history. Mac didn't even know exactly what period of history that was; it wasn't a subject that had ever interested him.

Was it the middle ages? Or the Romans, they had occupied Britain once, hadn't they? It was all hazy. A mass of unknowns clouding his mind. He needed an expert to consult. To look at the inscriptions and tell him their significance, if any. And if there was significance, then the right academic would be a valuable asset to the team, provided they had the stomach for it. Not many did.

"Anything I can do to help, sir?" a man asked.

Mac recognised the voice of PC Hunter and didn't look round.

"No," he replied.

"Just standing out there, thought if I could make myself useful..."

"Standing out there is right where I want you, constable," Mac said firmly.

"Between you and me, sir, I don't think this is one of Allen's," Hunter said.

Mac stopped what he was doing. A flare of rage spiked within him. He put the phone down and looked back over his shoulder.

"And how would you know?" he said, quietly.

"I just hear things, eh?" Hunter replied, glancing towards the door. "Like I hear AC might be interested in you."

"I've already had a warning from your boss on that, cheers. Now get lost," Mac snapped.

"Aye, well. Just so you know. In case...you know, you might need a mate," Hunter said.

His eye met Mac's and held. There was a smile on his face, but it didn't reach his eyes. He was chewing something, jaw moving like a cow. Mac seethed, hating bent coppers more than the worst criminals he'd come across. Maybe worse than Mark Souter. No, Mac couldn't hate anyone worse than him. Part of the problem was that he used to be one himself. Didn't matter that he'd not been on the take. He and a bloke called Strachan had appointed themselves judge and jury, circumventing the Procurator Fiscal. But it was all the same in the end. You were either straight or not. He rose and walked up to Hunter, who stood his ground with hands tucked into the armholes of his stab vest.

The grin was insolent now, telling Mac that he was part of a different chain of command. One that didn't go through the Police Scotland. Mac glanced over Hunter's shoulder, towards the door, and let a slight smile tug at the corner of his mouth. Hunter glanced in the same direction and Mac deftly plucked a hair from the back of his head, where it protruded from the rim of his cap. Mac stepped back as Hunter clapped a hand to his neck, staring at him with the kind of wide eyes that usually presaged violence.

Mac held up the hair and then deftly sealed it in an evidence bag he took from the inside pocket of his jacket, where he always kept a spare.

"Now, if I think you or your boss is interfering in my investigation, this DNA turns up somewhere it shouldn't," Mac said, putting the bag back into his pocket.

"You can't do that," Hunter snarled.

"You're a bent copper, pal. You know I can do anything I want. You're also so low down in the food chain that you're not going to be missed if I decide to fit you up. You won't get an expensive Stockbridge solicitor like that ned downstairs. Now, get back to your post."

Hunter clenched his fists, taking a breath as though preparing himself to strike the senior officer. Then self-preservation took over. Mac didn't blink as he watched it play out. Had the guy gone for him, Mac wouldn't have held back. His car keys were clenched in one fist, casually palmed when he had put the evidence bag back into his pocket. He would have done some damage had Hunter gone for him. A good chance to vent some frustration and justify it as self-defense. He almost wished Hunter had taken a swing.

CHAPTER TEN

As Mac left the building and got back to his car, an email appeared. It was a diary invite to the press conference. The email came from the HQ Public Relations department in Glasgow. Mac had been expecting it but not looking forward to it. Briefing the press was a necessary part of policing, but in a case like this it was a grudging necessity. Details had to be kept close to the chest or there would be a free-for-all. At the moment, the story was of interest to the Scottish press and media, but would be unlikely to be noticed UK wide. Unless details leaked out about the mutilations. He drove, putting the phone in its hands-free cradle and calling Reid, knowing his commanding officer would want to be brought up to date with the fine detail ahead of the press briefing. As he waited for Reid to pick up, he checked himself in the rear-view mirror.

Dark hair tousled, but not as if he'd just got out of bed. He could get away with it. A woman had once told him his kind of hair was made for fingers to be run through it and frequently looked like that's just what had been happening. Dark eyes, half lidded, the way they went when his mind was elsewhere. Stubble, that would be fashionable if it were deliberate, would need to be shaved smooth. Mac checked his serious face in the mirror, the one that was expected when a police officer was talking about murder. The one he'd had to practice over and over until he got it right. It was good enough. Serious but with compassion and the hard edge the public expected from its police force. Public relations was all about coppers being approachable, known within their communities and knowing that community in return. But when it came to violent crime, what the public really wanted was someone ruthless and tough as nails. You had to be scarier than the bad guys.

The trouble was Meredith Blakely, civilian head of the Police Scotland PR team, had a thing about photogenic cops. Mac had tuned out of some senior leadership team conference call about PR and how, unfortunately, the public responded better to good looking officers. It would be funny if she hadn't been deadly serious. And she thought Mac's particular brand of tall, dark, and deadly played well. She was in her forties, married, but not so you'd notice. Good looking, but pushy. Mac didn't check the email to see if she had nominated herself to attend. It seemed like she almost always did when he was involved, though she claimed it was because of his rank. As he left the estate and headed back to the Niddrie Road station, he idly wondered if he should just make a harassment complaint.

"Mac, got the invite through?" Reid said, answering the call after the twentieth ring.

"Got it. On my way now."

"Where are we on the case?"

"Melissa is running down the ID. Got some potential leads on a blood stained item found at the scene, a canvas. We think it was blank and covered in someone else's blood, hung there as a message. Nari is chasing up forensics and Kai is doing his usual with the digital evidence; victim's phone and building CCTV."

"That better give us something. We paid a lot of money for that software and it hasn't paid for itself yet."

"If it gives us a killer, that should satisfy the Commissioner."

"Nothing satisfies him if it involves spending. What's your working hypothesis?"

It was very early days in the case, but Reid knew Mac well enough to acknowledge that he would already be working on a theory based on the evidence found so far. Mac hesitated and Reid pounced.

"Tell me what I'm not going to like hearing before I end up reading about it in the Daily Record, right?" he said with Glaswegian directness.

"A dealer working for Allen made the 999 call. He's got an expensive Stockbridge solicitor, and a flat kept for him while he was doing time."

"Was our victim a junkie?"

"Don't know until we get post mortem results and an ID. But Hance has the guy armour plated, which is odd if this is nothing to do with him."

"If the press asks about a gangland connection, stonewall it," Reid said.

"You think?" Mac replied with a degree of sarcasm.

Silence in reply was an unspoken rebuke. Mac could picture the bared teeth and rolled eyes at the other end.

"Meredith Blakely is on her way out to you to go over your statement. It'll be the usual, as little as possible. But if Hance Allen is involved, it sounds to me like a junkie out of his depth and punished."

"That's one possibility," Mac agreed.

He wasn't about to suggest to Reid that the mutilation might be taking the form of Celtic inscriptions. Nor that the theory originated with Kai's girlfriend's tattoos. Reid wouldn't take kindly to that kind of speculation, and Mac didn't want to be ripped up one side and down the other for fifteen minutes. Better to keep quiet until he had something concrete.

"Good. There'll be cameras there, so make sure you look the part," Reid said and hung up.

Rubbing at his chin, Mac decided to spare himself some grief and pick up some disposable razors. Driving past the station, he pulled in at a supermarket half a mile down the road. A girl was sitting on the ground beside the entrance. She wore a woolly hat over greasy hair and a dirty blanket was wrapped around her knees. A McDonalds' cup stood on the ground at her feet. A gust of wind blew it over, but she didn't notice. Mac observed the unnatural pallor and saw the sweat trickling down the side of her face, despite constant shivering and a single figure temperature outdoors. She looked like she could still be at school. He slowed, knowing he carried no cash to give her, knowing that if it did, the money would feed the habit that had left her shivering and sweating.

A store security guard was coming out of the shop. Mac

reached into his coat and pulled out his warrant card, holding up a hand to stop the man in his tracks. The girl looked up as Mac crouched beside her. Shoppers coming in and out of the store studiously ignored her.

"Alright, love?" Mac said quietly.

"I'm just going," she mumbled, shifting in her blanket.

"It's OK. I'm not here to move you on," Mac said, trying for reassurance.

The girl reminded him of Áine, Siobhan's daughter. They couldn't have been that far apart in age, four or five years, maybe. The idea of how easily someone could end up like this sent a chill through him. The girl watched him warily as Mac showed her his ID, backing off the store security with a dark-eyed stare.

"You homeless?" Mac asked.

"Aye."

"What are you on?"

"Whatever I can get," the girl said.

Mac wanted to ask her how she'd ended up there, but there wasn't time for her life story. She was clearly hurting, probably run out of money to get a fix and in too much of a mess to go on the game.

"Well, I'm not going to give you money. I know what you'll use it for..." Mac began.

"I won't. I swear. I won't. I just want something to eat," the girl insisted, coming to life at the mention of cash.

"No. But I know some people who can get you off the streets. Find a bed for you."

He watched the hope that had briefly kindled in her eyes fade. She returned to a state of defeated lethargy.

"Why?" she said, dully.

"Because it's what you need. Might not be what you want, but it's what you need, eh?" Mac said, keeping his tone light, like he was trying to tame a feral animal.

"She can't stay here, mate," the store security said, hovering.

"She won't be, right? Someone will be by to pick her up," Mac said, straightening. "And you're going to stay right here with her until they do."

"I need to get back..."

"You need to do as I tell you," Mac cut right across him. "She'll be off your premises soon enough."

The security man nodded, taking up a position on the far side of the doorway to the girl, watching her warily. Mac went into the shop, skimming through his phone for a specific person, then hitting dial. He had bought and paid for razors and shaving gel by the time he'd organised something for her. A charity helping the homeless in Edinburgh and a case worker there who'd moved on since their brief fling and Mac's reluctance to commit to her. Moved on enough to take his call and promise to head out straight away for the girl. Mac added a sandwich and a drink to his shopping, then used the customer toilets to shave his *high-boned, sharp cheeks and strong jawline.* Mac scoffed. He had Meredith Blakely to thank for this ridiculous description, and had been the butt of many a joke as a result. On the way out, he gave the sandwich and drink to the girl, telling her someone was on the way and she'd be indoors that night.

Walking away, he felt a fool. He couldn't help every rough sleeper he came across. Not even all the rough sleeping girls who looked the same age as Áine. It was a drop in the ocean.

But that was police work. He remembered a story about some king who thought he could hold back the tide. English or maybe Scottish. He couldn't remember. It didn't matter. By the time he reached his car, his mind was back on the case.

CHAPTER ELEVEN

IF CLIO OPENED THE WINDOW of her office and leaned out far enough without falling two stories to the concrete yard below, she could catch a glimpse of Holyrood Palace down along the Canongate. Her office was a cupboard on the third floor of Moray House, which had thrilled her when she first started working at the University of Edinburgh. It looked as though it had stood since Tudor times, stone almost black from pollution, windows tall and leaded.

It was the home of the History Department's Centre for Celtic Studies, overlooking a pleasant quadrangle at the rear of the building and was one of the oldest structures on Canongate. It was also poorly heated and poorly connected. So, she kept an oil fired heater under her desk in flagrant disregard for health and safety regs. Maia had shown her how to use her phone as a hotspot, which enabled Clio to get around the constant connectivity drop outs.

A helpful IT man from the university had installed a

booster, then had asked her out. The booster certainly helped, but she'd pleaded a hectic schedule regarding a date. And kept pleading it when he asked the second and third times. She fully expected the booster to be removed from where it was plugged into a socket in the wall beside the door, any day now in retribution. After oversleeping yet again, she'd forgotten to make herself a packed lunch. She normally made one for Maia too, but they usually came back untouched.

Such had been the disturbing revelation at McDonalds, almost a week ago, that she hadn't thought to pick herself something up from there. Or something for Maia, for that matter, though she knew the school would send out a snippy tweet if they found any child being given fast food by a parent. She and Maia had already been the inspiration for one such tweet. As a result, her stomach was currently growling. There was a pile of unmarked essays from her undergraduate class to her left. A smaller pile from her post-grad class just beneath it.

The rest of the desk was taken up with books, photocopies of pages, journals, and scribbled notes. Her laptop reigned over the chaos, showing bloody images of ancient Celtic glyphs carved into flesh. The cupboard office was at the landing of a small, rickety staircase which itself was a major thoroughfare. Every time she heard someone clomping past, she reached for the lid of the laptop, ready to slam it shut.

If Karen happened to come by, Clio did not think she would react well to these horrific images of her dead son. There were enough gossips in the small faculty that if any of her other colleagues saw it, the news would spread. She could think of no sound academic reason for her to be translating the early-Pictish era glyphs. Ramsay had offered more money

71

when Clio had looked ready to walk away. She would have done too, had the amounts not begun to double.

Now, she was sitting on two hundred quid to discretely translate glyphs which Alex Martins had been cutting into his own body over a prolonged period, as well as a range of street graffiti, which appeared to be of the same language. Or not. It was proving frustratingly difficult to translate, like encountering a language you understood being spoken in a dialect that rendered it almost unintelligible. But not quite.

Those not quite moments were the reason she was not thinking of her hunger and why she was looking up in panic at every sound on the stairs, too engrossed to have heard the person coming until they were right outside. After about a hundred such shocks, she closed the lid and sat back in her chair, leaning it onto its back two legs and balancing there, looking at the stain on the ceiling that had been a leak last year.

Then came the knock at the door. Clio almost overbalanced, catching the edge of the desk just in time. She gathered her notes together and turned them over, placing the pile of undergraduate essays on top of them.

"Come in!" she called out.

Karen Martins entered, and Clio thanked the universe for her lucky timing.

"Karen! How are you?" Clio said, standing.

"Morning, Clio. Yes, busy as usual. I'm helping to curate the new Pictish Edinburgh exhibition at the National. It is growing arms and legs. Two things really, I won't keep you. You've obviously got your hands full."

Karen Martins was in her early fifties but had the soft skin and round face of a woman ten years younger. Her eyes were hazel and her lips luscious and full. Pouting was a natural expression for her, and when she smiled, her mouth looked positively cherubic. The size of the faculty meant their head took on her fair share of lectures and Clio had a feeling those classes were well subscribed by male students. Female too, for that matter.

She didn't look like an academic and Clio supposed that was because as faculty head, she had to be a politician just as much as a teacher.

"Yes, I have to get these graded by the Easter break..." Clio began.

"And your latest book finished? I mean the...romances," Karen said with an arched eyebrow.

Clio flushed. "Never on company time, Karen. You know that."

Karen barked out a laugh. "Actually, I'm a bit of a fan, so I'm tempted to say, what the hell!"

Clio was taken aback that Karen Martins was a reader of historical romances. Clio had been writing them as a sideline to academic work for fifteen years and had disclosed it upon applying for the job at the university. Karen had never mentioned it before.

"Right," Clio said haltingly.

"But no, extracurricular is just that," Karen said, switching from jollity to seriousness in the blink of an eye. "On that subject," she continued with a smile. "I wanted to check in with you to see if you've had any contact with a journalist named Ramsay Jones?"

Clio felt icy fingers on the back of her neck. Karen was

looking directly at her, lips pursed. Her lipstick was dark and her hair, pinned up on top of her head, was coal black. She tilted her head slightly to one side and drummed her fingers against the sheath of papers she held to her breast.

"He got in touch. He said that you had given him my name."

"Yes," Karen said, but extending the vowels to spell the word with five. "I did at first. I found what he was proposing to be tasteless in the extreme. I know the pictures are out there after the police leaked them, but still..."

She looked away, face momentarily twisting, and Clio felt a pang of sympathy. She was about to go and give her a hug when the soft hazel eyes pounced back on her.

"I don't think it would actually be wise for any member of this faculty to get involved," she said flatly.

"Oh...well that's good because I...haven't given him any opinions," Clio said truthfully.

There was something in her boss's manner that told her it would not be received well if she admitted she was hard at work on the problem.

"Good. Best to block him. Shut him out. It can only bring the University into disrepute. On the other hand...co-incidentally...or possibly not...a police officer has contacted me."

Karen stopped, having begun looking through the papers she carried. She lifted out a sheet and turned it so that Clio could see.

"He was looking for a member of the faculty to consult with over some symbols found at a crime scene."

Clio looked at the paper, but all it contained was a name and a mobile number, all in Karen's distinctive scrawl.

DCI Callum McNeill, Serious Crimes Unit.

"Does this have something to do with...what the journalist wanted to know about?" Clio asked.

"I doubt it. How could it?" Karen replied.

"Just that I've been here for five years and no-one has ever asked for my opinion, even within my own field. Now two come along at once."

"Nothing more than coincidence, I expect. Don't read too much into it. Ramsay Jones is a ghoul trying to drum something up from Alex's..."

Karen's eyes went distant; her pout wavered until she seemed to come back into the room, eyes sharpening.

"I understand," Clio said, wanting to spare Karen the pain of having to say it.

"Alex's suicide," Karen said calmly and deliberately. "You can't come to terms with something if you can't speak it aloud," she said with conviction.

"I've read that. It was a long time before I could speak about my mother's cancer, even though she survived it. I just couldn't bring myself to talk about it."

"Hmm, yes," Karen said, looking around the room, then back at Clio. "Suffice to say we can't refuse a police request for help. But, for the other..."

"I'll ignore him," Clio said, which earned a tight smile.

"Good. Glad we're on the same page. An office is going to be available on the first floor next year. Duncan Crieff has decided to retire. Maybe we could get you out of the cupboard into a proper room, eh?"

Clio beamed and tried to tamp down the feeling of quid pro quo she was left with. It reminded her she would likely not rise higher in the university echelons. Politics was not for her. Karen moved toward the door.

"OK, well, good to catch up, Clio. Keep up the writing, all of it." She tapped the side of her nose with a smile, and Clio laughed. "Be sure to give that police officer a ring and see how the faculty can help. If it's discovery of bones on a building site somewhere, then push it off to Graeme, he'll end himself with excitement. Still goes on about how he was on the Yorvik dig as a student."

Karen rolled her eyes and breezed out of the room without waiting for a reply. Clio picked up the paper and looked at the name thoughtfully.

CHAPTER TWELVE

THE INVESTIGATION FELL into a routine for the next few days. Mac was the first to their commandeered office every day and the last to leave. Melissa, always the office manager, ran the daily huddles where the team reviewed their actions and gave progress updates. It became almost mundane; going over witness statements, forensic evidence, cross-referencing, and filing. Mac considered it the most dangerous time of any investigation, the moment when the team began to forget the bloody horror of the crime itself and saw only the administration. Crime scene pictures remained up in vivid colour as a reminder. Mac needed it as much as the others. It was too easy to nod off at the desk, metaphorically. To stop seeing the detail and the bigger picture, so immersed were they in the mundane.

"Got him!" Melissa called out, breaking him out of another session trawling the metal forums for mention of an obscure Edinburgh band called Omega.

She appeared at the door of his office, a proud smile painted across her face. Melissa never could manage cool. But Mac smiled back, never quite managing not to when she looked like that.

"ID?" he queried.

She nodded. "Finally got a senior manager at Lothian Social Services to commit to a straight answer. God, as a bureaucracy, they put us to shame!"

Mac stood, scooping his jacket from the back of his chair. Since moving into his new office, he'd made it more amenable to himself. The litter was gone and the desk and computer clinically sanitized. He'd waited until the team was gone before doing that himself, having already banned the contracted cleaners from the office until the investigation was over. Leaks were to be avoided in all cases, but particularly one as nasty as this. Coppers were leaky enough on their own without throwing in underpaid civilians with inadequate background checks.

He followed her out. Kai and Nari were on calls, following up on statements taken at Bute Tower, looking to build a network of people who might have known the victim and his movements. He shrugged his jacket on as Melissa grabbed hers. There was a rapport between them that Mac didn't quite have yet with the other two younger officers. Melissa knew that telling her boss she'd got someone to ID a victim meant heading out to meet them and see the ID in person. Mac liked to see the reactions, look a witness in the eye when he asked about his victim. Melissa knew that and also knew she'd be going along. Mac didn't even pause as he walked between the rows of desks towards the door. Melissa followed, hurrying to keep up with Mac's long-legged stride.

"So, who've we got?" Mac asked.

"A caseworker, but not from social services. The manager I spoke to, a guy called Martin Stapleton, put me onto an addiction charity they work with. Said one of their caseworkers would be able to identify Richard McCullough, if that's who our victim is."

Mac sighed as he pushed through the office's double doors and strode along the corridor. Uniformed officers got out of the way as he led Melissa past interview rooms and down a set of stairs to the ground floor.

"That chimes with the tox screen from the postmortem. He was a user," he said.

"Looks almost certain. Either an active user or recently in recovery. Why so glum, guv?"

Mac looked about and lowered his voice.

"Drugs mean Hance Allen and zero chance of closure. If this is Allen, we'll have to fight our own side as much as his to get anywhere."

"But there's still the mutilation. If that is symbolic..." Melissa speculated.

"Then we might be onto something. Here's hoping," Mac replied. "You drive," he told Melissa. "If we get a positive ID, I've got an idea where to go to find out more about his associates."

They left the station through a fire door that led out past the bins and along a narrow brick alley between buildings. It was a quick route to the car park without having to go out the front and around the building.

"What's that then, guv?" Melissa asked, already pulling up the address they were heading for on her phone.

"The best record shop in the east of Scotland," Mac said. "Though I'll have to grovel. I didn't exactly end things well with the proprietor."

"End things?" Melissa asked with a ghost of a smile.

Mac grimaced, reaching Melissa's hatchback as she clicked it open.

"That's all you're getting. Call it the excitement of making some progress getting the better of me," he replied.

Melissa laughed. "Consider it filed under discuss later with Nari and Kai."

"You're fired," Mac said, deadpan as he got into the car.

Melissa had arranged to meet the charity worker at the hospital mortuary where the body was being kept on ice. The post mortem had told them what was obvious at first sight. Death through catastrophic blood loss as a result of stab wounds. The remnants of an opiate in his system strong enough that it wasn't the kind obtained with a prescription. No food in the last twenty-four hours. Signs consistent with fasting, probably not intentional. Just the self-neglect of a drug user. They headed for Morningside, with its yellow sandstone edged in black from the traffic fumes. Old buildings and green spaces. Lawyers, accountants, private dentists, and places with royal in the title. Like the Royal Edinburgh hospital, whose mortuary held the body of who they assumed was Richard McCullough. After flashing the badge to access staff parking and enter via a discrete rear door, they made their way into the bowels of the sprawling building.

Floors were tiled and smelled of disinfectant. Doors had no handles but swung in both directions at a shove of the shoulder, or a trolley. Mac thrust hands deep into pockets, feeling the unpleasant organic nature of the place. A place where bodies were reduced to tissue and fluid, which was then sluiced away. Outside one of the pathology labs was a bench seat and on it a man who sat with hands on knees and an expression that said he wanted to run. He had a pockmarked face, pinched and hard but with startling blue eyes. His hair was a faint gold fuzz, and he wore jeans and a t-shirt.

"Mr. Darren Cluny?" Melissa asked, like a friendly HR manager greeting a job applicant.

"Aye," Cluny said, standing and wiping his hands on his jeans before grasping the handshake Melissa offered.

She introduced Mac, who nodded curtly.

"I've done this a few times. Never really get used to it," Cluny said, licking his lips.

"It's just like ripping off a plaster. One quick tug," Mac said.

"Aye, I'm hoping it's not Richie. Really hope it's not," Cluny said,

"Why's that?" Melissa asked.

She stood just to one side; drawing Cluny's eyes to her while Mac observed his reactions.

"I thought I was getting through to him. It was early days, but he'd hit rock bottom, you know?"

"How so?" Melissa asked.

"He was in a band, but they split up when the singer died. Suicide. Richie blamed himself. Said he should have done something about it but was too wrapped up in his own world to notice how desperate his mate had got. The guy had been his best friend since school."

"Let's get this over with, shall we?" Mac said.

He led the way through the double doors and into the lab.

81

A body lay covered in a white sheet on a metal table, hideous in its suggestive shape. A lab assistant in a white coat stood by the head, ready to do the honours. Mac stepped aside as Cluny approached with trepidation. The white sheet was pulled back and Cluny turned the same colour. He stared and then looked away, nodding.

"That's him. Richie McCullough."

He got himself out of that room quickly, almost running. Mac nodded to Melissa, who went after him as he stopped by the lifts, one hand to his mouth, the other wrapped around his midriff. Mac took out his phone as Melissa put a hand on Cluny's back and spoke to him softly. He searched for a number and dialled. A man answered.

"Raid the Grave," he said.

"Hi Von, it's Callum," Mac said. "She in?"

"Hey, Callum, my man!" Von replied, American accent becoming obvious. "Where you been, buddy?"

"Around. She in?"

"I wouldn't be talking to you if she was. You did a number on her, man."

"Not intentionally, Von."

"She didn't see it that way. She stepped out for a coffee. Be back in…"

"Listen, I need some info. You up to looking into her file for me?"

Before Von could answer, there came the sound of a door and a female voice in the background, though Mac couldn't make out what was said. Then it became very clear.

"You want something? Come and ask me for it," she said, then hung up.

Mac sighed. Melissa was walking back, making notes on her own phone. Cluny was gone, the lift ascending.

"Not much that we hadn't already surmised, guv. He didn't know McCullough all that well. Said he had an interest in paganism, though. He wasn't aware of the name for it, by the way, that came from me. Just said that McCullough used it like a crutch to get him through the addiction. You know, like some people turn to Jesus. He was all about the old gods. That was a quote from something McCullough said once; 'The old gods were watching.'"

Mac nodded, seeing the inscriptions on the walls of the building and carved into the flesh of Richard McCullough. Thought about how long ago it had been since people followed that kind of religion in this part of Scotland. Edinburgh was old, he knew that. He was sure the Castle wasn't even the oldest part. That it was built on something even more ancient. Suddenly, he wished for something as simple as a dealer murdering a junkie who couldn't pay.

"Let's get back to the station. Then I want you to find a next of kin. Check in with Kai and Nari. I'm going to do some research of my own, see if I can't track down his bandmates," Mac said.

CHAPTER THIRTEEN

AN HOUR LATER Mac was in his own car, heading north towards the heart of the city, the Old Town. The traffic was crawling and so were the pedestrians, roads and pavements clogged. While waiting in a backed up queue at lights, Mac noticed the black Volvo. It had caught his eye a few hundred yards back, closing up to him rather than letting another car out of a junction. Initially, it was a blip on his internal radar, a new-looking saloon car that had been behind him at two different sets of traffic lights. At first, he dismissed it. Noticed it again three cars back as he drove along Nicholson Street towards South Bridge. Then he caught them turning left behind him, seemingly going their own way. But he clocked the driver looking at him instead of the direction the car was going.

Short fair hair, sunglasses even though it looked like rain, white shirt with long sleeves. The car reappeared as he was approaching the university, joining ahead of him. A passenger turned to look back over his shoulder. Mac grinned and lifted his fingers off the steering wheel to give them a wave. If they were following him, they weren't much good. He took his phone from his pocket and snapped a picture of the registration. Then he cut across traffic without indicating, earning an angry blast from an oncoming bus. He put his foot down as he drove down the middle of Infirmary Street. Parked cars to either side reduced it to a single lane. A brief glimpse of a fair head turned suddenly, as though the driver of the car in front had just spotted his manoeuvre.

Tan buildings of great antiquity rushed by and a man and woman with backpacks jumped back as they peeked from behind a parked car. He braked just in time for the right-angle turn onto High School Wynd. The city was constricting around him; the buildings getting taller, the streets narrower. He felt claustrophobic as the cobbled lane descended towards Cowgate and the murky sky retreated. Whoever was following him could either do a U-turn in the middle of the street or drive along for another quarter of a mile before they could turn around. That close to the High Street, the traffic would stick to them like tar, and Mac could be anywhere by the time they got back to where they had lost him. He turned left onto Cowgate, heading back towards South Bridge, which crossed Cowgate twenty feet above. Just before the bridge, he turned into a cobbled close barely wide enough for the Audi. Twenty yards along was a car park belonging to a pub. A light drizzle spattered the windscreen. Beyond it was a black wall of slick stone covered with ivy.

Weeds fought for air through gaps in the cracked concrete. A bold sign visible in his rear-view mirror proclaimed *Live Football*. Mac took out his phone, breathing hard. Partly it was exhilaration, partly it was anger. If these people were AC, then what would be their purpose in none too covertly observing him? Was this to do with a serious assault back on Skye he'd never been nicked for? Or something to do with his past association with Laird Strachan? Strachan had slipped through AC's fingers by dint of the fact that he'd thrown himself from the balcony of a tower block. He took out the phone and called Kai.

"Guv?"

"Busy?"

"No, not really..."

"Well, you should be. I am. I need you to check ANPR for a reg."

He snapped out the plate number, pulling up the picture on his phone. Kai went quiet as he accessed the national Automatic Number Plate Recognition database. Mac heard typing and watched the rain gradually obscure the back alley car park. It was getting heavier, beginning to drum on the roof of the car.

"Got it. One of ours. Hold on; let me check it against the police vehicle's register. It's registered to an AC unit, guv."

Mac nodded to himself grimly and hung up. Reid had heard right. AC were sniffing around, but the fact that he was being followed didn't tell Mac who their target was. It could still be either him or Reid. His boss was far from lily white despite his years as an Anti-Corruption Detective Chief Inspector. Mac had served under him there after helping in Operation Archer that had taken down several high ranking but corrupt officers. Laird Strachan had been amongst them. Mac had been lucky to get out of Strack's orbit just in time.

But as far as AC was concerned, a dirty copper was never clean. No matter what he did. No matter what he achieved. Mac sat for a while, brooding. Now two of his team would link him to AC, Nari, and Kai. He would have to speak to both of them or the trust would be lost. Better to transfer them off the team at that point.

He opened the car door and kicked it wide, then slammed it shut with his heel. This wasn't what he needed right now. The McCullough case was shaping up to be a complex one. An itch at the back of his mind told him it wouldn't be the last time he'd be tailed. If he'd been suspended pending an AC investigation before being assigned the case, couldn't care less. Do your worst. But to be suspended now that he had his teeth into it. That was pure torture. It riled him. The knowledge that he had snapped at those closest to him, his team, riled him even more. They didn't deserve it. He stalked up the hill, hunching his shoulders against the rain. Hands dug deep into his pockets. He stopped at a black door. A sign above proclaimed *Raid the Grave,* but apart from that, there was no indication of the nature of the property within. He pushed open the door. Inside was a hallway just large enough that his shoulders brushed both walls. A dank courtyard beyond was surrounded on all sides by brick walls, barred windows and a rusty metal staircase descending from a second-floor fire door. To his left was a door with a glass panel in its upper half and a sign hanging from a plastic sucker saying *Open* in gothic script.

Beyond was Mecca. *Raid the Grave* was a record shop, home to an independent label and to Evie Black. No sign of her only staff member, Von Parker, a hulking Texan. Evie glanced up from behind a till opposite the door. Something wet and visceral was playing loud, vocals inhuman and growling. The space between the door and the till was taken up by boxes on trestle tables, packed with vinyl, cds and tapes. Posters covered every inch of the walls and windows. Natural light was an enemy. Evie was reading a book, but lowered it when she saw Mac. She watched him with long-lashed, dark eyes that Mac remembered so well. There was a time those eyes had been hard to look away from.

"Hi, Evie," Mac said, trying for casual.

Evie raised an eyebrow. "Who said you could come back in here?"

"I'm a paying customer," Mac said with his best boyish grin.

It was the kind of smile that women of a certain age fell for. Evie wasn't that age.

"I reserve the right to refuse service."

Mac grunted non-committally, circling the tables and approaching the till. She was in her thirties with short, spiky black hair. A round face that would have looked innocent had it not been for the black eyeliner and matching lipstick. Instead, it looked knowing and sultry. Piercings studded her nose and one eyebrow. White scars crisscrossed her forearms and were displayed without shame. Her t-shirt was printed with an obscene publication and showed a good portion of midriff. When he approached, she put down the book and folded hands covered in rings over knees covered in fishnets.

"I finished my community service order last month," she said.

"That wasn't my fault," Mac protested.

"I get busted a week after getting dumped by a cop?" Evie said, dripping with sarcasm.

"Coincidence. I'm not in the drug squad. And I didn't think I dumped you."

She stood up from the stool she'd been sitting on, planted her hands on the counter.

"What would you call it?"

"I didn't think it was that serious between us," Mac said.

"You didn't give it a chance."

"I didn't know either one of us wanted to give it a chance," Mac replied.

He was at the counter now too, refusing to back down and only half believing that Evie didn't have a right to be angry. He meant what he had said, but knew he could have handled it better. At the time, the wound left by Siobhan was fresh and Evie had always shown an interest. He'd stopped it when he realised he was using her as a crutch.

"If you treat a regular like this, I'd like to see how you treat strangers," Mac attempted levity but got a black stare.

Evie sniffed and resumed her seat and her previous activity.

"I'm busy. You want to buy something, get stuck in. You want advice on what to buy, Google it."

"Neither. I want to pick your brains."

"Buy something then."

He suppressed a sigh that he knew would start a fight. Once upon a time, he and Evie had been able to pass half an hour talking about music. Two people who didn't like people enjoying each other's company. That was well and truly gone. The bridge nuked, and the ashes scattered. He turned away, flicked rapidly through one of the boxes and came out with three EPs. He put them on the counter and took out his phone.

"Contactless?"

"Yep," Evie said, giving nothing back.

She fished out a small white card reader and put it on the counter, typing in a pin and the amount. She pushed it towards Mac. He paid with his phone.

"There used to be a band called Omega. Local boys, I think. You remember them?"

"What have they done?"

"Disbanded, but I'm trying to find their names. I know one of them, Richard McCullough."

Evie arched an eyebrow. "Probably shouldn't be helping the fuzz. Doubtless you're trying to fit them up for something. Polis!" she made the last word sound like an expletive.

"Don't even know them or I wouldn't be asking. Their entry's been deleted from Encyclopedia Extreme, pretty sure there used to be one. And you know almost as much about the underground as I do."

Mac was playing to the vanity of someone who prided themselves on their esoteric knowledge. As psychology went, it was pretty blatant and Evie was smart enough to know that. But that didn't mean she had the will not to want to prove her superior knowledge.

She gave Mac a disparaging look and turned away, showing a skirt that barely covered her backside. Mac looked and Evie, looking back over her shoulder, caught him looking. He met her eyes and steadfastly refused to stop looking. Evie went through a curtain of beads hanging in a doorway behind her. She came back with an A4 sized notepad. The pages were crinkled and stiff, covered in scrawled notes. She started turning pages, dark eyes occasionally flicking up to Mac. By the time she found the entry she was looking for, there was the ghost of a smile tugging at the corner of her mouth.

"Omega. Rich McCullough, guitars. Jacek Andrysiak, drums, Gaunt on vocals..."

"Gaunt! That's it!" Mac said as the name he hadn't been able to remember clicked back into his mind. "You have a real name for Gaunt in your wee bible there?"

She snapped the notepad shut. "Nope. Band is no longer active and haven't been for a long while. Something bad happened to one of them. Overdose or something. I don't know. Gaunt moved on. Went abroad somewhere. Down under last I heard. Lots of conspiracies about them. Always are with black maniacs, if they're doing it properly."

Evie's eyes flicked up and down Mac's slim figure, back to his face. The full lips tugged upwards more, briefly. She bit her lower lip.

"Sorry," she said.

"What for?" Mac replied.

"For being rude. You know, you don't look like polis. You never did."

"What do polis look like?" Mac asked.

"Old men with a beer belly and a suit from Asda. Or young tossers in uniform with Napoleon complexes." Evie replied.

Mac smiled, looking into his suit jacket as though checking the label.

"Good deals from George these days," he said.

"Nah. That suit fits you far too well," Evie said, eyes flicking up and down Mac for at least the second time.

Mac held her eyes for a long moment. She was attractive and part of the attraction was the fact that she was an outsider. Like him. He was used to attention from women, aware that his propensity for glowering at the world was taken for brooding. He was tall, dark, and silent. Women seemed to like it. For a moment, Mac wanted very much to put aside work and ask this woman out for a coffee. Wanted to talk music again, not murder. Her eyes opened a little wider, lips parted, like she was waiting. Anticipating. But he knew Evie Black. Knew the games she liked to play. Could see the trap coming a mile away.

"Well, thanks for your help," Mac said, turning away.

"Don't forget your records," she called after him.

"Right." he turned back and took them from her.

Her smoky eyes found his and locked on. She took matters into her own hands.

"Not even going to ask me out?" she said with a hint of coquettishness.

"No," Mac said as he left the shop without looking back.

CHAPTER FOURTEEN

THE RAIN HAD PASSED OVER. Leaving the shop, Mac tossed the three randomly selected records onto the passenger seat of the Audi. A traffic warden was walking up the cobbled hill of Robertson's Close towards South Bridge. He looked over at where Mac was parked. Mac folded his arms and stared back. The man hurried his stride. Mac's phone vibrated in his suit pocket and he leaned against the wet car as he took it out.

"Mel," he answered.

Evie Black had moved aside a corner of a poster and was looking out of the shop window.

"I took a call from the University. A Professor by the name of...Clio Wray. You put in a call to the Dean, did you?" Mel said.

"I wanted an expert to look over the graffiti at the site and a transcription of the mutilations. I asked her to provide an expert in Celtic language or whatever."

"Well, Professor Wray is keen to help. Want me to ask her to come in?"

"Is she at the University now?"

"I assume so. Said her office was Old Moray House."

"That's not far from where I'm standing. Call her and tell her I'll come to her."

Mac hung up, still looking towards the window of Raid the Grave. He thought of Siobhan and felt guilty. It annoyed him. He spun through a search of his last calls and came up with the number of the shop. Let it ring a few times as he locked the car and walked away. The landline handset had been right next to the till, so Evie was playing her own game in not answering. Mac hung up, putting his phone away as he turned onto Cowgate, heading towards Holyrood Road.

Old Moray House wasn't far, and Mac wanted to walk. In his pocket, he felt his phone buzz with a brief notification. There had been long enough since his hang-up for Evie to check the missed call and then text the number. He didn't look to see what she'd said. He could wait. The Old Town crowded him, pavements multi-coloured with tourists wearing Day-Glo cagoules and carrying umbrellas. Students were the other main traffic, moving in groups that laughed and talked as loudly as the tourists or solitary, headphones locking them away from the world.

Cutting down Gullan's Close, he had to turn sideways to let two young girls in ripped jeans get past him. University buildings loomed to either side, the newer buildings crisp and clean in sandstone tan. The older buildings had all the wrong tones of green and brown from the traffic fumes that ate at facades not meant to be subjected to acid. He turned over the developing facts in his mind as he walked, head down, hands in pockets. A drugs connection. Reid would want that pushed hard. The Police and Crime Commissioner would be pushing him in turn. The press went crazy for gangland deaths and being seen to be tough on the trade made for easy political points. Mac wished McCullough hadn't been an addict. It would have left him without a motive, but he could do without the political pressure. He would have to take steps to investigate. That meant bringing in Chaz Pollock, who was already lawyered up. It was a mess and wouldn't get any neater. On the other hand, the Celtic angle was opaque but interesting. It occurred to him as he headed towards Canongate along the narrow close it wouldn't be sensible to show a probably elderly academic crime scene pictures. He reached for his phone, swiping the screen awake, and stopped. The buzz hadn't been from Evie Black. It was from Siobhan.

Call me please

His mind was full of bloody Celtic imagery, a body with savage stab wounds. It spun at three words from a woman he hadn't spoken to in three months. Was she still at her mum's in Corstorphine? That wizened old witch who had never liked him because police work kept him away from her daughter and granddaughter when they needed him. Was Siobhan regretting ending it? His first instinct was to call her, to arrange to meet. Surely, she wouldn't text if she didn't want to meet. Not with such urgency. Then the city caught up with him. A commotion up ahead, raised voices, a man, and a woman. The policeman took over. Mac walked along the close, wet, mildewed stone almost brushing his shoulders. A block of flats, probably student accommodation, rose beyond the wall on one side. An older building, slate roofed and gaunt, rose to the other side. The close kinked to the left and as he turned the corner he saw a man, hood over his head and mask covering his face.

He was wrestling for a bag with a girl. She wore yoga pants that showed every freckle and a baggy t-shirt. Her hair was long and dark. She clung to the bag tenaciously until the man shoved at her and she hit the wall, losing her grip. He took off running. Mac didn't waste his breath on shouting for him to stop. He was at a dead run within two steps, phone still clutched in one hand, forgotten. The sound of running footsteps was loud in the confined space.

"Mikey!" someone called urgently.

The hood turned and Mac saw the mask had a skull design on it, white bones on black. The kind of fashion accessory that didn't exist before the pandemic. Now it was everywhere. Eyes went wide above the mask. They lingered on Mac for a second too long. An uneven cobblestone caught his foot, and he stumbled, came down hard on one knee. Mac closed the distance, grabbed for the baggy hoody the mugger was wearing. The man turned and lashed out with his right hand. There was something hard and heavy in it which caught Mac across the temple and blanked his sight to white. When his vision returned, the man was running down an even narrower close that intersected Gullan's Close and ran parallel to Canongate. Mac knew it was a dead end. Standing, he touched his right temple. His fingers came away bloody, and he swore.

He was still swearing as he followed the mugger into the narrow lane, unbuttoning his jacket as he went. The sound of running footsteps came to him from behind and when he looked he saw the woman, girl really, standing with mouth open as though about to shout. The hooded menace was coming back. He'd reached the end of the lane and realised there was no way out. The walls were high to either side and at the end was a gate with inward turned prongs at the top. The University of Edinburgh didn't like trespassers. Mac saw a heaving chest, wide, wild eyes. He stood between the mugger and freedom. The girl stood behind him, which meant Mac also stood between her and harm. Either way, he wasn't for moving.

"I'm a copper. Don't be an idiot, son. You're in enough trouble," Mac said, stopping.

The man kept moving slowly, but Mac saw the eyes go wider for an instant then narrow; the arms move out from his sides. The bag was dropped. The moron was getting ready to rush him. When it came, though, Mac was ready. He ducked and took the charge on the shoulder, hearing the wind rushing from the man as his own speed drove the air from his lungs. Mac stood while simultaneously jerking his head up. He felt the man's teeth snap shut as the back of his head caught the underside of the mugger's jaw. Mac held onto the front of the hoody and felt the body weight sliding backwards, held him up long enough to bring a fist into his side. Then, letting him go, Mac brought up a knee which connected neatly with a temple. All over in a few seconds. Nothing elegant. Dirty, grunting street fighting and Mac had learned to do it with the savagery of a wild animal almost before he could talk.

He stood back, breathing heavily between teeth clenched in rage. The man was groaning, stirring on the wet ground.

Mac reached for his phone, having replaced it in his pocket when he had followed the mugger into the lane. When he took it out, he saw the extra damage, a crack going from one corner to the next and a multi-colored blaze of pixelated static. He stabbed at it, but it didn't respond. Then something heavy and hard connected with the back of his head, knocking him to his knees. The girl stood behind him, her bag held in both hands by the straps. Mac stared at her in disbelief as she went to the aid of her own mugger.

"Come on, Mikey!" she said urgently.

"Hey! I'm a police officer!" Mac bellowed.

"You're on camera. Police brutality!" the girl retorted, holding up her own phone.

"I was trying to help you," Mac said.

"I didn't ask for your help, pig," she said as she ran away, her boyfriend, for that's clearly who he was, staggering beside her.

Mac swore loudly and profusely. He picked himself up, wincing at the pain in his head, dabbing at the blood from his temple. His suit was stained with water and unmentionable substances. The phone was thrown against a wall to explode into crystal shards and he stalked out of the lane. For a moment, he considered retracing his steps to the car. But it would take longer than it would to go to Old Moray House on foot. Siobhan came back into his mind, but he pushed the thought of her aside. He couldn't speak to her now. Not until he got a new phone. He also couldn't show this old prof the pictures either, they were on his phone. As he emerged onto Canongate, heading east towards Holyrood, the locals studiously ignored him. The tourists looked, but not for long.

No-one was keen to meet his eyes. And everyone, bar none, gave him a wide-berth.

There was a modern intercom system on one of the conical stone gate posts. A door set beside it. He saw the name *Prof. C. Wray* and hit the buzzer. A youthful voice answered.

"Yes?"

"DCI McNeill, police. I believe my office called ahead," Mac said.

"Yes, come on up. First door on your left, up the stairs. I'm on the first floor landing," Clio replied.

The door clicked and Mac pushed it open.

CHAPTER FIFTEEN

"OH, MY GOD what happened to you!" was Clio's greeting to Mac as he opened the door of her office.

He immediately regretted his decision to keep this appointment. But, without a phone to let Professor Wray know why he was cancelling, it risked putting her back up. And who knew when the next gap in her diary might be, even for a police investigation? He was looking down when he stepped into the office, self-conscious of the state of his clothes and his face. When he looked up from under his brows, he stopped. Clio was not what he had expected. She was early forties, attractive, a strong jaw outlining round cheeks and dark blue eyes. Very attractive. She was up out of her seat and crossing the room to him, a matter of a couple of short strides in the tight space, snagging a wooden chair as she went. It was the folding kind with a cushion tied to the back. Mac noticed the odd detail; it just seemed out of place in a university.

"A mugging," he said, rummaging for his warrant card. "I'm…"

"DCI McNeill, I presume?" Clio said, sitting back on a corner of her desk and dislodging a pile of papers.

She jumped up, trying to catch the cascade, but didn't manage it. She had a good bum, Mac noticed, perfectly shown off by a pair of tight fitting black jeans. He caught the hint of ink in the small of her back where her jumper and the t-shirt beneath rode up slightly. He looked away before she turned back, struggling with an armful of paper.

"Sorry, bit disorganised. I'm an academic, after all. There's a reason for the stereotype of the mad professor," she said, grinning.

Mac found himself disarmed by that smile. It was cheeky and carefree. Combined with the poky, cold office, and sense of barely controlled chaos, it lent Professor Wray a sense of vulnerability which was in contrast to her confident manner.

"Who would dare mug a police officer?" she asked, putting down the papers and sitting behind her desk.

"The victim," Mac commented, then waved a hand as though to dismiss the comment. "It doesn't matter. I apologise for turning up looking like I've been pummelled through a hedge. My phone is out of order and I couldn't call ahead to cancel."

"That's alright," Clio said. "A bit of drama to take the edge of a day spent marking. I'll never say no to a bit of excitement."

The disarming smile came again. Mac wondered if she knew she was doing it, if she did it deliberately. That was the kind of thought only a copper had. Cynical and paranoid.

He'd only just met the woman. Maybe that crack on his head had done some damage.

"I'm afraid I'm not prepared for the meeting I wanted to have with you. I had planned to show you some images of what we believe are a series of Celtic inscriptions," Mac said, trying to regain control of the situation, putting on his best senior officer voice.

"Yes, Karen mentioned something about that. A crime scene were the words she used, I think?"

"Right. That would be Doctor Karen Martins?" Mac asked, taking out his notebook and a pencil, flipping through to the page where he had noted the details.

"Yes. Wow, I didn't think a modern policeman would use one of those. I thought it would be all phones and apps these days," Clio said.

"I tried it and then my phone ran out of charge right before I was due to use it to give evidence in court. Once bitten, eh?" Mac said wryly.

Clio laughed. "Oh no. Did that really happen?"

"God's witness," Mac said gravely, hand on heart. "How much did Doctor Martins tell you about the help I needed?"

Mac's eye was drawn to a corner of paper sticking out of the pile that had fallen to the floor. It was a printout of a photograph. He could see reds in various shades and some dark lines, curved and hooked. Without letting his gaze linger on the paper for too long, he looked at his notepad, sketching the shapes he had glimpsed but without letting on what he was doing. Something about those shapes was familiar.

"Exactly that. Some inscriptions at a crime scene that require translation," she said.

"Right," Mac replied, watching Clio closely now.

She sat with hands folded in front of her and looked back. But her interlaced thumbs fidgeted, moving back and forth.

"I didn't mention the word translation in my email or when I spoke to your boss. Where did that come from?" Mac said.

Clio's mouth opened and she sat back. It shut again, and she looked at her closed laptop, drummed her fingers on the top.

"What else would you want an academic to do with ancient inscriptions?" she said.

Mac smiled. "I suppose so."

Instinct was making the hairs on the back of his neck stand up. This cute professor with a hint of a Yorkshire accent was hiding something.

"Would it be possible to get a cup of coffee or tea?" Mac asked. The oldest trick in the book, but he wanted to sneak a look at the pile of papers, needed Clio out of the office to do it.

Her eyes danced to the page he had noticed. Colour flooded her face, and she picked up the stack, shuffled it and placed it on the other side of the desk, screened from sight by a pile of books.

"I'm afraid our budget doesn't stretch to a coffee machine," she said. "And the kettle in the kitchen is broken," she added, utterly failing to sound convincing.

Mac closed the notebook and gave Clio a long, level look.

"Would you like to tell me why you're suddenly so jumpy and what you're hiding from me in that pile of papers?" he said.

For a moment, he thought she was going to brazen it out. It wouldn't be difficult. Mac couldn't initiate a search without a reason and forcing Clio to show him the papers would constitute a search, unless she handed them over freely. But not everyone knew that. Sometimes people just assumed that a police officer had to be obeyed at all times. Not often and not among the criminal fraternity. But it was always worth a shot. Clio collapsed like a pricked balloon. She pulled out a sheaf of papers, handing them over and covering her face.

"I'm in so much trouble if Karen finds out about this. I've probably broken the law as well but, I needed the money."

Mac hid the excitement he felt. The images on the papers were so close to the crime scene that was plastered across the walls of his team's office that they could almost be from the same place. Inscriptions of circles and horizontal lines, some scored through vertically. Carved into flesh. Clotted blood, dark and lined in brighter red. Hacked into an arm. Mac frowned. The wrist in the picture had been cut vertically. Richard Mc-Cullough's wrists hadn't been cut. This looked like a suicide.

"Where did you get these?" he asked, flipping through the papers.

He came to an image of inscriptions daubed across a wall; the blood dribbling down towards the floor, making the inscriptions hard to pick out. In the top corner of the image was a white square, or at least one corner of it. Mac squinted. It looked like a canvas. This was too much. Too lucky. Too much of a coincidence. The universe just didn't treat coppers like this. Clio was hesitating, and Mac looked up. Something in his eyes made her push herself back from the desk until she bumped into the wall. She licked her lips.

"A journalist asked me to do the same thing that you want me to do. Look at some pictures of what he claimed were Celtic or Pictish inscriptions and translate them."

"This is a crime scene," Mac said flatly.

"It's a suicide," Clio replied, a touch defensively.

"How the hell do you know?"

"Hey! I didn't take them. I was given them. And I know it's a suicide because I know who's in the picture."

"And?" Mac prompted.

"His name is Alex Martins. He's Karen's son. Was, Karen's son."

She was beginning to look distressed and Mac realised he may have played the detective too hard. He needed this woman to be talking freely and without fear of consequences. A law might have been broken in the obtaining of these pictures, but he didn't care. He wanted the person who took them.

"Clio. Is it OK if I call you Clio?" Mac said.

Clio nodded curtly, lips compressed. Which was a shame because she had full lips that looked very sexy. But not when she was scared, evidently.

"Clio, you're not in any trouble. This all just took me by surprise. I have crime scene pictures and they're very similar to this. Do you see why I would be so keen to know where you got them?"

"Yes, yes," Clio said finally. "Look, I lied...the kettle is working fine. Do you still want a coffee? I could do with one."

Mac laughed. It was genuine and heartfelt, and it brought a smile to Clio's face. Sudden footsteps on rickety wood sounded outside the door. Clio was out of her seat, practically vaulting across the desk in a second, snatching the pictures out of Mac's hands. The footsteps went up the stairs without stopping, fading away along the corridor above. Clio breathed a sigh of relief and then overbalanced. She had been holding herself up with one hand, the other grabbing for the papers. Now, she fell forward and directly into Mac. He dropped the papers and caught her as she tumbled, ending up with her across his lap and looking up at him. Their faces were inches apart and Mac's hand had landed, completely accidentally, on her right breast. When he realised, he snatched his hands away as though burned, and Clio tumbled to the floor. He shot out of his chair and stooped to try and help her up, just as she tried to get herself up. Their heads came together with a re-sounding smack.

Mac sat down again sharply, holding his forehead as Clio leaned against the leg of her desk in an identical posture. For a moment, they looked at each other and then both burst out laughing.

"I hate this room!" Clio cried. "And if Karen finds out I took these pictures from that journalist, she'll sack me."

"She won't find out from me. I'm parked not far from here. Bring this stuff and we can go somewhere less..."

"Public?" Clio said, reaching out for a hand up.

"I was going to say claustrophobic," Mac replied, pulling her up. And messy, he said to himself.

CHAPTER SIXTEEN

CLIO PUT HER PAPERS into a large holdall she produced from under the desk, removing some clothing from it first. Mac noticed shorts and a t-shirt. She added her laptop onto the pile and then zipped up the bag and slung it over her shoulder. She led the way out, back down the stairs. A woman was just letting herself into the building and she looked up. Mac noted dark hair and pale skin, older than she looked and not bad looking at that.

"Hi Karen!" Clio said brightly. "This is DCI McNeill. I said I would accompany him to the station to help with his investigation."

Karen looked past Clio to Mac, who smiled disarmingly.

"Thank you for volunteering your staff for this Doctor Martins," Mac said, guessing that the woman was the Doctor Karen Martins he had exchanged emails with. The same Karen Martins whose son was the gruesome subject of the pictures in Clio's bag. And somehow linked to the death of Richard McCullough. Maybe.

"I didn't realise it would involve official questioning," Karen said, eyes direct and unafraid.

"No, it's nothing like that. The material we need help with is highly sensitive. I'd rather Professor Wray reviewed it in person," Mac said. "We won't keep her long."

Karen Martins pursed her lips as she stepped aside to let the two out of the narrow door behind her.

"Can you give me any more information about the nature of your inquiry?" Karen asked.

"I'm afraid not. But your faculty's help is much appreciated," Mac replied, stepping out of the door.

"I would offer to help myself, but I'm afraid my schedule just won't allow it," Karen replied.

Mac gave a polite smile, wondering what kind of academic schedule rated more important than helping with an official police inquiry. Maybe the suicide of her son was still too fresh in her mind. He hadn't volunteered the nature of the crime scene, only that he needed an expert in Celtic symbolism. But if the same kind of symbolism was present at the scene of Alex Martins' death, that might mean it was too close for comfort.

"I'm sure Professor Wray is also an expert in her field. She'll do fine."

"She is. Almost as much as me," Karen replied, smiling tightly. "But like I said. Schedules. Don't keep her too long, Inspector."

With that, Karen Martins strode away and Mac heard her clattering up the stairs as the door swung shut. For a moment, he stood, pondering the exchange. Then he turned away and caught up with Clio. They retraced his steps through the out-skirts of the Old Town to the car park where he had left his car. Clio kept up a stream of semi-interesting narrative on the history of the district and the older buildings they passed. Mac was content to let her, wanting to delay getting into specifics of the case until they were somewhere more secure. As they arrived at the car, there was no sign of Evie in the window as he looked up towards the shop. Clio picked up the records as she opened the passenger door. The cover art was brightly col-ored and highly lurid. Mac took them from her and tossed them into the back.

"Your taste or a teenage son?" Clio asked, getting in.

"You have to be a boy to appreciate metal?" Mac asked.

Clio flushed. "That was inexcusably chauvinistic of me. Sorry. Unconscious bias and all that."

"They're mine, impulse purchase," Mac said.

"I'm the same, but it's vintage maps with me," Clio said.

Mac wasn't looking to further the small talk, but this drew his attention. The idea appealed to him in a way he couldn't really explain.

"What sort of maps, like ordinance survey?" he asked.

"Maybe, but my primary interest is a lot earlier than the 1800s. I had my eye on a reproduction of a medieval map dat-ing from about the 1400s. More of a piece of speculative art than an example of cartography. It had ley lines marked on it and covered this part of Scotland."

"Ley lines?" Mac asked.

"Lines of power occurring in nature. Believed to run from specific foci, like Stone Henge, for example. Castle Rock here in Edinburgh would be another. Not science as such, so I don't exactly make a big thing about it. But I have an open mind to most things. Anyway, I couldn't tell you more about that particular piece because I was pipped at the post. I had it reserved and everything and someone came in and offered the dealer twice the price." Clio grimaced and shrugged. "Probably too much to spend on something frivolous when you've got a tween in the house, anyway."

Mac decided to end the small talk, putting aside his own interests, dismissing it as an attraction to Clio herself. His bloody libido had had a mind of its own since Siobhan had left. He turned in his seat to face her, leaning on the armrest of the driver's seat. He laced his fingers together and looked at her frankly.

"Could you tell me now about the journalist and how he came by those pictures?"

Clio told him all she knew about Ramsay Jones. Mac made rapid notes, adding his own questions as they occurred. Questions that Clio wasn't in a position to answer. Like how Jones had got hold of police photographs of a suicide scene in the first place, because that's what they had to be. No-one else would go into a blood-soaked room containing a mutilated corpse and stop to take pictures. Clio showed him all the pictures she had printed off and those on her laptop. Alex Martins had been scarred in a similar way to Richard McCullough. The walls had been marked with blood in the same way as the graffiti in Bute Tower's stairwell. Then there were the other pictures. A picture of a tattoo, complex and ornate and unmistakably similar to the inscriptions at his crime scene and Alex Martin's suicide scene.

Another showed graffiti, the underside of a bridge somewhere. Impossible to tell where from the pictures. The side of a building. A road sign.

"He wouldn't go into too much detail," Clio said. "Only that he was working on a story and all the images were linked. He hinted at a theory he had, but wouldn't give me any definitive information. Just wanted to know if this was a language and, if so, what it said."

"Is it?" Mac asked.

"I believe so, yes. Those horizontal and vertical lines are a form of Ogham, which is found in the west of Scotland and Northern Ireland mainly. Those curving symbols are common to this part of the country and can be traced back to pre-Roman Pictish tribes from this area. Both would fall under what you would describe as Celtic."

"I'll need to keep these," Mac told her, shuffling the papers together. "They look like police pictures, so shouldn't be in the public domain."

"But I've taken money to translate them," Clio protested.

"Good. When Ramsay Jones comes to you for your findings, I would like you to contact me," Mac said. "If he owes you any more for your work, I'll let him pay you before I take him in for questioning." He gave her a grin and a wink.

Clio actually blushed. "Do you suspect him of something? You haven't said much about what you wanted me to help you with."

Mac reached to the seat behind Clio and plucked a rucksack from the passenger footwell. He placed the papers in it and zipped it closed.

"I have a murder scene which looks similar to what you've already seen. I don't know that Mr. Jones has done anything, but he's a person of interest now. At least until we've established what he knows about Alex Martins and how he got those pictures."

He started the car's engine. At this point, Clio's help had fallen down the priority list for Mac. The connection between Alex Martins and Richard McCullough had to be established. Their deaths were too similar. Mac wanted to see what records existed for the suicide, who investigated it, what evidence was collected. What the connection was between the two men.

"Are you up for coming to the station to look at the pictures of my crime scene? It's not pretty, so if you'd rather not..."

"I'm not squeamish," Clio said firmly. "And I've come this far. Karen can be a bit of a dragon, but she's a decent person, and she went through hell when Alex died. Ended up in hospital for over a year, and no-one knows why he did it. If there's any way that your case can help shed some light, then I'm in."

There was a determination in her words and a resolute set of her chin that Mac approved of. He couldn't compel her, only appeal to a sense of civic duty or dangle the opportunity for good publicity, whether for an individual career or the reputation of the institution itself. From those three motivations, you could usually find at least one that worked as leverage. But Clio seemed to have some higher ideals. It was refreshing. He nodded.

"Let's get you to the station, then."

"Funny you should have those records. That's the sort of thing Alex was into. I met him a few times. He was a musician, sort of Goth type," Clio said. "Karen played me one of his tapes once. Sounded like a hellish noise to me, but she was proud of him." Mac was reversing out of the space, turning the big car in the narrow lane. But something was resonating within him like a tuning fork. A musician, there was the connection. Funny how life worked sometimes. Trawl through statements and talking to people, get nowhere. Then have a five-minute conversation with a total stranger and find out more about your murder victim than you could discover in a week of investigation.

CHAPTER SEVENTEEN

KAI AND NARI were still out when Mac got back to Niddrie Road. Melissa was there, and Mac introduced her to Clio. But only after he'd assured Melissa he was ok, she'd taken one look at him and become the mum of the office. If he'd let her, she'd have probably sent him home. He had warned Clio before they stepped into the office about the gruesome nature of the pictures. When confronted with blood, gore, splatter, and a lot of red, Clio went a bit pale but seemed to zero in on the in-scriptions. She became distracted, putting down the bag she had carried from the car, followed by her jacket, without really looking where they were going. Mel picked them up off the floor and hung them on the nearest chair. Clio was looking closely at the nearest set of photos taken from the building's stairwell, mouth moving silently. Mac exchanged glances with Melissa, who looked intrigued.

"A couple of messages for you guv," Melissa said. "From

the same number and routed here through the switchboard. A Siobhan McCready?"

Mac remembered the missed call that he couldn't return because his phone had smashed.

"Can you show Professor Wray anything she wants in the context of the symbols? She's going to be our expert," Mac told Melissa.

"Actually, it's Doctor Wray," Clio said without turning round. "But Clio's fine."

Mac walked into his glass walled cubicle, closing the door and then the blinds that covered its upper half.

He picked up the phone on the desk and dialled Siobhan's number by memory. An Irish lilt came onto the line after a few rings.

"Hello?"

"Siobhan! Its Callum," Mac said. "Sorry, I was working. Didn't have a chance to reply."

Now that he had her on the phone, he felt ridiculously nervous. Like a schoolboy. He settled behind his desk, sat back in the chair, and then leaned forward, unable to relax.

"Oh, yeah, that was a while ago, Callum. I'm sorry I was in a panic and..."

"What happened? Is it Áine?" Mac leaped straight to the only thing he could think of that would panic Siobhan.

He had a sinking feeling, which wasn't to do with the thought that Áine might be hurt or in some kind of trouble. Part of him had wanted the message from Siobhan to have been the precursor to a steamy reunion. That she had broken down and been unable to resist him, given in to some fevered fantasy. It had been juvenile. Far more likely that Siobhan needed help and reached out to the only police officer she knew personally, wanting to get that help directly instead of waiting for an overworked, under-resourced force to respond.

"It was. She wasn't at school. I dropped her but the school told me she didn't show up for registration. But we found her now. I'm sorry to bother you..."

She sounded regretful, uncomfortable too. Mac felt a flash of anger but suppressed it. It wasn't her fault he'd got his hopes up. She'd done the right thing. It didn't matter how things had ended between them after three years. If Áine was in danger, he would have been there if it was three in the morning.

"It's OK. Where was she?"

"She and her friend Katie took a bus into town for the day. One of my friends, Phoebe, saw them and called me. Something and nothing."

"It's not like Áine though," Mac said.

"No, she's been acting up since...for the last few months. Probably puberty."

"Right. Want me to talk to her?"

There was a silence at the other end, the hint of a frustrated grunt, then a sigh. He knew the combination well. It always happened when Siobhan was angry and trying to hide it.

"No, I don't think you should talk to her. I don't want to give her any false hope. And if you show up out of the blue..."

Mac felt the bite of frustration, feeling that Siobhan was contradicting herself, deliberately trying to score points.

"You called me. Presumably to help look for her."

"As a policeman. Jesus, Callum!" Siobhan bit back. "It's not the same as you appearing out of nowhere for a heart-to-heart. She's going to think we're getting back together and we're not."

It was emphatic. As emphatic as Siobhan had been the night she'd ended it. Mac felt the same angry resentment, the same helpless sense of injustice. His eyes rose to look out where Clio had taken a photo from the board to lay it on a desk, drawing something on a piece of paper next to it. Melissa was taking down other pictures, seemingly at Clio's direction. Her eyes met Mac's for a moment, the communication unspoken. It looked like Clio was onto something; she was working intently as though she had a definite purpose. The look from Melissa said as much. Too late, Mac realised that Siobhan had finished talking, and he'd tuned out for half of it.

"Are you even listening? I take it you're in the office? You don't have a landline at home. Am I distracting you from work right now?"

There was a very dangerous edge to her voice now. It was sharp enough to do damage and he could hear the crystal fragility in her tone that would break into anger at any moment.

"I am. No, you're not," he replied.

"So, are you going to answer me?" Siobhan demanded.

Mac had no idea what the question had been. His mind had shifted to the case and the possibilities if the bizarre shapes had meaning. A ritual killing perhaps.

"I didn't ask a question, Callum," Siobhan said.

It was worse than anger. Her voice sounded tired, defeated. Mac closed his eyes, gritting his teeth and holding back the anger at Siobhan's games. He was no good at game playing. He couldn't read the signals and it had always infuriated him when an argument seemed to degenerate into traps being laid and points being scored.

"Look, I should have just called 999. I'm sorry I panicked and came to you. It wasn't fair. Bye, Callum."

Mac stayed quiet as the line went dead. He'd wanted to say her name, to make her stay on the phone, but couldn't bring himself to. He wasn't about to reduce himself in that way. She'd left him. With infinite control, he replaced the receiver. For a moment he stared at the computer display on a corner of the desk, showing the Police Scotland logo. Then he pulled the keyboard towards him, stabbed in his credentials and checked his inbox. Emails from Blakely complimenting him on his press briefing and suggesting a follow up, as well as a draft suggestion of a social media message to get the word out there that the police were across everything. A terse message from Reid, wanting to know why he wasn't answering his phone. Mac kept skimming. Post Mortem on Richard Mc-Cullough. Nothing he didn't already know about. Updates from Nari, nobody at Bute Tower was talking. As far as his neighbors were concerned, he never went out, spoke to anyone or did anything. He was a recluse.

He wasn't. Mac knew the signs of witness intimidation. People knew not to talk to the polis. They knew that Chaz Pollock had been spoken to. Knew he was protected and no-one wanted to get involved. Better to pretend that McCullough never existed. They all thought it was a drug dealer's revenge, clearly. Mac felt the familiar sense of cold anger that people like that were willing to let criminals like Pollock or Allen get away with anything. They couldn't see how keeping quiet did nothing but perpetuate the terror they lived under in the first place. Or maybe they were the smart ones. When the criminals had their hooks into police officers, how could you trust the very force who was supposed to protect you? Pushing his chair back from the desk, he strode out into the main office.

"You have something interesting, Doctor Wray?" he asked.

She looked up. "Clio, please. And yes. There are some shared characters between the marks Alex made on himself and the marks on your dead body. And the more I look, the more I'm seeing. Here."

She put two pictures side by side and then a third sheet of paper where she had drawn out a clean copy of the shape. To Mac, it was a collection of lines, like a tally. Meaningless. But Clio's eyes were bright. Melissa had turned in her seat and was watching keenly as Mac perched on a corner of the desk.

"The thing is, these are not just random shapes. If I'm right, which I think I am, these are from an obscure dialect of Pictish runes. They were found about ten years ago in caves under the castle, here in Edinburgh. And since then on artifacts found at a dig just outside the city, under the foundations of a building being demolished. The resemblance is uncanny. Too esoteric to have been images a young boy just stumbled over on the internet. I think Alex knew what he was doing and so did your killer."

Mac stared at Clio with eyes that would have made anyone else think he was about to accuse them of something. Clio stared right back, wide-eyed and red-cheeked. She looked like a little girl who'd just figured out the answer to a puzzle, gleeful in her victory. The terrible nature of the puzzle had passed her by in her excitement at solving the mystery. Mac thought she had missed her calling. This was a born detective if ever he'd met one.

"What does it say?"

"I don't know at the moment. I need to do some more research."

Mac nodded. "We need to know more about Alex Martins," he said. "We need to talk to his mother."

Clio's face fell. "Really? Oh hell, I'm going to get fired, aren't I?"

CHAPTER EIGHTEEN

MAC WANTED TO GO and see Karen Martins immediately. Melissa reminded him about his head and the fact that he looked like he'd fallen down and rolled in a puddle. Several times. He grinned ruefully, willing to be mothered while riding high on what felt like a solid lead. He left Melissa to the task that had occupied her all day, tracking down next of kin for Richard McCullough, someone, anyone to tell that he was gone. There was something unbearably sad when no-one could be found. Clio seemed happy to stay in the station, shown the vending machines and the toilets. Mac was happy for her to immerse herself as much as she wished, thinking through his justification to Reid for letting a civilian into the investigation. Having no mobile helped, he could delay telling his boss this latest step. He drove home, changed, and then headed back to Old Moray House.

Karen Martins' office was locked. A colleague with a shock of white hair despite a relatively youthful face popped his head out of a door and informed him that Karen was gone for the day. Gone home early. Mac had flashed the badge and been directed to an admin office where a home address was dutifully supplied. Karen Martins lived outside of Edinburgh in a village called Ratho, not far from the airport. There had been no sign of being followed since giving the Anti-Corruption unit registered vehicle the slip earlier. Mac kept a sharp eye out, though. His mind wandered to the kinds of things AC could be interested in. They didn't like that Kenny Reid had left them to go back into operational policing. There were some in AC who considered it a betrayal. It certainly wasn't a forward move in Reid's career. So, maybe they were looking to apply pressure on Mac to get at Reid. Some senior officers in AC would love to get something on their old colleague. Mac wasn't exactly milky white either. He'd never been bent, as such. But he'd come close a few times. Then there was his life before the police force. As the rain began to fall in earnest, while he made his way west along the M8, his mind went back to that road covered in sheeting rain. Watching Mark Souter winding along, hunched, head down. A killer who'd spent the night enjoying himself while Mac's sister was in the ground. If he was going to be crucified for a crime he'd committed as a youth, then he wished he'd finished it. Except he knew that it would have eaten him up inside. Some men could kill and carry that weight around with them. Or else just not feel it. Mac knew himself well enough to know that the burden of that guilt would have killed him.

Ratho was a small village of old cottages grouped around a handful of streets. The main road was lined with a bungalow terrace on one side, old worker's cottages. Newer builds occupied the other side, probably open fields until the fifties. Those houses only looked new compared to the other side of the street. Sat nav guided him out of the village and along a road that ran between wide open expanses of farmland. A church was visible above trees in the distance. He almost missed the turning, the road sign announcing a concealed entrance almost hidden by the misting curtain of rain. Turning quickly, the Audi scraped a hedge on one side and Mac found himself on a single track lane with a bungalow visible at the end. It was sleek and modern, a bespoke build of tall windows and long timber planks, interspersed with expanses of grey stone. Mac didn't know much about architecture, but he had a nose for wealth. And this place stank of it. He pulled up onto a gravel drive.

The front door was, thankfully, under a stone porch. To its left was a long, sheet of glass looking into an open plan living room. Very Scandi in its looks, white, grey, and light colored wood. Minimalist. He pressed the button on a video doorbell, noticing a garage to his right.

"Yes?" a voice came over the intercom, a man's voice.

"DCI McNeill, Police Scotland," Mac said clearly, holding up his warrant card to the lens. "I was hoping to speak to Karen Martins if she's home."

"What for?"

The man had spoken three words, but with such a tone of haughty privilege that Mac knew they weren't going to get along. A certain kind of person wasn't fazed by a police officer. Innocent people, it was said, had nothing to fear from coppers. That was clearly untrue. Everyone should have a healthy fear of the polis. But, a certain class of person, usually public school and university educated and always with money, seemed to believe they were somehow above the law. Barristers were bad for it. Politicians worse.

"That's for me to know, mate," Mac said between gritted teeth.

"I beg your pardon."

"This is a murder investigation. So, are you going to open the door or do I have to start getting suspicious?" Mac retorted.

The man must have been right behind the door because it opened a moment later. He was tall and slender, wearing a fleece and jeans and bare feet. He looked offended, but Mac wasn't for giving him an inch. It was unprofessional; he knew. And would probably result in a complaint to the Police Complaints Commission. To be added to the file. He didn't care. The PCC was toothless and no-one with Mac's record was getting reprimanded over being rude to a snotty nosed member of the public. It made Mac unwilling to put up with anything. He stepped into the hall, which was high-ceilinged, light, and airy.

"Her work said she'd come home. I'd like to speak to her," he said.

The man called out Karen's name over his shoulder, face going red. Mac took out a card with his name, rank, and number on it.

"Here, for the complaint. That's M-C, not M-A-C. Two L's."

He stepped further into the house, noticing the art on the walls. Paintings on square canvases that looked familiar. They were abstract. Colourful and full of energy. An interesting contrast to the Scandinavian calm that the rest of the house exuded. Ahead of Mac was a staircase, and he saw Karen Martins appear around a corner, descending towards him. She wore a baggy jumper and joggers, no makeup and hair pinned on top of her head in a messy pile. Quite the contrast from the woman Mac had met at the university. She stopped halfway.

"It's alright, Charles. Go back to work."

"What the hell is this about, Karen?" Charles spat with surprising venom.

"Alex, of course," she replied calmly, giving him a look that matched his venom and upped the ante.

Not a happy marriage, Mac observed. Probably bound together by the money one of them brings to the table and the other doesn't want to give up. He works from home. Architect, maybe. Built the house himself.

"Come up, DCI McNeill," Karen said, turning and not waiting to see if Mac would follow.

He walked up the stairs as Charles disappeared behind a slammed door, prompting a dog to bark angrily somewhere in the house. At the top of the stairs, he followed Karen to a mezzanine lounge overlooking the expansive living room downstairs. She sat on a sofa, drawing her feet up, and looked at him, waiting. Mac took an adjacent chair.

"I wanted to talk to you about your son, as you surmised," Mac said.

"Should I be angry at Doctor Wray? I told her not to help that gutter so-called journalist who was sniffing around."

"No. She's helping us with the matter I contacted you about. We found out that a journalist had obtained police photographs through an internal investigation," Mac lied smoothly.

"Well, that's a relief. Clio is an excellent academic. An asset to the faculty. But I will fire her in a heartbeat if I find out she's gone against my instructions."

"I need to ask you why your son killed himself," Mac said, cutting to the chase.

"You don't waste any time," Karen commented. "How the hell should I know why he killed himself?"

"Or why he had apparently self-harmed before doing it," Mac said.

"Again, if I knew the answer, maybe I could have helped him. He was a very disturbed boy. He lived in a...fantasy world. Obsessed with it."

"To do with Celtic mythology, perhaps?" Mac suggested.

"Clio has been helping that bloody journalist, hasn't she?" Karen demanded, sitting forward.

"I can assure you she hasn't," Mac said calmly.

"Look, I spent more than a year in a psychiatric hospital after what I found..." Karen looked away, putting her hand over her mouth. "I found him. I went into that nightmare of blood and...I found my son. My boy...dead!"

There were tears in her eyes and she squeezed them shut tight.

"I'm sorry to open old wounds. I wouldn't ask if it wasn't important."

"The coroner ruled death by suicide. The marks on his arms were self-inflicted. The flat was locked and chained. I had to get a locksmith to take the door off the hinges. Why do you want to look at this again?"

There was a plaintive wail to her voice that spoke of grief buried in a shallow grave, but only just. He felt bad about asking the questions he had to ask, immediately regretted getting the working class chip on his shoulder with the man at the door. The husband, presumably.

"I'm not investigating your son's death. I'm investigating a murder and the same symbols found on your son's body and in his flat were found at the scene of the murder."

"How on earth did you find out about Alex to make this connection," Karen said, suddenly.

Mac hesitated, wondering at the question, but knowing that grief made people behave irrationally. Even old grief.

"As I said..."

"Oh god, what does it matter? I'm sorry. It's the shock of the police coming to the door after all this time." Karen was all over the place, from tears to cold control in the space of a heartbeat.

Mac kept a well-practiced sympathetic face on. Karen sighed, smiled weakly.

"Would you like some coffee, DCI McNeill?" she asked.

"Yes. Please," Mac replied.

She nodded and rose, leaving the room to return with two steaming mugs a few minutes later. Mac had his notepad out. She resumed her seat, sipped the coffee, and began to talk about her son.

CHAPTER NINETEEN

"HE WAS A MUSICIAN. Since the age of six, he wanted to play the guitar," Karen said, cradling her coffee cup.

She sat at the end of the sofa, legs, once again, drawn up beneath her and a bright yellow cushion on her lap. She stared into space as she spoke, eyes haunted. A golden retriever padded up the stairs and came towards her, ignoring Mac. She absently stroked its head, and it jumped up onto the seat beside her, tongue lolling. Mac sipped coffee that was hot and bitter, and said nothing.

"At first it was Elvis, that was my music. Then all the seventies era that his dad was into. Pink Floyd, Genesis. All that complicated over-blown orchestration. By the time he was a teenager, it was like he was obsessed with...horrible themes. Death and devil worship and...it was horrific. He decorated his room with posters that I couldn't bear to look at. Got a pentagram tattoo when he was under age. Fifteen for Christ's sake!"

"I expect that didn't go down well," Mac said quietly, showing empathy.

"We went crazy on him. Charles, that's my husband, wanted to sue the tattoo parlour but Alex wouldn't tell us where he'd had it done. I wanted to go to the police," she laughed bitterly. "They didn't want to know. Not a crime committed, apparently. Bloody child abuse if you ask me!"

Mac stayed quiet but could imagine a desk sergeant somewhere suppressing laughter at Karen Martins. When there wasn't enough resource to pursue serious crime, a tattoo parlour giving ink to a boy barely underage wasn't going to get much traction. He kept his face neutral. Karen's anger made her dark eyes go wide, her lips pout. She was sultry and very attractive, even now. Mac mentally kicked himself for his maleness. Not the time or the place.

"He moved out. For four weeks, I was frantic. But, we heard from one of his friends who told us where he was. He was staying with an older boy named Richard."

"Richard McCullough?" Mac asked.

"Yes. They had formed a band together with a Polish boy. Alex was the youngest. They were sixteen or seventeen. Richard had a council flat in some god-forsaken place. Jack was still at his parents', but I gather he was hardly ever there."

"That would be Jacek Andrysiak?" Mac interjected again, pencil held ready.

"I don't know. They called him Jack. Maybe. He was Polish," Karen said dismissively.

"So what happened next?" Mac prompted, keeping his voice low and steady.

"Alex flushed his life down the toilet. He dropped out of

school. Played in his band. Ignored us because we were so negative all the time," she said this with scorn and another harsh laugh.

"When was this?" Mac asked.

"Well, he had just turned fifteen when he got that bloody tattoo. The first of many. Just after his sixteenth birthday, Charles and I were really trying to reach out to him. We tried to be positive and supportive, even though we were horrified by his choices. But it led to him opening up to us a little. I think he was self-harming by then. I caught a glimpse of... something on his arm and I was so terrified I couldn't bring it up with him. Didn't want him to vanish again. Anyway, about two years after he left, he told us that his band had a recording contract with a local label in Edinburgh. They'd found a lead singer by then and they were making a record. He was so...triumphalist about it. Like it vindicated every decision he'd ever made and which we'd criticised. Oh god, I just wanted to protect him and I couldn't!"

Karen's voice broke, and she hid her face in her hand. The dog raised its head at the distress in its mistress's voice. Mac put his coffee mug on the floor to one side. Karen's hands were shaking to such an extent that the coffee in her cup slopped over the rim. She barely reacted as the hot liquid touched her skin. Mac moved slowly and carefully, removing the cup, and put it onto the floor. As he did, her fingers tightened around his own. She looked at him, eyes liquid and vulnerable. He let her hold on to his hand without moving closer. Only a few feet separated them and she held his gaze for a long moment, lips slightly parted.

"Can you go on?" he asked.

Karen blinked and slowly withdrew her hand. Mac suppressed a sigh of relief.

"He was wrong. The so-called label was a one-woman operation; the contract wasn't worth the paper it was written on. Alex went further and further into this fantasy world he'd concocted. All Satanism and Celtic gods. A Mish-mash of mythology and religion. Nonsense. Then on the 1st of November 2021, I went to see him. He'd moved into a flat of his own and had sent me a cryptic text. Jack had also reached out, saying he was worried about Alex and Richard. They'd both been using drugs. Abusing drugs. I had to break into Alex's flat and I..."

She looked away but reached out as she did. Mac took her hand instinctively and squeezed it. Seeing her vulnerability reminded him of his own. Of the loss he was feeling all over again after Siobhan reaching out and then her fresh rejection. It would be so easy to just put his arm around Karen Martins. To offer comfort. So easy and yet so complicated. It would poison the case. Instead, he patted the back of her hand like a priest giving comfort to a widow. Again, rebuffed, Karen withdrew her hand.

"Did you ever meet Richard McCullough?" Mac asked.

"Once," Karen said, wiping her nose with the back of her hand. "Alex was so excited about this bloody record deal. He asked me to be there when he and the other boys signed their first ever contract. It was a backstreet record shop. Can you believe that? Not even a record label with offices somewhere respectable."

"Can you remember what it was called?" Mac asked.

"Something to do with...graves," Karen said. "I remember

there was this huge American there. And a girl who had a very high opinion of herself."

A chill ran down the back of Mac's neck. Evie Black knew both Richard McCullough and Alex Martins. She must have done because she had signed their band to her home-made label. Which meant she was playing him.

"Was my son's death a suicide?" Karen said, looking at him.

"I have no reason to doubt the coroner's findings," Mac assured her. "I am just looking into similarities that have come to light. Namely, the Celtic inscriptions which your son marked himself with. Did he leave anything that would give you any understanding of this...fantasy world of his?" Mac asked.

Karen shook her head. "I couldn't bear to look at anything from that period of his life. I burned it all," she said.

"Any insight you can give me? Was there anything meaningful about the symbols that I've seen in the pictures?" Mac persisted.

"None. It was nonsense. Alex took elements of the Celtic mythology he'd gleaned from the internet and built a framework all around some kind of apocalyptic vision. Everything was fueled by the drugs."

She shook her head, hugging the cushion closer to herself. Mac could see the grief still close to the surface and a husband who was not supportive. This was a woman craving comfort. He had to get out of there before she turned those eyes on him again.

"Thank you, Mrs. Martins. I realise how difficult this has been, but you've been very helpful. I won't bother you any longer. Anything else I need can be obtained from the official records. I'd also like to say how sorry I am for your loss."

Mac stood and Karen gazed up at him, surprise on her face. She pursed her lips and then rose herself, folding her arms beneath her breasts, which only emphasised them.

"You don't need to see me out," Mac said quickly, retracing his steps to the front door.

The dog escorted him, wagging its tail and nudging his hand with its cold nose. He ruffled its fur as he opened the door, making sure it couldn't run out. The rain had stopped, and he did not look back as he walked to the car and got in. Only then did he let out a long breath. A disturbed youth immersed in a world of his own making, exacerbated by drug use, kills himself in a gory and bizarre way. His friend is murdered in a manner reminiscent of that suicide. Revenge? Someone blaming Richard McCullough for Alex Martin's death? That would make Karen Martins a suspect, but Mac's instinct told him that was ridiculous. She was a mother, her grief for her son genuine, and she was obviously blaming herself for his death. A woman trapped in a loveless marriage and craving comfort and love beyond it. Not a sadistic killer. As he started the engine, he wondered if he should try and get a look at Karen Martins' psychiatric report.

CHAPTER TWENTY

As THE ENGINE FIRED UP, Mac reached for his phone, then swore as he remembered smashing it against the wall. It felt like being thrown back twenty years. How had police investigations been conducted without instant access to information or your team? It would have to wait. He needed any information gathered by the coroner regarding the suicide of Alex Martins. But he couldn't do anything about it in the middle of the Lothian countryside. An email when he returned to the office and the team would be moving on the information by tomorrow morning, but it was frustratingly slow. He drove away from the Martins' house into a sky already darkening past purple. Evie Black had lied to him. That couldn't go unchecked. She was either covering up something or playing a game with him. Either way, he couldn't let it go. Mac's hands tightened on the wheel as he headed back to Edinburgh. If this was just a silly game, it was at the expense of a murder investigation. Not clever Evie. Not clever at all.

It would be after six by the time he got back to Edinburgh, closer to seven by the time he fought through the rush hour to the office. The team would be gone by then. But he knew that the time spent getting to Niddrie Mains Road would be time he could focus on the new information. As he drove, he switched on the CD player, not remembering what was already in there. Something low and crushingly heavy filled the confined space. Jagged riffs. Funereal pace. The sort of music that calmed his brain. His conscious mind focused on the road while his subconscious lost itself in the music and mulled over the facts.

A young man of disturbed mind abuses and kills himself. A friend and colleague is murdered in a way that mirrors the suicide. A canvas, possibly from Alex Martins' flat, is placed at the murder scene. There to be found. Which would ultimately lead back to Alex Martins through the DNA on the canvas. A message left in a dead language. It all depended what that message was. If this was the beginning of a series, then he might already have the name of the next victim. Jacek Andrysiak? He hit the wheel, slipping out of his state of mindful concentration. He should be sending officers to find Jacek Andrysiak. He might be a suspect or in need of protection. The strobe of headlights coming the other way helped soothe him back into the focus state. Hands moved on the wheel automatically, guiding him by muscle memory.

If no witnesses could be found confirming visitors to Richard McCullough and the CCTV was inconclusive, then it would come down to those bizarre inscriptions. Ramsay Jones, the reporter who'd approached Clio. He was another lead. A clever man seeing what the police had failed to find or someone more involved? A petrol station appeared out of the night, garish with its neon and bright colours. He pulled into a parking space and walked in, taking out his warrant card.

"DCI McNeill, Police Scotland. I need the use of a phone, please," he said to the youth working the till.

The kid looked at the badge with wide eyes, stammered, and then opened a door with a combination lock behind him. Then he remembered the other combination lock on the door that kept customers from getting through to the office. That door closed and locked as he let it go after Mac entered. Mac waited as he fumbled with a bunch of keys. Finally, he was admitted into a back office store room and directed to a phone on the wall. Mac dialled the Police Scotland HQ switchboard and asked for Niddrie Mains Road CID. Kai answered after a minute of ringing.

"Kai, it's McNeill."

"Hi, guv. You just caught me. I've been hanging on for you."

"Got something?"

"Maybe. A blurred image on a car park camera taken from about twenty metres distance. But I think it's McCullough at a car. Big, dark SUV. Maybe a Land Rover from the shape."

"Not his?"

"No, looks too expensive even on the poor video from this camera. Anyway, I'll try and clean it up and see if we can get a plate on the vehicle. I'm also looking at any other camera in the area to try and track it into the estate."

Mac was thinking of Allen's drug dealers. Moving around in large, expensive cars. Usually a crew in the back. They knew McCullough was a user, so it would be no surprise if it turned out he was meeting a dealer in a car park. It just didn't fit with the case as it was developing. The continual hints of drug involvement were beginning to grate. He either wanted proof Hance Allen was behind it so he could go after him or proof this was something darker. One or the other.

"Is Doctor Wray still there?"

"No, she had to go get her daughter from school. She left some notes for you though, and Melissa got a new phone couriered in. It's on your desk."

Mac laughed silently. Melissa always looked after him, even when he was being a bad tempered sod.

"Great. I'm on my way in after a brief detour. Go home, Kai. Good work today."

He bought a sandwich and a bottle of water on his way out and sat in his car for fifteen minutes refueling before heading to his next stop.

It was fully dark by the time he pulled up in front of Raid the Grave Records. His car blocking the narrow alley. The windows of the shop were dark but there was a light on in the flat above. He tried the outer door. Locked. Stepped back and looked up. Faint sounds of music. Curtains closed and lights on. Evie was home. Mac went back to the car, opened the door, and planted his hand on the horn for a count of five. Nothing. Another five count. Someone briefly came to the window of a flat next door. A shadow moved against the curtains of Evie's flat, but she didn't look out. Another blast of the horn. Ten seconds. More movement in Evie's flat, but the curtains still didn't move. She was clearly pissed off with him. He remembered the narrow passage beyond the outer door, rusted fire stairs leading to the courtyard and the close leading out to South Bridge.

He walked up the remainder of High School Wynd, out onto Infirmary Street and then South Bridge, stepping from the gloom of the side streets to the stark orange of street lights. He walked past a sandwich deli, a mobile phone repair shop, and a beauty salon. All closed and shuttered. He almost walked straight past a door set back from the pavement after the beauty salon. A large, wheeled bin had been left in front of it. He pushed at it, moving it a few inches. Put his back into it and shoved it to a slow roll that stopped a few yards down the street. Tried the door it had been hiding. At some point, the lock had been forced. The door swung open on a lightless passageway. There was an almighty stench from there. Vomit. Along with other unmentionable bodily fluids, he didn't want to think about. It stoked his anger at Evie. If she hadn't lied to him, hadn't played her silly game, he wouldn't be back here, wading through some tramp's doss house.

It was so dark there was no way of knowing what he was putting his feet into. He walked through, pushing the thought from his mind. The only warning he had was a suggestion of motion from above. A shadow moving against the orange tinted night sky above the courtyard. Then something hit him in the shoulder with the force of a pile of bricks. Pain stabbed into his right shoulder and he crashed back against the wall of the passageway, one foot slipping out from beneath him. He caught the sound of a grunt, like someone jumping to concrete from just high enough to make it a painful landing. Even through the agony in his shoulder, his mind was working. There had been someone on that fire escape. They hit him with something before jumping the last few feet and hitting the ground hard.

The street fighter instinct kicked in as he felt whoever it was running past him. Jumping over him. He lashed out hard with his right hand, stabbing rather than swinging. It made contact. He pushed himself away from the wall, hand smearing through something wet, aiming with his shoulder and looking to pin his assailant against the opposite wall. Instead, something hit him in the mouth so hard his head smacked against the wall behind him. Black out. When he came to, Mac had no way of knowing how long he'd been out. There was a stabbing pain at the front of his head that told him he'd hit the back of it hard. The close was still black as pitch, but he had the sense that he was alone. Painfully and with some foul language under his breath, he levered himself up. His head was spinning, and he was close to vomiting. Maybe concussed. Swallowing the bile rising in his throat, he took a deep, shaky breath and stepped into the courtyard. He looked up. The fire door at the top of the staircase was open, and a light was visible through it.

Slowly, more because of his throbbing head than a sense of caution, he began to ascend. At the top was a corridor. At one end it turned a sharp corner and descended a few steps. Beyond that was a common passageway that led past three doors. The first was the door to Evie's flat. A concrete staircase led up from the building's front door, coming out between Evie's flat and the one next to it. The light he had seen was coming from her flat. The door was open. Mac felt dread, stomach churning. He entered, careful not to touch the door frame or anything inside. He didn't call out to Evie, not wanting to alert anyone who might still be inside. Her flat comprised a hallway that led to the left, opening out into a living room directly above the front of the shop. Two doors opposite him as he stepped inside led to the bathroom and the only bedroom. He knew the layout because he'd been here before.

Living room was empty and unmarked. A door led from the living room into a kitchen, which was neatly kept and also empty. Too small to afford any hiding places. Mac snatched a tea towel hanging from a hook and used it to turn the handle of the bathroom door. The first thing he saw as he let the door swing open was the blood smeared over the walls, the sink, the bathroom mirror. Smeared into familiar shapes. The shower curtain was pulled around the bath, which was behind the door. Using the tea towel, he tugged the curtain back. Evie lay in a full bathtub. He couldn't see her face; it was covered by a plastic bag tied firmly around her neck. But he knew it was Evie, recognised the tattoo over her left breast and another on her navel.

CHAPTER TWENTY-ONE

MAC DIALLED 999 from Evie's landline. He identified himself as a police officer and requested DI Barland be notified, as well as DCS Reid and a SOCO team. After giving the address, he hung up. Wincing at the pain in his head, he went through kitchen drawers and cupboards, keeping the tea towel between his hands and direct contact with surfaces. Eventually, he found a box of latex gloves in amongst bottles of cleaning products. He put on a pair and went back to the bathroom, taking the added precaution of thrusting his hands into his pockets. Crouching beside the bath, he leaned in and tried to absorb everything he could about the body. Waving tendrils of blood hung thick in the water behind her head, indicating a possible head injury as a cause of death. There was no sign of stab wounds as there had been with McCullough.

No mutilation of the body from what he could see. Her head was above water, arms on the sides of the tub. Her breasts floated and he could see her stomach though the water was murky with blood. Not so murky that he couldn't make out the tattoo in the shape of a spider. There was something else, occasionally visible through the blood-thick water, then hidden. Something running the length of her thighs. Carefully, he dipped a hand into the water to disturb it and get a clearer look. The word *witch* had been carved into the flesh of her left thigh. It didn't take long for the blue lights and sirens to descend from South Bridge. Mac went down the fire escape to meet the first responders, slipping on one of the steps and only just catching himself on the railing. A uniform was coming through the close, lighting the way with a torch.

He saw the slip and hurried forward.

"DCI McNeill?"

Mac didn't even try and place the officer. He waved the help away, eyes narrowed against the pain, and nodded sharply, wincing at the fresh explosion in his head.

"Get up there and secure the flat. No-one goes in until SOCO arrives. And no-one from the other flats comes down these stairs or through the close. My team is on the way," Mac ordered.

The man didn't waste time asking questions, but took the fire escape stairs two at a time. His partner was coming through the close and Mac stopped her with a raised hand.

"I was assaulted in here and managed to land a punch. It's likely to be the killer. Secure the close from the street. No one in or out."

He stumbled again, going back through the close. Maybe it was the head injury or maybe it was the nauseating smell in the dank passage, but when he emerged onto South Bridge, his stomach flipped. He had the presence of mind to stumble a few paces away before doubling over and vomiting. His skin was clammy and a freezing sweat stood out on his forehead. The sight of Evie loomed before his eyes and he couldn't shift it. Earlier that day, he'd flirted with her. Then had actually thought about seeing her. She'd been on his mind when he went to see Karen Martins, making him more than usually aware of the Dean's flirtation. Now Evie was dead. And there was no question that this was a series. A serial killer. His stomach tried to leave his body again, and he doubled over, vision blurring and swimming.

By the time Melissa turned up, he was sitting in the back of one of the squad cars that had arrived, head back against the headrest, eyes closed.

"Guv?"

He opened his eyes and squinted at her.

"Jesus. You look like..." she began.

"I know. Hearing that a lot today," Mac replied. "I hit my head. Think I'm concussed."

"Then we need to get you checked out."

"No way. This is a fresh crime scene. The killer did this to me. They were leaving as I was arriving."

"Mac, you can't do much good with a head injury. And you might do some damage. I've got this. Kai and Nari are on their way," Melissa said firmly.

A crowd had gathered on that portion of South Bridge. Uniform had set up a cordon, and the public was beyond it, looking in, taking pictures, gossiping, and speculating. Scene of Crime Officers were going in and out, anonymous in their white paper suits. Blue lights strobed everywhere and did nothing for Mac's pounding head. Melissa got into the car

143

next to him, leaving the door open. The stench emanating from her boss was making her gag. God knows what he'd rolled in in that alley.

"Want to tell me what happened, guv?" she asked.

Mac was finding it difficult to concentrate. He frowned. "Evie was playing me, the little fool. Lied to me. She knew more than she was telling about McCullough, Martins, too. Think she was holding out just to punish me for dumping her. I came here to have it out with her. Find out..."

It took an effort, but his fuddled mind realised Melissa was worried. She was looking around, face creased in concern.

"What is it?" Mac said.

"I don't think you should say any more until you've had your head checked. I don't think you know how it sounds," Melissa said.

Mac tried to follow her logic but failed. "I'm just telling you how I came to be here. The door was locked, so I came around to the back entrance. There's a fire escape that leads up to the flats above the shops."

"You knew the layout of the building," Melissa said intently.

"Yes, I've been up there before."

"You had a relationship with the victim," Melissa said, again with peculiar intensity.

"What the hell is this, Melissa?" Mac demanded.

There was a sharp rap on the car's rear window. An over-sized signet ring on an index finger was being used to tap. Mac saw an overcoat. Melissa glanced up just as Detective Chief Superintendent Kenny Reid stooped to look in. He had the loose face of a bloodhound, eyes pouched and cheeks sagging.

But there was still a squareness to his face emphasised by the barrel chest of an ex-boxer. The eyes were clear blue and sharp.

"Right, Barland, you've got a crime scene to manage. Get on it. I will make sure this idiot gets his head looked at," Reid snapped.

Melissa threw Mac a regretful look. "Yes, sir," she said, getting out of the car.

Reid crooked a finger at Mac. "You come with me. My driver will take us along to the nearest A&E."

Mac shook his head and wished he hadn't. "Guv, I can't..."

"Can't? Can't? What's that then, French or something? 'cause it's not a word in my vocabulary, son. Move it," Reid replied.

He strode to an unmarked car parked behind the one Mac was sitting in. Mac gingerly levered himself out of the car and staggered to Reid's. His boss was already positioned in the back and the driver had started the engine. Mac almost fell into the seat beside the DCS.

"What happened, son?" Reid said, suddenly gentle in tone.

Mac explained as best he could, despite the fog that was clouding everything. Reid nodded to the driver, and the car began to move.

"I overheard what you said to Barland. I don't like to hear words like played, dumped, or have it out with when we're talking about a murder victim. It's the kind of thing you expect to hear from a suspect during an interview. Do you understand, Callum?"

Reid was using his first name. That meant he was in serious trouble. Mac remembered all the times his father had called him Callum instead of Cal. He put a hand to his head, trying to find clarity.

"Yeah, Evie and I had a fling. It was nothing serious. But she was withholding evidence. She lied to me about knowing the first victim. I had a right to be angry," Mac said, wearily.

"If the press gets wind of it, that's not how they'll see it. Not after all the crap that's been coming out of the Met in the last few years. And what do you mean, the first victim?"

Mac could feel those cold blue eyes like a pickaxe to the head. "Same MO as the McCullough crime scene. Mutilations and Celtic symbols scrawled everywhere. They carved the word witch into Evie's thigh. This is a serial killer, Kenny, and they're not done yet."

Reid swore profusely, obscenely and for a good minute. He leaned forward, tapping the driver on the shoulder with a gnarled finger.

"You heard nothing. Understand? Anything said in this car gets into the press and I'll have your job and then your pension."

The driver must have been assigned to Reid for a while. He didn't bat an eyelid at the aggression or the threat, just said "Right, sir," and continued to face forward, concentrating on the road ahead.

Reid sat back, face set as though he were chewing on a piece of concrete.

"Serial. You're sure?"

"Yes," Mac replied. "And unless I'm a suspect in the McCullough killing, I can't be a suspect in this one. Despite my prior relationship with the deceased."

"Get yourself married, son. Then this kind of thing won't happen," Reid snapped.

Mac barked a laugh, knowing that Reid had been married three times and infidelity had been a problem in each one.

"It could be said that you killed her and tried to link it to McCullough to cover your tracks," Reid suggested.

"Who will say that?" Mac asked. "I'm SIO on both cases. I'm not investigating myself."

"If it gets out, I will be under pressure to assign this fresh case to someone else," Reid pointed out.

"Then don't let it get out. They're linked and I'm going to get him," Mac replied.

Reid lowered his voice so that Mac could barely hear him. "There's still the issue of Anti-Corruption."

"You've had a red notice for me?"

"No. Nothing. But I think I'm being followed," Reid said.

It was a measure of the trust between the two men that Reid would admit that to Mac. It would be unlikely in the extreme that he would say the same to any other subordinate.

"So am I," Mac replied. "Earlier today."

Reid swore again, baring his teeth for a moment as he glared out of the window.

"So, it's an undercover operation. By bloody incompetents, if we've both spotted the surveillance." Reid sounded just as angry about the incompetence as the fact that he was under surveillance.

"Unless they wanted us to see them. Some kind of mind game," Mac suggested. "The kind of thing you and I used to come up with."

Reid laughed without humour. "The current crop of AC

officers aren't up to our standards, son. That unit has gone to the dogs since I left."

Mac chuckled, and Reid shot him a bludgeoning look. "What's so bloody funny?" he demanded.

"Only you would face an AC investigation and wish they were conducting it more effectively."

"Yeah, well. I'm a perfectionist, son. If someone's looking to take me down, I want to know it was the very best."

The car pulled into the A&E drop-off zone for the Royal Edinburgh Hospital. Mac opened the door, but Reid leaned across and pulled it shut.

"Right, you've already been stupid enough to tell Barland about your relationship with this victim. Don't tell anyone else and keep it off the paperwork. Get yourself checked out and take a couple of days off. That's a bloody order. Disobey and I'll suspend you. Barland can run it until you're recovered."

Mac gritted his teeth and forced himself to nod. "Yes, sir."

"And don't give me that insubordinate back chat," Reid replied, reading an insult into Mac's tone. "Now get out of my sight."

Mac opened the door and got out of the car.

"Take care, son," Reid said as Mac slammed the door shut.

CHAPTER TWENTY-TWO

MAC HAD EVERY INTENTION of disobeying his orders and risking suspension. Which Reid wouldn't have hesitated to do if the roles had been reversed. He waited three hours in A&E before giving up. He bought two packs of paracetamol and hailed a cab, intending to go back to the office. Feeling the dried blood in his hair and a pain that made him want to empty his stomach again convinced him to change his destination. A shower and change of clothes first, then into the office and check in with Melissa and the team. Back at his flat, after showering and bagging up his clothes, he lay down for a moment across the bed and didn't wake until mid-morning. He sat up slowly, feeling hung over and squinting against the bright sunlight spilling through his bedroom window. But, despite the hangover, his head was clearer. He winced when he recalled how he had run his mouth off in front of Melissa, telling her about how angry he'd been at Evie. Even drunk, he wouldn't have been so stupid.

Another shower to sluice away the last of the concussion and wake himself up. The thought of food made him nauseous, so he skipped it, dressing and making a coffee. His laptop was in the office. The longer he was at home, the more out of the loop he was becoming. It was an uncomfortable feeling, especially with a serial killer out there. A particularly sadistic one. He forgot he had left his car outside Raid the Grave Records the previous night and then remembered that he hadn't yet replaced his broken phone when he reached for it to call a cab. What a bloody shambles. Literally. He left the flat and started walking until he saw a cab that he could flag down and gave the address of the station on Niddrie Mains Road. He carried the clothes he had been wearing the night before in a bin bag to be examined by forensics. In a separate, sealed bag was a sample of his blood matted hair. He remembered it had looked like Evie had suffered a head wound. There was a good chance the same weapon was used on him, which meant there might just be DNA from the killer present. A slim chance, but he'd take what he could get at this point.

Edinburgh was damp but under a blue sky, untroubled by the pewter grey of rain clouds. Pavements and roads looked as though they'd been sluiced clean, leaving them shiny and fresh. Like someone had reset the clock and started the city again, brand new. Yesterday had been a killer, but Mac hadn't been beaten. He was up on his feet again and ready to seize this case by the throat. Reid wasn't going to take it away from him because of his connection to Evie. Mac wasn't the kind of man to take a case personally. So many ended up unsolved that it was madness to become that obsessed. But part of him hated the idea of a killer walking the streets. Perhaps because Iona's killer had never been caught. In his darker moments, Mac had looked up Mark Souter. He'd done it by trawling social media, not wanting any official connection between them to exist on any police database. Souter was still alive and still on Skye. Still walking free.

He'd not looked for over a year, not wanting to risk the temptation to go over there. It was the ultimate test. Maybe this time he wouldn't be able to stop himself. Seeing a middle-aged Mark Souter, a middle age that had been denied Iona, might be too much. Mac stared out of the taxi's window at the city rolling past and blanked his mind, forcing it back to the case. There was a thrill in him despite everything that had happened. Another killing was another crime scene. Another chance to gather data and evidence. Another chance for the killer to slip up. One hair. One drop of blood or saliva. That would be all it took to pin someone to a crime scene, and that was half the case. It should be almost impossible in this era of forensics for anyone to commit any crime and get away with it. No matter how clever or well prepared, how could you avoid leaving something behind? Something microscopic would be all he needed. Providing he could find it.

The entire team was assembled at Niddrie Mains Road. They all looked up at his entrance and he held up the bin bag.

"My clothes from last night. I need someone to take these down to forensics and get them processed for DNA that doesn't belong to me."

"I'll handle it, guv," Nari said, getting up from her desk.

Mac handed her the clear evidence bag containing his hair and clotted blood. "Might just be mine, but if the killer used the same weapon on me as Evie Black, there might be some cross-contamination," Mac said.

Nari nodded, taking both bags in one hand, and grabbing her coat from the back of her chair with the other.

"I didn't expect to see you today, guv," Melissa said, carefully.

"Rumours of my death have been greatly exaggerated," Mac said wryly.

He took off his jacket and dropped it over the back of a chair, then sat. "So, brief me. What did I miss while I was gaga last night?"

Melissa glanced at Kai, looking uncertain, but Mac just stared her out, wanting no further debate. It took her a second to pick up on the message, then she was all efficiency.

"Victim suffered blunt force trauma to the back of the head, which might have been the cause of death. However, the forensic pathologist noted signs of cyanosis on the lips which would indicate suffocation or, given where she was found, drowning. He hasn't committed as the head wound is serious, but she might have been stunned by the blow to the head and then dragged to the bath where she was drowned. Or just killed outright by the trauma and placed in the bath. We know our killer likes to present a tableau."

So, Melissa had picked up on the commonalities between this and the McCullough murder. Mac nodded approval, both for her summary and the unspoken assumption.

"There was mutilation of the body post mortem. No sign of any blood-stained clothes in the flat."

Mac's eyes narrowed. "If she was dressed when she was attacked, there'd be no way she could avoid something getting on her clothes. And whoever lamped me last night definitely wasn't carrying anything."

"Exactly," Melissa confirmed. "Which could indicate she was naked already. Which would further suggest..."

"That she possibly had an intimate relationship with her killer," Mac finished.

"Working hypothesis is that she let the killer into the flat, having arranged to meet him..." Kai began.

"Him?" Mac interrupted. "We don't know that it's a man."

"Was she bi-sexual?" Melissa asked.

She asked Mac directly, then realised her mistake. She knew Mac had a prior relationship with the victim, Kai didn't, and Melissa knew Mac wouldn't want that information spread. She blushed but couldn't take it back. She continued looking at Mac. He glanced at Kai, who was paying attention.

"Full disclosure then. I knew Evie Black. I...dated her to use the current parlance. It was something and nothing. Over before it began. This doesn't go further than these four walls and nothing in writing. Anywhere. Right?"

Kai nodded, and Melissa looked away. "My DNA might be found in the flat. I was last there a couple of months ago. But Evie was a cleaning maniac, so the place will have been deep cleaned a few times since then."

"That's good. We don't want to muddy the waters, eh?" Kai said.

It was an astute observation, and Mac gave him a nod. He could be tough on the young DC because of his outward shallowness and sometimes lax attitude. But, Mac had to remind himself, there was a reason he had taken Kai on. There was a sharp mind there. And, in addition to his technical skills, Kai was a people person. He made connections about relationships and found subtexts that the rest of the team, and Mac in particular, might miss.

"No, we do not."

"We've lifted Evie Black's computer and phone, but there are a lot of papers in her flat and the shop. It's all boxed and moved to secure storage. We'll start going through it today. The obvious connection between McCullough and Black is music..."

"It's more than that, Kai. I spoke to Doctor Karen Martins, Clio Wray's boss. Her son Alex was in a band with Richard McCullough, and they were signed to the label operated by Evie Black. Alex committed suicide in a manner very similar to our crime scenes. They are all connected," Mac said.

"Was there anyone else in the band?" Kai asked.

"Good question. Yes, a guy called Gaunt who, according to Evie, moved abroad not long after Alex's suicide, and another named Jacek Andrysiak. Maybe Polish. Who's still around somewhere. We need to find him. He's a person of interest. Kai, you have something?"

Mac had noticed Kai swiftly turn back to his computer at the mention of Jacek Andrysiak.

"Maybe, maybe. I've been going through the McCullough's phone and social media. No mention of Jacek, but I have seen some messages to a number that's just saved as Jack. Goes back about four years, most of it the usual stuff. Chat about football, music, arrangements to meet up. Then there's a row about two years ago. Jack seemed pretty angry at McCullough. Blamed him for something and the name Alex is mentioned."

Mac got up, crossing to Kai's desk. A computer window was open, resembling the display of a phone and showed lists of text message conversations. Kai opened one and scrolled through the messages until he reached the one he was interested in. It was dated November 5th, 2021. Mac felt the hairs rise on the back of his neck. It was dated four days after Alex Martins' suicide.

This is ur fault. You gave him the stuff. You did this - came from whoever McCullough had saved in his phone as Jack.

Get off your high horse. You sick or somethin? You were the 1 who messed his head up wiv all that devil stuff. I just wanted to play guitar in a band. You 2 were the ones obsessed with death and all that crap. He started self harmin cause of what you put in his head - was the reply.

"I didn't make a connection 'cos I didn't know about Alex Martins. But this isn't the only agro McCullough had. There's another thirteen conversations where he was having a go at someone, mostly begging for money, and raging when he couldn't get it. Usual junkie stuff," Kai said.

"So, Jack blames McCullough for Alex's death. The mother blames him too for getting her son addicted to drugs. She was also angry at Evie Black. I got the impression she thought Evie was stringing her son along, letting him believe he was going somewhere."

"So, she's a suspect too?"

Mac shrugged. Instinct told him that Karen Martins wasn't the type to inflict sadistic violence, but they had to follow the evidence. "Let's see if she's got an alibi..."

A phone rang, and Melissa picked it up. She listened for a few seconds.

"Clio's just arrived. She's downstairs."

Melissa looked at Mac and they both had the same thought. Now that her boss was a potential suspect, they couldn't have her around.

"Want me to speak to her?" Melissa asked after a moment.

"No. I'll do it," Mac replied. "Kai, get started on tracking down Jacek Andrysiak. That's J-A-C-E-K A-N-D-R-Y-S-I-A-K. Melissa, when I get back, you can walk me through the rest of what we know about last night's crime scene. Oh, and see if you can get hold of Karen Martins' psychiatric report. She had a breakdown after finding her son's body and told me she spent a year in a hospital."

"On what grounds? As the case stands, the report isn't essential to the investigation. Karen Martins' isn't, strictly speaking, a suspect. A person of interest, possibly, but that's it. And it's tenuous at best. She's a grieving mother who fell apart after finding the body of her son, after he mutilated then killed himself. We'll never get a court order on that basis."

Mac sighed and scrubbed a hand through his hair.

"What about Public Interest Disclosure? Withholding the info could put others at risk." Mel just stared at him. "Yeah, yeah, I know. Just do what you can. This case is shaping up to be a headache of the first order. I just want to know we've explored all avenues."

Mel held up her hands. "Okay, fine, I'll do my best. But don't hold your breath."

He left the office, heading for reception. For some reason he found himself full of regret that he was going to be dispensing with Clio's services.

CHAPTER TWENTY-THREE

CLIO WAS SEATED in the reception area next to a skinny man in a tracksuit and a bored expression on his face. Clio, by contrast, seemed to take in everything around her with great interest. Obviously a person unused to being inside a police station. He flattered himself that her face lit up when she saw him coming through the security doors into the waiting area. She stood, smiling, and Mac couldn't help but return it.

"Morning, Inspector!" Clio said, brightly. "Did you get my messages?"

That stopped Mac. Melissa hadn't mentioned Clio trying to get hold of him.

"Ah, no. My phone was broken," Mac said.

"Yes, you mentioned that when you came to see me. I thought you'd have a backup or something," Clio said, hoisting her holdall onto her shoulder.

"No, Police Scotland's budget doesn't stretch to more than one phone each. I still need to get my replacement up and running," Mac said with a smile that he hoped was jovial.

He turned to the desk sergeant. "Any rooms free?"

The sergeant checked a computer screen. "Two is free, sir."

Mac punched in the access code for the security door and held it open for Clio. "Can I have a word?" he asked.

Clio frowned but went through ahead of him. Mac directed her to Interview Room Two. It was small, furnished with a plastic-topped table and two chairs. A panic button ran around the walls and it was lit by uncomfortably bright strip lights in the ceiling. Not for the first time, Mac wished these rooms came with dimmer switches.

"Take a seat," he said, pulling out a chair for Clio and taking the one opposite.

She looked confused, and with some surprise, Mac felt bad about being the cause. Her face remained pretty, despite being creased into a frown. He realised he had become used to seeing a quirky smile and a spark in her eyes. But he wasn't her friend. He barely knew her, and this had to be professional.

"Why so formal, Mac?" she asked, reverting to the name he'd given her permission to use now that they were alone.

"Clio, the investigation has moved on considerably since yesterday. I'm not sure the work I asked you to undertake for us is going to be needed going forward."

He hated the cold, emotionless tone, and the robotic, corporate words. It wasn't the first time he'd needed to cut off emotions and move on. The police force required that ability, especially in its senior officers. You learned not to think about the trail of devastation left in your wake.

"Oh, that's disappointing. And a little annoying, if I'm honest. I put my job on hold to help you," Clio replied.

"I know and I do appreciate all your efforts," Mac said.

"That's it?" Clio asked, an edge to her tone now.

She was looking directly at Mac, eye to eye and refusing to look away. He noticed the bracelet she wore, made of interwoven leather and bearing a motif of trees and flowers. He hadn't noticed it before. She wore a t-shirt under a well-used denim jacket. The t-shirt was worn and baggy, the collar shapeless and revealing two necklaces against a smooth expanse of pale skin. Mac was aware of all this in his periphery as well as the light, slightly floral scent of her perfume. She didn't wear makeup, but didn't need it. Maybe he was still suffering from the aftereffects of the concussion because sitting so close to her, he found his mind wandering.

"I'm afraid so, Doctor Wray," Mac said, slipping an extra layer of formality in to gain some distance.

"Oh no, I'm sorry, *Mac*," Clio said, emphasising the nickname. "You don't get to go all formal on me. I'm owed an explanation. You bring me in and ask me to look at some truly horrible things, claiming you need my help. I get totally absorbed in it, spending hours researching, and risking my job, I might add, and now you're just throwing me out? I don't think so."

Mac found it curious that she was so annoyed by this. The inconvenience she had been put to was one thing. But this was different. He was starting to feel like this was a breakup.

"Did you even read my last message?" Clio said, standing.

"No, I told you, my phone is broken. I haven't signed into the new one yet. But, rest assured, I will read everything you've been kind enough to send me."

"Fine," Clio said, clearing her throat.

She grabbed her bag, strode to the door, and then stopped, one hand on the handle. She turned back to Mac. "No. Do you know what? I will not let this go just because you've treated me appallingly. It's too important."

She marched back to the table and dropped her holdall on top. Unzipping it, she took out a cardboard folder full of papers. She extracted the first two and placed them on the table.

"What am I looking at?" Mac asked.

He could see that they were inscriptions, photocopied from somewhere. They looked similar to those found at both of his crime scenes.

"These tell me you're going to have two more killings. Three in total. Maybe more but three at a time," Clio said, stabbing a finger at the symbols.

Mac stared at her and read the angry honesty on her face. She believed what she was saying. Was convinced of it. Her blue eyes bored into his, bright as the sky. There was a light gloss on her lips and he caught the smell of some fruity lip balm. The insane urge to kiss her flared within him before he brutally stamped it to death.

"Sit down," he ordered.

Clio obeyed, lips parted and breathing slightly heavily. Her eyes were wide with something akin to excitement, or possibly he was reading it completely wrong and she was just bloody furious. Mac wondered how many missed calls and messages he would find when he switched on the new phone and it downloaded the information from the old virtual SIM.

"Explain it to me, please, Clio," he said quietly and with intensity.

She couldn't possibly know she'd already been proved partially correct. Another death had come a week after the first. If there was no doubt about what she was saying, there could be another one soon. Maybe in a week's time?

"It's an obscure dialect found in this part of Scotland, almost exclusively, and used by the natives who lived here, the Votadini," Clio began. "They lived on top of what's now Castle Rock, specifically way back in the Bronze Age. I originally thought it was a more standard dialect found throughout Northern Europe, Wales, and Ireland, but couldn't make sense of it in that context. Then I thought of the Votadini. I did a research paper on the Iron Age remains found at Cramond. Anyway, once I started seeing the symbols in those terms, it started to make sense. These symbols, in particular, were found on the body. The Celts believed the number three to be sacred. This symbol represents the season of Imbolc. Basically, the time of year between the winter and vernal solstices."

Mac wasn't following the terminology and when Clio saw this, she began to explain further, but Mac put up a hand. He leaned forward over the picture. Clio did the same; their heads were just inches apart, eyes intent on the paper.

"Just give me the meat, Clio. If I need to, I'll read up on the rest. You're saying the murderer planned their killing to coincide with a particular time of year?"

"Yes!" Clio looked up just as Mac did.

Mac was suddenly aware of her proximity. He sat back, crossing his legs and folding his arms, impervious and professional. Clio remained bright-eyed and thrilled.

"This symbol represents the trinity, the Celtic trinity, the

161

number three which they saw all around them in the natural world. And this one represents Bealtaine."

Mac's eyes skipped over the paper, taking in the strange words and wrestling with the concept. He had shifted his mind to the idea that McCullough and Evie were killed by someone in connection with Alex Martin's suicide. A vengeful mother killing those she believed responsible for the death of her son, perhaps? Or a bandmate who had seen his musical future go down the toilet as his friends dived into drugs. Then there was the journalist, Ramsay Jones, who had access to information that he shouldn't. Now, he found himself mentally resetting completely because Clio was suggesting a much more esoteric motive.

"This sounds more like a ritual to me. I've been looking for different realistic motives anchored in the here and now with all this stuff..." Mac waved a hand at the papers, "...as mere window dressing. But what you're telling me is all this stuff is actually the point."

Clio nodded emphatically. "That's exactly what I'm saying. I think the killer is communicating. I think the deaths are a..."

She stopped suddenly, sitting back with a troubled look on her face. Mac watched her and waited.

"A sacrifice," Clio said finally.

"A human sacrifice? To what?"

"Look, there are many deities in Celtic mythology, Mac. Another question might be *for* what?" Clio said.

"You mean not a...a tribute, but a transaction? This killer wants something?"

"I don't want to destroy my credibility completely by using the word, but I think it's a...spell," Clio said, flushing as she said it.

Mac let out a long breath, watching Clio for a moment, trying to gauge if she was actually on the level. She could be the killer, stringing him along for the sheer fun of it, revealing her cleverness. A spell, for Christ's sake. What did she take him for?

"If I didn't want to offend you more than I already have, I would ask you where you were last night. About eight?" Mac said.

"At home, face timing my mum, actually. With Maia. What's significant about eight o'clock last night?"

"Maia?" Mac asked.

"My daughter. Want my mum's number so you can check my alibi? It sounded like you were looking for one? Has there been another death?" There was a distinct chilliness to her voice, which dismayed Mac.

"Look, Clio, I'm sorry if I upset you earlier. I honestly believed these markings, all this stuff, was more than likely a red herring. But from what you've told me, I have to consider that you're right. I have to keep that possibility open. Especially if there's a third murder coming like you suggest. Will you keep working with us?"

"Third? So, there has been another one? Oh my god! This is a serial killer?" Clio exclaimed. "I was right?"

"You may be right," Mac admitted. "I think I need you on the team because there's no way I'll ever make sense of this lot."

But he was seeing the first signs of fear in Clio. The eyes wide with sudden realisation. He could almost follow the train of her thoughts. Until now, it had been an academic

163

problem. She could tell herself that's all it was, even knowing the reality of the situation. But, if her theory was proved right, then there was a very dangerous, disturbed individual out there. And she was helping to catch him. Mac knew what would come next, could feel Clio slipping away from him. It would hurt the investigation. And the rest.

"Is Maia safe if I continue to help you? Am I putting her in harm's way?" Clio asked.

Mac considered lying to her. Telling her what she wanted to hear, giving the usual police assurances that were based on no solid fact except the need to keep panic at bay. The kind the public were told every day. But he couldn't.

"Only if the killer knows you're helping us. That doesn't have to be found out by anyone. My team are solid, Clio. We can move you to a different location to do your work. Or you can do it from home or your own office. I can keep you and Maia safe."

Except someone did already know. Karen Martins, and she had both motive and the historical knowledge. Mac pushed down the twinge of guilt. Clio was running a hand through her short, brown hair.

"I'll have to think about it. Just give me twenty-four hours," she said.

CHAPTER TWENTY-FOUR

MAC WATCHED CLIO leave the station. He'd mentally U-turned after her revelation. If there was going to be more of this cryptic Celtic crap, he wanted an expert on staff to decipher it. It gave him some trouble that he knew he was lying to her. Especially with a kid involved. He could get another expert, but found himself reluctant to. That was selfish, and he knew it. On the other hand, he could make sure she and her daughter were protected. That made Karen Martins the priority. If she was cleared, then Clio was safe. There would be no way the killer could find out that she was helping. Her boss was the only one who knew outside of the police, and Mac knew his team was secure. There would be no leaks from inside the SCU. He headed back up the stairs to the office.

"How'd she take it?" Melissa asked.

"She didn't," Mac replied. "I asked her to stay on after hearing what she had to say. Long story short, these inscriptions may be more significant than we thought. She thinks there'll be another death. Three at a time."

"At a time!" Kai exclaimed. "How many does she think there's going to be?"

"She's not a fortune teller. She's just relaying to us what the symbols mean and three is a significant number. So, we have to consider the possibility that it's significant to our killer too. We've had two deaths a week apart. Let's assume we're now fighting to prevent another one in a week's time."

Both looked shocked. But that faded quickly. Kai's eyes went to the picture boards, reminding himself of just how twisted this guy was. Of what they were trying to prevent happening to someone else. Melissa shook her head, taking out her phone.

"I'm going to tell Cazzy I'll be late tonight," she said.

Mac nodded curtly. Kai sighed somewhere behind him. Neither of them needed to be told to work overtime. They knew that the extra hours put in now could literally be life and death for someone. Nari walked in and sensed the charged atmosphere immediately.

"What's happened?" she asked.

Mac perched himself on a desk at the front of the room and brought them all up to speed regarding the conversation he'd had with Clio. He included her worries about her safety and particularly that of her daughter.

"We're not going to draw attention to her by having official protection assigned. So far, no-one can know that she's been working with us. We need to get our suspects in ASAP and start testing alibis. Kai, you're on Andrysiak. Find him and get him here. Nari, there's a journalist out there called

Ramsay Jones, freelance. Clio said he offered her references from the Guardian and the Independent, so chase up the editors and find him. He at least should be staying somewhere relatively local. Speak to him where he is so we don't spook him. If he's reluctant to talk, then arrest him and let me know. Kai, your suspect may not be a UK national, so has to be considered a potential flight risk. So, when you find him, don't waste time. Just get him in a cell. If he's innocent, we can apologise later. I just don't want him skipping the country."

Nari was making notes frantically. Kai nodded, turning to his computer.

"And me, guv?" Melissa asked.

"You and I are going to see Karen Martins again. You speak to the university and find out if she's in the office today. I'll be with you in a minute."

Mac left his team bustling and went into his cubicle, picking up the new phone that Melissa had arranged. It was plugged in and fully charged. He sat down and fired it up, working his way through the setup required by the security software installed on all Police Scotland tech. Finally, he was in and the phone was pulling all the messages that had piled up since his other handset had been so cruelly abused. A message from Evie caught his eye. He opened it. It was short and came with a picture. She'd forgiven him then, unless the picture was to show him what he'd never be touching again. His finger hovered over the delete button. If AC found out he was investigating the murder of a woman he'd been involved with, deleting it would be a highly compromising action. On the other hand, the picture on his phone was a guarantee of the case being taken off his hands. "I'm sorry, Evie," he said softly. He hit delete.

Clio knew she was being followed. A man walking his dog had caught her eye as she'd driven past. She couldn't look away and the man stared back. Clio's pulse hammered. She felt a cold sweat break out as she craned her head to look back at the man. Then she saw the car behind and the driver, a woman, who stared straight at her. She turned at random, palms sweaty on the wheel, and the driver turned too. She took another random turn, ending up face to face with a bus coming down a one-way street. The woman driver sailed past at the end of the street behind her, looking. The bus driver honked and pointed to the no entry sign that Clio had missed. She felt tears prick her eyes as she fumbled to put the Mini into reverse. And as she shot out of the side-street, narrowly avoided a car coming the other way.

It swerved into the opposite lane to avoid her, and the driver gesticulated. Passersby were watching now. Had they been watching her already? With shaking hands, she somehow got the car straight and pulled into the kerb. It was a double yellow in front of a no parking sign, but she didn't care. She rested her head on the steering wheel, holding onto it with white knuckles. A logical part of her mind knew that she was drawing attention to herself. People were staring at her because she was staring at them. But it wasn't the logical part of her brain that was in control. Fear was driving her. Terror. Not for herself, but for Maia. It had suddenly become very real for her. Not a clever academic puzzle, made attractive because of the drama of working with the police on an actual murder case. She was helping catch someone who had killed twice and would kill again. Someone who did not want to get caught. At least not until they had completed their work. What would they be likely to do to her or Maia if they found out she was making a material difference?

"I could lie. Tell Mac that I can't make any more sense out of it. That it's all just nonsense," she said to herself.

The idea of just backing out, ghosting the journalist and police both, going back to her mundane life was attractive. In fact, the urge to drive away and never look back was almost overwhelming.

"Life's too short. Too short to take stupid risks," she said aloud.

A flash of color at the window caught her eye. A traffic warden was standing there, looking at her reproachfully. He was pulling out the machine he wore at his waist, moving to the front of the car to look at the number plate. Clio opened the door.

"I know there's no parking here, but I've just had some terrible news and I'm quite shaken up. I don't think I can drive safely at the moment."

She held up a hand, which trembled visibly. It felt like her face must be pale. Felt like her blood sugar had crashed through the floor. The traffic warden pursed his lips, hesitating.

"You need an ambulance?" he asked in an accent that said English wasn't his first language.

"If I did, I'd still be here tomorrow," Clio said, sitting on the edge of the driver's seat and putting her head in her hands.

The man appeared in front of her and, for one terrifying moment, she convinced herself that he was the killer. That he'd been stalking her this whole time, and this was where

Maia became an orphan. He put a hand into his pocket and took out a packet of boiled sweets.

"You look white as a ghost. The sugar will help," the man said.

Clio hesitated, then took one. It was pink and red stripes and tasted of strawberries.

"I'll walk around the block. Slowly," the man said with a wink.

Clio smiled around her sweet. It might have been her imagination, but she felt better already. The shakes were subsiding. She reached up for the stone contained in one of her necklaces. It was jasper, known as the supreme nurturer, sustaining and supporting in times of stress. Touching it had always brought comfort when she was feeling anxious. She got fully back into the car, staring out of the windscreen but not seeing the street beyond. She was seeing Mac's face, his dark, earnest eyes. Hair that made her want to tidy it for him, brush it back with her fingers into some kind of order. The kindness she had just been shown had changed her perspective. That man had given her a break just when she needed some compassion. This evil killer, whoever he was, would kill again. The message was clear. Three deaths for Imbolc then, come Bealtaine three more? Mac hadn't asked what she meant when she showed him the symbol for Bealtaine. Though Clio knew. It was part of the Celtic calendar, analogous with spring and two or three months away.

If her help could save another life, possibly more, then she had to give it. Had to trust Mac that he could keep her and Maia safe. A buzzing in her pocket broke into her train of thought. Fishing out her phone, she saw it was Karen.

"Hi Karen," she answered, putting on as bright a tone as she could manage.

"Clio, just thought I'd check in and see how you're doing, noticed you weren't in the office."

"Yes, sorry. It's this police thing," Clio said, checking around that no-one seemed near enough to listen or overhear.

"Really? I thought that would be a few hours' work at the most. Is it going to take much longer?"

"I think so. I don't really know how much I can say, but..." Clio hesitated, genuinely unsure of what, if anything, she should disclose. "I don't think I'm allowed to say anything. I've got plenty of work from them to tackle, but it is a few days' work, at least."

There was silence on the other end for a moment.

"Has it got anything to do with Alex?" Karen finally asked.

Clio's heart almost stopped. "Alex? No, Mac hasn't asked me anything about that."

"Mac?" Karen asked. "No, never mind. It's just that a policeman came to see me last night asking about Alex," Karen said. "And I did say to you it wouldn't be good for the university to help that journalist. Didn't I?"

There was an edge to Karen's voice that could have cut Clio's throat.

"You did. Karen, what they asked me to look at was from a crime scene. A very recent crime scene."

She waited, mouth dry, wondering how much trouble she was in.

"Let me speak to the Vice Chancellor. We might need to speak to the University's solicitors if this is going to take you away from your work. Just in terms of what we're obliged to provide," Karen said. "Leave it with me. Will you be in the office today?"

"I thought I would work from home, if that's ok?"

"Home? Yes, I suppose so. I'm doing the same. OK, well, I'll be in touch."

Karen hung up. Clio breathed a sigh of relief.

CHAPTER TWENTY-FIVE

"PENNY FOR THEM, GUV?" Melissa said as she drove them both out of Edinburgh towards Ratho for the second time in as many days.

Mac had handed his keys to a uniform at the station with instructions to recover his car from High School Wynd and return it to Niddrie Mains Road. He felt vulnerable without it, unable to get about with the freedom that he wanted. Such losses were trivial in the grand scheme of things, but they bothered him out of all proportion. Like losing his phone. But his mind wasn't on that. It kept going back to Clio. Melissa had begun calling her by her first name within 24 hours of meeting her. Mac would use her title in front of others, but in his head she was Clio already.

"Doctor Wray is a civilian, and she's becoming instrumental in helping to catch this killer. That puts her and her family at risk," he said. "I don't like it."

"Neither do I. Clio is a lovely person. I almost wish she were going to be around more often," Melissa replied.

"Cazzy will be jealous," Mac replied.

"Clio isn't my type. Thought she might be yours, though," Melissa said.

Mac looked at her. Just looked, and she grimaced. "Sorry, guv. Just sometimes, I think you need someone to look after you." She put her hand up for a moment. "There, I said it. I know I'm not allowed to, but I said it. Fire me."

For a long moment, Mac was silent and unsmiling, watching the beginnings of rain against the windscreen. "I couldn't fire you, Melissa," he said finally. "You'd sue."

Melissa laughed, and Mac grinned. "Cazzy would sue Police Scotland back to the stone age that's for sure. But that's what I mean. You need a Cazzy. She looks after me and you don't have anyone like that."

"I look after myself. Do I strike you as the kind of man that's easy to live with?" he said, indulging the personal talk for a moment.

Normally, he would have stamped on it. Pushed her away and maintained the distance. He wondered if this wasn't the effect of being hit on the head. Or maybe the much bigger injury he'd sustained when Siobhan walked out. Taking herself and the child that Mac had allowed himself to think of as his own. Thoughts of Siobhan and Áine brought a stab of pain that he brutally repressed.

"No, you don't," Melissa said. "But neither am I. I think I drive Cazzy mad sometimes with my need for everything to be in order and in its proper place. She tells me I'll never cope with a baby about the place if I can't stand a bit of mess."

Mac considered his own well-ordered flat. He didn't have time for cleaning, which is why he paid someone to do it for him. But if he'd had the time, he knew it would be done with forensic thoroughness. The idea of a small bundle of chaos being let loose in it made him uncomfortable. An older child was different. Áine had been ten. No, she'd been eleven or twelve. Maybe thirteen. It wasn't that he couldn't remember now, he'd never committed the fact to memory. Siobhan had told him, and it had promptly been deleted as irrelevant. Christ, no wonder she'd left. He grunted a reply to Melissa, then decided to change the subject. This conversation was going nowhere.

"Karen Martins is likely to be hostile. I've spoken to her once and she'll probably think there's nothing more to say. Or ask why we're insistent on dragging it all back up again. Her husband is entitled and arrogant. Don't let him get under your skin," he said, more for something to bring the conversation back to professional matters than because Melissa needed to know.

She nodded and made no comment on Mac's shutting down of the personal chat.

"I'll lead. I've established some kind of rapport with her," he added.

Melissa gave him a sharp glance. Mac was waiting for a reaction and saw it, though he didn't acknowledge it. If Melissa wanted to think he was some kind of womaniser, then let her. The rain was thundering down by the time they reached the Martins' house just beyond the village of Ratho. The sky was dark despite it being lunch time. A couple of lights glowed warmly in the face of the starkly modern facade of the house.

"Wow, I like this," Melissa commented. "Clean lines and modern."

"Always thought of you as a rose cottage type," Mac commented.

Melissa laughed. "Too messy. Give me contemporary with decking and a contained garden any day."

She reached into the back for an umbrella, but Mac stopped her.

"Let's walk to the door and get ourselves soaked. It'll give us a reason to ask for a towel. You can go get one and have a snoop around."

Melissa grinned. "Right you are, Holmes," she said, dropping the umbrella.

"Just before we go. Did you put in a requisition for Karen's hospital report? I know it's unlikely she's the killer, but she's the only one outside of this team who knows Clio is helping us. I don't want that risk for her and her daughter."

"I understand, guv. I'm across it."

Mac nodded his thanks and got out of the car, resisting the instinct to flinch from the cold water. Melissa covered the distance to the front door with hunched shoulders. Mac walked as though it were a balmy, sunny day. At the doorbell, there was the usual rigmarole with the master of the house. Mac bullied him into opening up for them. Fleece, a different one, sandals over thick grey hiking socks. Charles Martins stood with one hand on the door. A single glance dismissed Melissa and then withered in Mac's direction.

"Karen is not here," he said belligerently.

"The University said that she was working from home today," Melissa said. She had phoned Karen Martins' office before they left the station.

"She isn't. She left this morning for work and I haven't seen her since," Charles replied.

"It's drookit out here. Would you mind if we came in?" Melissa said.

"Yes, I'm busy," Charles replied.

"Is everything alright, Charles?" a voice came from behind him.

A man appeared in a doorway holding a mug of something hot. He wore a gray shirt, black trousers, and a white rectangle at his throat.

"It's fine, Gordon. These officers were just leaving," Charles said. "They wanted to speak to my wife."

"Actually, a word or two with you would be just as good," Mac said.

As he spoke, he stepped forward and to the side. Charles instinctively stepped back, though he had every right to stand his ground. If he had, Mac couldn't have forced the issue. It was all about assuming the other person would back down and projecting that. One of the magic tricks of the police. Melissa followed.

"I'll fetch a couple of towels," the priest said.

"Actually, just point me in the right direction. I need the loo, if that's OK, Mr. Martins?" Melissa said.

Charles nodded, slamming the door. He pointed down a hallway.

"There's a WC, third door along."

Mac looked in the opposite direction. He could see the living room, overlooked by the mezzanine level that he and Karen had sat in. It would put the WC out of sight and let Melissa slip out for a snoop.

"Let's take a seat," Mac said, striding into the living room to be greeted by the dog.

"I'll put the kettle on. It's not long boiled," the priest said.

"And you are?" Mac said, taking a seat on a large corner sofa.

The room was open plan and occupied the full width of the house. Tall windows in front and behind allowed in plenty of natural light. The floor was hardwood and apart from the sofa there was a black leather bucket chair, another chair of wicker and a coffee table that looked like it was made of driftwood.

"Reverend Gordon Brunt, friend of the family."

Brunt came forward, offering his hand, long-fingered with large knuckles and prominent veins. He smiled warmly and Mac shook the hand without standing. Charles Martins had perched himself on the edge of the wicker chair, hands clasped between his knees.

"I can't think what you want to talk to me about," he said.

"Any idea where your wife might have gone?" Mac asked.

"None."

"She have a mobile phone?"

"What? Yes, of course she does. Why?" Martins seemed confused, face creased into a puzzled frown.

"Do you?" Mac asked.

"Naturally, but..."

"Then you can tell me where she is," Mac pointed out.

He couldn't make him, couldn't take away Martins' phone

without a search warrant, but he could bully the man into it. It wasn't as if he was asking for the phone. Just for Martins to check his wife's location.

"Oh, right," Martins said, penny dropping.

He fished in his jeans pockets and took out his phone, waking it and putting in a pin code.

"What do you do for a living, by the way?" Mac asked.

"I'm an architect," Martins said distractedly.

"How do you take your coffee, officer?" Brunt called from the kitchen.

"Filter, if you have it. Milk but nondairy, two sugars. Tea if you only have instant," Mac called back.

It was rude, but it would hopefully keep the priest out of the way for a few minutes.

"I can't find her. Her phone might be out of charge. I've only got her last location," Martins said.

"May I see?" Mac asked.

Martins turned the phone towards Mac. It showed a map with a grey circle in the centre, labelled Karen. Mac frowned, pressing the circle showed that her last location had been logged at just after 8 am that morning. The location was the middle of Edinburgh; in fact, it was the Old Moray building of the university.

"What time did she leave this morning?" Mac asked.

"Same time as usual, about half seven. Look what's this about?" Martins said.

Mac ignored the question but just stared at Martins, saying nothing. It wasn't that he was trying to intimidate the man. His mind was elsewhere, but who knew what a silent stare might dredge up from the depths? Besides, the man was annoying him. Martins looked away, looked back, looked away again. Then he abruptly stood.

"I resent this. I've done nothing wrong!"

"Tea and coffee," Blunt announced, coming into the room from the kitchen carrying a tray and three mugs.

"Is Karen in the habit of letting her phone run out of charge overnight? That's when I charge mine. I think most people do," Mac commented, accepting his coffee. Instant with dairy milk by the looks of it. Well, what do you know, a passive aggressive priest.

"Yes, of course she does."

"So, her phone hasn't run out of charge since 8.07 this morning," Mac said. "Either she's broken it, dropped it in the toilet or something, or switched off the location. Why would she do that?"

"How would I know?" Martins was pacing the room now, clearly agitated.

"Is this an interrogation officer?" Brunt asked politely. "Because I'm a qualified solicitor as well as a minister, just so you know."

"No, no. I wanted to talk to Karen and Charles has been trying to help me figure out how to find her," Mac said amiably.

"Well, she clearly isn't here, so why don't you speak to her employer..." Brunt began.

"What was your relationship like with your son, Mr. Martins?" Mac asked, picking the moment of greatest impact for the question.

Martins had been at the window, but now he whirled, eyes wide. "What the hell is that to do with you?"

"Did you know that he had been self-harming?" Mac asked, pinning Martins with a hard stare.

"No. I mean, yes, I do know. I didn't at the time."

"So, you weren't that close?" Mac persisted.

"No! Ok? Is that a crime now? I failed as a father. Satisfied?"

Brunt stood and walked to Martins, placing large hands on the other man's shoulders. "Don't get overwrought, Charles. You weren't a failure. You were a good father. You are a good man with nothing to feel guilty about."

"Alex's friends seemed to blame you for his self-harming. Why would that be?" Mac asked, smooth in the lie.

Mac's instincts were driving him. There was something about Martins' immediate defensiveness and the assured confidence of the minister that just didn't smell right. Maybe it was his automatic suspicion of anyone claiming the title of priest. The cynicism of an atheist copper.

"It wasn't my fault!" Martins shouted.

CHAPTER TWENTY-SIX

AT THAT POINT, Mac heard Melissa walking down the hallway into the living room. It was the perfect timing, when Martins was already on the back foot. She had probably been listening to the conversation and had timed her entrance for maximum disruption, sensing that Martins just needed a push and to even the numbers.

"What wasn't your fault?" Mac asked quietly.

"I was cleared!" Martins spat.

Melissa quietly took a seat next to Mac, who leaned forward, intent on his prey. "Of what?" he asked.

"As a solicitor, I need to make it known I'm not at all happy with the tone of this conversation," Brunt said, turning away from Martins and standing resolutely between him and the two police officers.

"This is part of a murder inquiry," Mac said bluntly, deciding to deploy his nuclear option. "And I deem these questions to be important. If Mr. Martins wishes to make this formal, we can reconvene at Niddrie Mains Road Station, assuming he wishes you to represent him. Frankly, I might prefer that given how bloody defensive he's been the whole time."

Brunt raised his hands placatingly. "Look, let's not be hasty."

"Want me to call for a car, guv?" Melissa said, taking out her phone.

"No!" Martins said. "No. Look. I've done nothing wrong. You wanted to talk about my wife. I'm happy to answer any questions..."

"I did. Now I want to talk about you. What were you cleared of? If it's a criminal charge, I'll find out in the time it takes me to walk to my car, so there's no point in hiding it." Mac said, harshly.

Martins looked at Brunt, who returned an inscrutable stare, then shrugged. Martins licked his lips as Brunt sat down in the bucket seat, arms draped over the rests, hands dangling at the wrists. He was left standing by the coffee table, the focus of three pairs of eyes.

"I was accused of something a few years ago. Something I did not do, would never do. That boy had serious mental issues. He was a psychopath."

"What boy? Alex, your son?" Mac asked.

Martins almost fell into the wicker chair. "He was not my son. Karen had an affair, but he wanted nothing more to do with her when she got pregnant."

"What were you accused of?" Mac persisted, knowing the answer he would get.

Martins was squirming. He would not look up, staring at the floor and twisting his fingers.

"Of...of..." he choked, tailing off into silence.

"Of molesting the child. When Alex was about nine or ten," Brunt answered, speaking clearly and coldly. "The case was dropped and social services were content after a period of supervised contact that it was a fabrication told by a mentally ill boy."

Mac exchanged looks with Melissa. He let the new information percolate, seeing the case in a new light. The Celtic inscriptions and mutilations took on a new meaning. Window dressing to lead the investigation in an erroneous direction. Alex Martins making accusations against his step-father, sharing with his bandmates, maybe even Evie. Charles Martins trying to shut down the threat once and for all.

"And now I think you should go. This can have no relevance to any inquiry you're conducting," Brunt said.

Mac was beginning to lose his patience with the man. He had little time for solicitors in the first place, particularly when they put themselves in his way.

"You don't have any clue what I'm investigating..."

"Why, the man who was murdered in Craigmillar, I assume? And wasn't there another death in the middle of the city just yesterday?" Brunt said.

Mac stared at him, but Brunt stared back. "You surely didn't expect to keep a crime like that a secret, did you? Especially when a hero police officer, the one who caught The Angel Killer, is attacked? There are videos all over Facebook."

"Alex was self-harming. You've denied knowing that before he took his own life. How did it make you feel to realise he did that to himself?" Melissa spoke for the first time.

Mac hadn't signalled to her to speak but was glad that

she had. He didn't trust himself to speak and not rip Brunt's head off. Mel could apply a touch of caring maternity to the question which caught a lot of suspects off guard, especially males. Martins frowned as though genuinely puzzled by the question.

"Feel? But it wasn't my fault. I'm innocent."

Mac felt an itch on the back of his neck. A thrill ran through him as though an electric shock had been triggered. He'd spoken plainly and simply, but it was obvious Charles Martins believed every word he'd just uttered. However, it demonstrated a complete lack of empathy that was telling. Whatever else they were, the killer lacked empathy for his victims. No-one capable of such violence could possess an iota of compassion. Mac decided that Charles Martins was a psychopath.

"Where were you between the hours of eight and nine last night?" Mac asked immediately after Martins' protestation of innocence.

"Charles, I advise you not to..." Brunt began, reaching out towards Martins as though to separate him from the police officers.

"I'm only looking for the truth," Mac snapped. "If Mr. Martins is innocent of any offence, then he doesn't need to worry about telling the truth."

"I just don't want him to inadvertently incriminate himself. You are behaving in a very bullying manner."

Mac grinned. "Yes, I am. And the two of you are behaving like guilty men. What am I going to find out when I put your name through our database, Reverend?"

"Nothing," Brunt said.

There was a flat coldness to his eyes now. Any facade of the polite minister, helpful and jovial, had melted away. His blue eyes had the glint of steel after rain.

"I was here. OK?" Martins said, then turned to the priest. "Gordon, there's no need to get angry."

"I'm just trying to protect you, Charles."

"You were at home. With your wife?" Melissa asked, taking out a notebook.

Martins hesitated, just for a fraction of a second, but it was enough. Mac smelled the lie about to leave his mouth. The answer would be yes.

"Yes."

Mac wanted to smile, but he kept it to himself. He wasn't clear how this man would fit into the case, but he had three pieces of circumstantial evidence. The possibility that he was a child abuser, the certainty that he lacked empathy and that he had just lied about his alibi. It was enough to put him at the top of the list. His wife had occupied that spot, but it was a discomforting thought as far as Mac was concerned. He just didn't see it in her. He didn't immediately reply, and Melissa had the good sense to stay quiet. Mac didn't have enough to make an arrest. He could invite Martins to the station, but it was unlikely he would come while the good reverend was on hand to counsel a refusal.

"What were the two of you doing?" Melissa asked when Mac sat back in his chair.

"I don't know, watching TV probably," Martins replied.

"Watching what, in particular?" Mac asked.

Once upon a time, that had been an easy way to test a lie made up on the spot. The advent of streaming services made it harder to catch that lie. No more checking the suspect's story against a copy of the Radio Times.

"I can't remember. I dozed off. Karen chose it, so it was probably one of those shows about Vikings."

"Obviously, we'll ask Karen the same question," Melissa put in.

"When we find her," Mac said, his mouth quirking into a half smile.

"Can you think where she might be if she's not at work and she isn't here?" Melissa asked, her face a picture of innocence.

Martins shook his head, spreading his hands. "Who knows, these days?"

"You two having some martial problems?" Mac probed.

"None of your business!" Martins snapped.

This time Mac's smile was full, and he gave a small shrug, as though conceding the point gladly. "If she was seeing someone, and you knew who, then we could pay him a visit."

"If she was, and I knew for certain, she'd be divorced," Martins replied coldly.

Melissa looked at Mac. He sensed the same thing she did; he felt sure. This conversation had gone as far as it could. They might be able to squeeze more out of him in an interview room, but not here. Mac stood and Melissa followed suit.

"Well, thank you for all your help, Mr. Martins. We'll be in touch."

There was no mistaking the look of relief on Martins' face or the shrewd appraisal on Brunt's. Mac and Melissa left the house. The rain had stopped and the gloomy sky was broken by patches of light. A wind that came straight out of a fridge greeted them enthusiastically. Mac got into the passenger seat. Melissa drove them away from the house without a word, knowing her boss wouldn't want to sit in full view of Martins and Brunt and discuss what they'd just heard.

"Want to arrange for him to be brought in?" she asked.

"We don't have enough, but I'm going to get it," Mac said grimly. "He's guilty of something. Find anything?"

"I went upstairs. Apparently, without any of you hearing me. The dog followed. There's a staircase at the other end of the house that leads to bedrooms and bathrooms. They're sleeping in separate rooms. At least I found a master bedroom with women's clothes and shoes in the wardrobe, makeup and a hair dryer on the dressing table. Another bedroom two doors along had his clothes. I focused on her room, which had an en-suite. Clean and tidy, nothing obvious that I could see without rummaging."

"You didn't rummage?" Mac asked, as though surprised.

Melissa chuckled. "No guv, I didn't. Thought maybe an illegal search wouldn't look too good."

Mac shrugged. "I would have rummaged," he muttered, though he wasn't serious. Not completely serious.

"One thing that jumped out at me in the en-suite was a pair of scissors with blood on them. Just a spot and it looked old, down at hinge."

"Where someone cleaning might miss it," Mac said. "What kind of scissors?"

"Small and sharp. Craft scissors maybe," Melissa said.

"Maybe she lost her nail trimmer and cut herself," Mac speculated.

"Probably nothing, but it was all I could find without doing a proper search," Melissa said.

"We need to find Karen Martins. I don't believe her phone ran out of charge first thing in the morning, not for someone as senior in her work as she is. She didn't want her husband to know where she was going."

"I think she's cheating," Melissa said.

"So do I, and so does he, though he can't prove it. If he could, I think he'd divorce her in a heartbeat. And I suspect the money in that family is his," Mac replied.

He took his phone from his pocket and fumbled with it for a moment. It was a different model to the one he'd been using for the last few years, and that kind of change bothered him. He brought up Kai's number and hit the speaker button.

"Guv," Kai answered in three rings.

"We're leaving the Martins house in Ratho, heading back to the city. I'm going to the university and Melissa is coming in to work the Evie Black evidence. Any updates on Andrysiak?"

"Found his social media. Managed to figure out that he's been living in the west end of Glasgow for the last couple of years. And was able to track down an address and got the local polis to knock him up. No answer, so I authorised a break in."

He stopped, waiting to see if he'd gone too far. Mac respected the initiative his DC had taken.

"And?"

"Empty. I got them to live stream it to me. No clothes, food in the fridge is at least two weeks out of date. It's a flat in one of those refurbed tenements. I tracked down the agency that deals with the flat. Rent is paid up until next week and they've had no notice that our boy was thinking of leaving."

"When was he last active on social media?" Mac asked.

"On the media I can find, sixteen days ago. And he was active almost every day before that, at least a dozen posts a week on Insta, Twitter, Facebook."

"Alright, good work, Kai. We're going to need an alert put out for him. All divisions, ports, airports, you know the drill. Send me the paperwork and I'll authorise it."

"I'm on it, guv."

"Is Nari with you?" Mac asked.

"No, she's got a lead on that journalist you wanted. Gone to find him."

Mac exchanged looks with Melissa. It hadn't occurred to Kai to go with her and Nari wouldn't ask.

"I'll try her," Mac said, hanging up.

Nari's number rang out. He hung up and tried again. Then he swore. He phoned the dispatcher at Police Scotland HQ and requested a trace on an officer's phone. Then he gritted his teeth as the operator ran the number through the system. They finally came back with a location.

"Get uniform backup to that location. Where's the nearest unit?" Mac didn't like the answer he got. After a brusque order, he hung up. "She's in Corstorphine, and we're closer than the nearest uniform," Mac said, showing Melissa the address. "Get us there."

"You don't want to see if Karen Martins is—"

"No!" Mac snapped. "She'll have to wait until Nari has had the bollocking of her life."

CHAPTER TWENTY-SEVEN

THE ADDRESS AT WHICH Nari's phone was last active was outside a guest house on the main road through Corstorphine. The buildings were uniform tan sandstone, stained dark from the elements and the pollution. Bungalows and pleasant townhouses rose on a hill to one side. Hedges and flower beds predominated around residential properties while the A8 through Corstorphine took on the air of a high street through a country village. Guest houses, artisan bakeries and cafes. There was a distinct feeling of separation from the city ahead of them, as though this area remained the village it had been before Edinburgh engulfed it. Melissa saw Nari's car in the driveway of the guest house and pulled in behind it, her car sticking out onto the pavement. Mac was first out and heading to the front door. He pressed the buzzer. Then he knocked. Then he hammered with the flat of his hand.

If Nari was in there talking to Ramsay Jones, then the only reason she wouldn't answer would be if she couldn't. A sick instinct had settled in the pit of his stomach. He knew something had happened, blamed himself for not drumming this into his DS strongly enough. She was so independent and desperate to prove herself. And as a DCI he drove all of his team hard, expected a lot. Maybe too much. And it led to risks being taken. Melissa's face was creased with worry. She went to the side of the house and rattled a gate that blocked access to a lane running between where they were and the tall fence of the house next door. Then Mac heard movement inside. A glass breaking, the clatter of something heavy being dropped. Mac stepped back from the door and went in with a kick. The door flew open to rebound against the wall. Mac caught it with one hand and stepped inside.

"Police!" he shouted.

Then he saw Nari's feet on the floor. She was lying half inside a room to the left, a few yards ahead. Mac ran forward. She was face down, stirring weakly as though just coming around, lifting one hand to her head. Melissa was behind him.

"Get an ambulance and stay with her!" Mac barked, looking around for an assailant.

The sounds he had heard had stopped. Then Mac heard movement upstairs.

"Police! Do not move!" he roared as he headed for a narrow staircase that had been carpeted sometime in the seventies.

There was a cry of pain from somewhere and a half choked sob. The sound of fear and panic. Mac took in a small bathroom decorated in olive green. Three other doors and a further floor above. The doors all had locks. He tried the one that seemed closest to the noise, couldn't open it. It lasted no longer than the front door when he lifted his foot to it. There was a bedroom beyond, double bed and chintzy decor. A sash window was open and when he went to it, he saw the ridiculous sight of a young man clambering down an ancient drainpipe. He looked up, face boyish and round. Terror painted across his features. He had a bag slung over his shoulder, but he hadn't zipped it properly and papers were on the verge of spilling out.

"I'm a police officer. Get down off there before you break your neck," Mac ordered. "Ramsay, you're in enough trouble. Don't make this any harder."

No answer. A screw pulled loose from the wall and the drainpipe shifted out six inches. Jones decided to chance it and jumped the remaining seven or eight feet. He was lucky and missed the paved patio by inches, hitting a lawn and rolling. Mac turned and ran back through the house for the back door.

"Who the hell are you? What's going on here?" said a middle-aged woman standing in the ruined front doorway, two plastic supermarket bags on the ground either side of her. "I'm calling the police!" she finished stridently.

Mac ignored her but heard Melissa identifying herself. The back door was closed and there was broken glass on the kitchen floor. Jones must have run into the kitchen when he heard the car, found the door locked and panicked, ran upstairs thinking to climb out of the window. Mac kicked the back door open, not wanting to waste time asking for the key. Jones was halfway up a long, narrow back garden. A paved path ran between a lawn on one side and a flower bed on the other. A shed stood at the end of the lawn and a gate with two bolts beside it. Jones reached the gate and, after a second of futile tugging at the first bolt, he turned to face Mac. He had a knife in his hand.

"Don't come any closer," he spat.

Mac slowed but kept coming, taking deliberate steps to close the distance. He stopped outside the range he judged Jones would have if he swung the knife. It was a chef's knife, presumably grabbed in haste from the kitchen.

"Did you attack my sergeant in there?" Mac said quietly.

All his self-recrimination was shifting now to the man in front of him. The man who somehow obtained pictures of a gruesome suicide scene and tried to work it up into a profitable story for himself. The man who attacked an unarmed female police officer and now thought he could threaten the life of another. Mac's chest heaved, only partly from the exertion of running up and down stairs. His eyes locked onto those of Ramsay Jones, who raised the knife to point at Mac.

"I know what's happening. You think I don't know!" Jones spat. "I've been followed. You've had me under surveillance. I've got the evidence. It's over!"

Mac assessed the threat of the situation. Jones was cornered and desperate. But there were no members of the public nearby and he stood between Jones and Melissa, Nari, and the woman whose house Mac had just broken into. No one in danger but him. And Jones. His hands tightened into fists. Anger made rational thought difficult. He saw a man who attacked a woman and ran away. Tried to get away with it, then lashed out like a trapped rat, lacking the courage to face what he did. Spots of rain pricked his head. Suddenly, he was standing in the shadow of a bus shelter waiting for the man who had murdered his younger sister. An eighteen-year-old boy whose mother was dead and whose father had drunk a pint of rat poison a week before. It was no longer Ramsay Jones who stood in front of him but Mark Souter, Iona's ex-boyfriend. Police hadn't been able to get him for it. His family had closed ranks and given him an alibi.

Mac took a step closer as the rain pattered harder against his shoulders. Souter had thought he had got away with it, had been drinking and laughing with his mates in the pub. Mac wouldn't let him get away with it. Jones' eyes went wide as Mac came forward. He lunged with the knife, but Mac grabbed his wrist and twisted hard. He pushed the arm down and out and drove a knee into Jones' stomach. The blade clattered to the path and Mac kicked it away behind him. He grabbed Jones by the hair and yanked his head back before hitting him in the mouth. Jones fell backward, his head hitting the side of the shed, his arm still held in a white-knuckled grip. Mac stepped forward, looming over him, and seeing someone else. This wasn't Corstorphine, this was Portree on Skye, and Callum McNeill was about to take revenge for his sister.

"Mac, no!" Melissa screamed behind him.

Mac stared down at Ramsay Jones, who had a hand raised above his head to protect himself. Melissa was running up the path then, reaching Mac, she grabbed his upraised arm and hauled him back. She put a surprising amount of force into it, managing to drag Mac away, then putting herself between him and Jones.

"What the hell, guv? What were you going to do, beat him unconscious? This isn't the eighties!"

"He had a knife. He attacked Nari," Mac mumbled, feeling dislocated.

"You disarmed him and Nari will be fine. Paramedics have just arrived. Jesus, he could press charges."

This last was delivered in a whisper, not wanting to let Ramsay Jones overhear. Not wanting to give him ideas. Mac turned away, running a hand through damp hair. He felt like he had blacked out. The fury he had felt had overwhelmed him. It had begun as the pursuit of a man who had assaulted a police officer. It had become...something else, and the anger had ruled him.

"We've got him, ok? Assault on a police officer. Nari doesn't know what happened. He opened the door when she knocked and let her in. She said he was offering to make coffee as she went into the living room and then, wham. But, she'll be ok."

She had a hand on his shoulder and was looking into his eyes as though willing that point to be heard. Mac nodded, re-covering his equilibrium, and mentally kicking himself. The consequences of his loss of control could be huge. He swore.

"Did you smooth things over with the owner, or whoever that was?"

"Maybe. Or she'll make a complaint, she's the type. But, I don't think the problem is you kicking in doors to chase down someone who had attacked a police officer. Do you?"

Mac nodded. "No. You're right."

He saw two uniformed officers appear at the back door of the house and he waved them over, then pointed to Jones.

"Ramsay Jones. Two counts of assaulting a police officer. Take him to Niddrie Mains Road for processing. DI Barland will follow."

Their faces became set and cold when they heard the charges. Both were male and they would have seen Nari being looked after by the paramedics. Nothing more guaranteed to wind up a copper than one of their own being hurt. And male coppers worth their salt always felt protective of female colleagues, no matter the equality of the 21st century.

"What about the injuries, sir?" one of them asked.

"Resisting arrest. Be sure to bag the knife. He attacked me with it," Mac said.

Melissa waited until Jones was being led away between the two uniforms. "I think you should take the rest of the day off, guv. Want me to drop you home?"

"No, drop me at Old Moray House. I want to see if Karen Martins has made an appearance. If she's not there, I'll get an Uber back to the station."

Melissa was about to speak. Mac could feel it coming. He put a hand up, face hard. "No."

Melissa looked frustrated, hands on her hips, biting her lip. "Guv, I'm just going to say it. I think that bang on the head did more damage than you thought. I just saw you seriously lose it. Maybe I need to speak to Reid."

She stared at him, refusing to look away. Mac felt a flare of anger at the threat. He kept a tight rein on it, though. Melissa was compassionate and loyal to her boss and her team. She wasn't playing politics or being insubordinate. She was worried about him. Mac took a breath, looked away, and tried to look contrite. He nodded.

"You're right, you're right," he sighed, running a hand through his hair.

A wet lock fell across his forehead and he caught the lifting of Melissa's hand, as though she were about to brush it back. That made a smile tug at his lips. Melissa blushed.

"I'll come back with you and pick up my car. Get Jones into an interview room. We need to know what all of this was about," he waved a hand towards the house. "And we need to either eliminate him from the enquiry or not."

"You probably shouldn't be driving..." Melissa began.

Mac grinned. Full on boyish rogue. "Don't push it, Detective Inspector. Take the win."

Melissa chuckled and nodded. But it was half-hearted and Mac could see the worry she was trying to hide.

CHAPTER TWENTY-EIGHT

MAC WALKED INTO THE OFFICE while Melissa headed down to the cells to speak to the custody sergeant about Ramsay Jones. Kai was at his desk but looking tense, glancing over his shoulder then towards Mac's glass cubicle. Mac followed his gaze. There was a man in there, sitting on the desk. He had short, dark hair and a trimmed beard that covered the lower half of his face. He wore two pieces of a three-piece suit, minus the jacket.

"Guv..." Kai said.

"I know," Mac replied, patting his shoulder.

Few men of the age the stranger looked would have the nerve to walk uninvited into a DCI's office. Or greet him with the kind of smile usually reserved for an equal. It took a special confidence. Arrogance. The officer was Anti-Corruption. Mac had been in his place dozens of times. He walked to his office without breaking eye contact, strolled in, and took a seat at his desk.

"Detective Chief Inspector McNeill?"

"You know that. Who are you?" Mac said.

"Detective Inspector Franks, sir. AC 7."

"Well, Franks, I am entitled to be questioned by an officer of superior rank," Mac said.

"I'm not here to question you, sir. This is not an official interrogation relating to specific charges against you."

"Well, you've marched into my office during an ongoing murder investigation. You've disrupted my team in their work trying to catch a double killer. All for what? A chat?"

"Yes, sir," Franks said, apparently immune to sarcasm.

Mac felt on edge but held himself under rigid control. He folded his arms, looking up at the other man from under lidded eyes.

"Say what you've got to say. I caught someone following me the other day. Bloody incompetent as well. Whoever it was needs to go on a course."

"They wanted you to see them, sir. I wanted to be upfront and honest with you. Ask for your help right from the get-go. But I was overruled. My guvnor wanted to see what you were up to..."

"Don't good cop, bad cop me. It's transparent," Mac cut across him.

"Why so hostile, sir? We're on the same side, aren't we?" Franks asked with an air of injured innocence.

"I used to do your job," Mac said.

"I know, and you were good at it. My guv speaks highly of you."

"And who would that be?"

"Detective Chief Superintendent Logan."

Mac laughed. "So this is about Kenny Reid. He and Logan always hated each other. Your boss is starting another witch hunt. It's not the first."

"So what does that tell you about DCS Reid?"

"That he rubs people up the wrong way. He makes enemies," Mac said.

"That he's bent, sir," Franks said, leaning over Mac, hands planted on the desk.

Mac came up out of his chair like a rocket. Franks stepped back.

"That's a serious allegation. And you have to know I'm going to be telling him."

"You won't, sir. Because if you do, we'll know that we need to be looking at you just as hard. It's been noted that you worked for Reid in AC 3. Before that, you were linked to DI Strachan, who had links to organised crime. I'm here as an overture, right? To offer you an amnesty if you're willing to help us in our investigation," Franks said, becoming intense again.

His eyes were unblinking, and he wasn't shying away, putting a fist to the desk surface as though to emphasise his point. Mac had to respect his brass neck. There was no sign of nerves and he'd already said enough to get himself thrown out of the office and an official complaint lodged. Some officers would have just decked him.

"You want me to turn on Kenny," Mac said bluntly.

"Aye, we do. In return for keeping your own past just that... in the past," Franks said, his accent dropping for a moment into pure Aberdeen.

"Get the hell out," Mac said, quietly.

"If you call DCS Reid, we'll know, and you become fair game. Is there nothing in your past you don't want looked at too closely, eh?"

"Get out!" Mac roared.

Franks flinched but then his cool reasserted itself. He stepped back from the desk, locking eyes with Mac for a moment.

"Yes, sir," he said and left the room.

Mac watched him go. His car keys were on the desk in front of him, where the uniform who had dropped his car off had left them. He snatched them up just as Melissa walked into the larger officer outside. She said something to Kai and then looked up, saw Mac. She came to the door, knocked on the glass, and opened it.

"Guv, I didn't think you'd still be here. Everything OK?"

Mac smiled tightly. "Couldn't be better. I'm going to sit in on the Jones interview."

He saw the protest on Melissa's face before she'd opened her mouth. He drove a tank over it. "I'm letting you lead, Melissa. I've had a bump on the head, remember?"

She closed her mouth and her lips writhed as though she were chewing down the words she wanted to say to him. Mac had tried a light tone but knew it would just wind her up even more than if he were dictatorial.

"How are you doing with Jacek Andrysiak?" he asked Kai as he moved into the outer room.

"Local boys in Glasgow are looking in likely places. Message is out to all ports. If he tries to leave the country, he'll be arrested. I've had a bit more luck with the CCTV, though."

Mac grinned. Finally, some good news. "Thrill me," he said.

"Got footage from the mobile repair shop next to Evie Black's flat on South Bridge. Saw a dark SUV parked outside for about fifteen minutes before you arrived on the scene. Disappeared maybe thirty seconds before you came into shot. You remember seeing it?"

Mac closed his eyes, trying to visualise the events of that night. He remembered sounding the horn of his car and then walking up High School Wynd to try the back door of the building. Then there was nothing. A vague memory of sitting in a police car. Everything else was blank. It was the first time he had tried to think through the night step-by-step. The gap in his memory was frightening.

"No, there's nothing. But if the video shows the car was there, then it was there. Could you get the registration?"

"Not yet. It's a basic camera, monochrome and not much use at night. Picture gets bleached out by the lamp-post. But I'm trying to clean it up. Looks to me like a similar color and shape to the one I glimpsed on the Bute Tower footage."

Mac nodded thoughtfully. "Did it come back at all? After I went into Evie's building?"

"Nae, but I'm trying to track down where it went. Not that easy, still a lot of traffic on the road at that time of night and it's a common enough type of car," Kai said.

"Keep me posted, That's good work, Kai." Mac clapped him on the shoulder as he walked by.

Melissa fell into step alongside him. They descended the stairs to the ground floor and one of the five interview rooms located there. When they entered the room, Ramsay Jones was sitting in a paper forensics suit. A young woman sat next to him, a pad open in front of her. Jones' lower lip was split and swollen. He was dabbing a paper towel against it. When he saw Mac, his chair hit the floor in his haste to stand and get as far away as he could.

"Sit down, Ramsay," Melissa said patiently.

"I want him out of here. He assaulted me!" Jones babbled.

Melissa ignored him as she handed a tape in a container to the solicitor, inviting her to verify that the tape was sealed. She received a nod and broke the seal and put it into a tape recorder, which had been placed on the side of the table. The station had yet to be dragged fully into the twenty-first century. She introduced herself; Mac spoke up, as did the solicitor. Jones refused and Melissa spoke for him.

"For the record, as per the statement I have already given," Mac said. "The suspect has sustained injury to his mouth in an altercation in which I struck him twice in self-defense."

"You attacked me!" Jones screeched.

"You attacked Detective Sergeant Nari Yun," Melissa said calmly. "Striking her on the top of her head with a glass bottle and rendering her unconscious. Why did you do that, Ramsay?"

He stood against the wall, watching Mac with large, round eyes, clutching the paper towel to his face.

"I panicked," he said.

"What did you panic about?" Melissa asked.

"I...I don't know."

"Did she identify herself as a police officer?" Melissa asked.

"Yes."

"You invited her inside the guest house, number 78 Glasgow Road, Corstorphine?" Melissa asked.

"Yes. She asked to come in. Said she had a few questions for me."

"And when her back was turned, you attacked her," Mac said before Melissa could ask the question. She gave him a filthy look.

"No!" Jones snapped, advancing a few steps, only to retreat again.

"But that's what happened. She was attacked," Melissa said.

"Yes."

"By you?"

"Yes!"

Mac looked at Melissa, who looked back and shrugged.

"So, which part of the story are you denying, exactly?" Mac asked with mock confusion.

"That I planned it. You implied I planned it. I didn't," Jones replied. "I...I wasn't myself."

"Then who were you?" Mac said, unsmiling.

"I...I don't know. I...I thought she was...after me."

Again, a look passed between the two police officers. The solicitor remained silent, making notes.

"She *was* after you. She had been tasked with finding you. In connection to Alex Martins," Mac said. "So you were spot on, pal."

"There are people after me," Jones said, turning to lean against the wall, hugging himself.

Mac had a bad feeling about where this was going. Something caught his eye. When Jones put his arms about himself, his left sleeve pulled up. Mac glimpsed something on the back of his left arm, a couple of angular lines. It looked like a tattoo.

"What people, Ramsay?" Melissa asked.

"You wouldn't understand," Jones replied.

"We did our research. Talked to Dan Greene at the Guardian and Flora Ogunlayes at the Independent. They said you're a talented writer who always gives them well written, well-researched copy. You're one of their go to freelancers. At least, you were. Until about three years ago. Want to tell us what happened?"

She slid a folder across the table to Mac, and he opened it. Saw a hospital admission dated three years ago. Psychiatric hospital. Admission under Section 2 of the Mental Health Act 1983. Mac's practised gaze ran down the medical report, certain words jumping out at him. Paranoid schizophrenic. Post Traumatic Stress Disorder. Acute Childhood Trauma. When he looked up, Jones was focused on him. The sweating paranoia was gone. He looked calm, and there was sly intelligence in his stare.

"He's one of them," Jones said, pointing at Mac.

The paper sleeve with its elasticated wrist had ridden up his forearm and remained there. Mac got a look at a crude tattoo in the shape of a star, a pentagram, in fact.

"Nice ink," he commented.

"A symbol of protection."

"Right. An ancient symbol. I have one myself, right here."

He tapped his chest above his heart. It was a lie, but Jones didn't need to know that.

"Do you know Evie Black, Ramsay?" Melissa asked.

Jones shook his head.

"Who do you think DCI McNeill is with?" Melissa changed her tack. "You said he was one of them. Who do you mean?"

"The Illuminati, of course," Jones said as though it was obvious.

"I strongly feel that my client needs to be given a psychiatric assessment before this interview proceeds any further," the solicitor spoke up.

Mac could understand her concern. Jones looked unhinged and sounded worse. The kind of unhinged capable of killing two people and carving ancient symbols into their flesh? Why not? He'd shown he could behave violently and obviously believed in the power of ancient symbols.

"Why were you so interested in the suicide of Alex Martins, Ramsay?" Mac asked, imitating Melissa's soft tone, trying for paternal and caring.

"Because Alex was their first victim," Jones said.

"Where did you get the photos from, Ramsey? The ones of Alex's suicide?"

Jones had been moving closer as he spoke, edging towards the table. Now he grabbed the chair, dragged it back a few feet and sat. He huddled, arms together about his waist, feet apart, knees together. He looked like a child. A frightened child.

"From you."

"Me?" Mac asked, confused. "I didn't give them to you."

"Not you! The police. The police gave them to me. I paid them."

Mac and Melissa shared a glance.

"You said Alex was their first victim, Ramsey," Melissa said gently. "Who do you mean? Do you mean the police?"

"No."

"Then who?" Mac asked.

"Nothing my client says while in such a state of clear mental dislocation is admissible. I demand..."

"Who!" Mac said sharply, slapping the table with the palm of his hand and making Jones jump.

"The men who were abusing him!" Jones shouted.

CHAPTER TWENTY-NINE

MAC THREW HIS SUIT JACKET down onto the sofa as he walked into the lounge. The room was dark. There were strips of tangerine light from the lamppost outside from the half opened blinds. He walked to the fridge, feeling the ache in his back from hours of sitting in the plastic interview room chair. Opened the fridge. Two ready meal curries looked back at him. He chose the one that was least expired and put it in the microwave. Hunger had come and gone. All that was left in his stomach was a slightly nauseating, empty feeling. But sense told him he should eat. As the microwave hummed to itself, he walked to the stereo, switched it on and pulled open a drawer in the adjacent unit. By the orange sodium light, he picked out a cassette with a black j-card insert bearing the name Omega in white letters. Handmade artwork. He wondered who the band had got to do that for them. Ramsay Jones probably had some creative connections with his background.

He put the cassette into the tape deck and then hit play, turning up the volume. Finally, he let his body fall into the faux leather bucket seat beside the stereo. It was similar to the one in the Martins' living room, though he doubted he had paid anywhere near as much for his. As he undid the first few buttons of his shirt, his eyes drifted to the sofa. Many were the weary evenings he and Siobhan had curled up on that sofa together. He had stretched out, one foot on the sofa, one on the floor, head nestled amid the cushions that she had brought to the flat. Gone now. Listened as she told him about her day, listened and tried to let police work fall away. Tried. A wall of noise hit him. A melancholy melody woven from tremolo picking. Another more rhythmic riff overlaid. Vocals were harsh and incomprehensible. Snarling and dripping. Hoarse screams and whispers.

Ramsay Jones had talked. Against the wishes of his solicitor he had talked, while the over-stretched duty psychiatrist was waiting to assess his mental competence. Mac felt the burden of his words, the need to talk about everything he had heard. But there was no-one he could discuss it with. There never had been. A sound penetrated the homemade nihilism of Alex Martins' band. It was a pulsing vibration. Mac realised it was his phone. He got up and walked to where he had discarded his jacket. The ringing ended, and he saw the missed call came from Clio. He stood looking at the screen for a long moment. Then decided that Clio was better off out of the investigation. It was a dark morass and he could feel himself drowning in it. This was the kind of case that wouldn't let you sleep. Wouldn't let you focus on anything except itself. The sort of case retired coppers still pored over. Stole boxes of files to take home and study, hoping to finally spot that elusive missed clue and break the case wide open. The phone lit up once more. Clio again.

He swiped and put the phone to speaker, putting it on the arm of the chair and then paused the cassette.

"Jesus, what was that?" Clio asked.

"Alex Martins," Mac said wearily.

"Oh, you sound half dead. Is this a good time?"

"I feel half dead, to be honest. But now is as good a time as any. Have you decided if you're going to continue helping us?"

"Yes. I am."

It was a small victory, but it meant he now had something else to worry about. Two some ones actually, Clio and her daughter. But he couldn't solve this case without her. He suppressed a guilty sigh. "Good, I think it's the right thing to do."

"Yes, well, I talked it over with Karen tonight and..."

"You what?" Mac sat up.

"She came to mine. She's my boss. I've known her for years. Is there a problem?"

Mac sat back in his seat, rubbing his eyes, and regretting his reaction. Clio didn't need to know that Karen was a person of interest. He couldn't convince himself she was a killer anyway, and Clio could hardly avoid her own boss.

"No, sorry. Just tired and it's been...a tough day."

"Want to talk about it?"

Mac opened his mouth to refuse, but at that moment, the microwave pinged. He pictured himself eating directly from the plastic container, sitting at the breakfast bar. Then returning to his chair. Alone. Suddenly, he would do anything to avoid that scenario.

"We got hold of Ramsay Jones, the journalist?" Mac said.

"Oh yeah, I haven't heard from him since I took on the police work. How is he?"

"Mentally unstable. Paranoid schizophrenic. He knocked my Detective Sergeant unconscious and attacked me with a chef's knife."

"Jesus!" Clio exclaimed. "What happened? Are you ok?"

"Aye, I'm fine. Like I said, he's mentally unstable. Convinced there's a conspiracy out to get him. Illuminati, if you can believe it. Probably Freemasons too. He didn't hold back. Buys into every conspiracy from QAnon to faked moon landings. He believes Diana was murdered and Covid was deliberately manufactured to control the population. He met Alex Martins, became friends with him. They bonded at a support group that Ramsay set up during a stable period. For survivors of abuse. He said he was abused by his dad and Alex told him he was abused by his step-father and another, as yet unidentified, male."

Once he'd started talking, Mac couldn't stop. It was like a dam bursting. There was something about Clio that Mac trusted. Part of him was horrified at his candor, but he suppressed that feeling. The idea of stoically bearing the weight of what he knew alone was sickening.

"Allegedly," he continued. "We checked and while there was a complaint made by Alex Martins, he subsequently withdrew it, claiming it had come from a period of mental instability when he had gone cold turkey from meds he was taking for bi-polar disorder."

"Poor Ramsey, and poor Alex, he sounds like he was really messed up. I had no idea. Was it only the alleged abuse that made him like that? Not that the abuse isn't horrific enough."

Mac smiled bleakly. Some would simply dismiss Alex Martins as mental, call him a nut job, disturbed, dangerous. Clio had reacted like a parent, wondering what had turned the innocent little boy into a messed up adult. It appealed to him. He felt the need to badly hurt which ever sick adult had twisted that boy into what he became.

"That's what we're going to find out. I'm not done with Charles Martins. He's an arrogant sod, thinks he's above the law because he's got a bit of money and the right connections. Ramsay thinks he's the devil. He's terrified of him."

"Is Ramsay involved in your case?"

"Cases," Mac corrected. "A woman was murdered and the word witch carved into her body. And our usual Celtic symbolism scattered about."

Clio was silent for a moment. "I knew there'd been a second one. You intimated as much when we last met. Was she drowned?"

"How did you know?" Mac asked. "We haven't released that detail anywhere."

"It's a traditional method of execution for witches and not just in Edinburgh. That and burning."

"Ramsay Jones has self-tattooed at least one pentagram onto his body as protection against what he saw as evil."

"Oh, my god! My daughter answered the phone to him! I sat next to him in McDonalds!" Clio gasped.

"Relax, Clio. He's not our murderer. He's alibied for them both," Mac said, feeling the weight of the day bearing down on him once more.

For a while in that long interview session, it had looked as though they were onto something. Ramsay had become more and more unhinged in his rambling, appearing to grow into the image of a deranged serial killer. But they'd been able to establish his whereabouts, and both alibis were unbreakable. He couldn't have killed Evie Black or Richard McCullough.

"Thank god."

"So, we've eliminated a suspect. Progress," Mac said, wearily.

"You don't sound very happy about it."

"Nari spoke to some of the editors Ramsay had worked for in London. They had a lot of positives to say about him. He had a glowing future. But, he was so messed up by what happened to him, I don't think he'll ever achieve it. We had to discontinue the interview when the duty psychiatric officer arrived and now he's been sectioned for his own good. It's just..." Mac tailed off, unbearable sadness filling him.

"Tragic," Clio said, gently.

"Yeah. Some people just don't get a chance," Mac replied.

"You say that like you have some experience."

Mac hesitated, was silent for a long moment. "You see a lot as a cop..." he sighed and rubbed his face. "Actually no, it's more than that...my little sister, Iona...she was murdered. When I was seventeen."

"I'm so sorry, Mac. She never had the chance to grow up," Clio said, softly.

"None. Someone took it away from her. Took it away and never had to answer for it. To this day he's still walking free," Mac said.

"Is that why you joined the police force?"

"Maybe. I didn't straight away. Left home after my dad died and just...existed for a while. Walked a thin line for a bit, could have gone either way. But, something happened after I'd moved to Edinburgh and it made me choose a side. The right side. Maybe what happened to Iona was at the back of my mind the whole time. Maybe."

"You're a really hard man to get to know. Do you know that?"

"I've been told." Mac smiled.

"My ex, Maia's dad, was the opposite. Never left a single thought unspoken and thrived on being the centre of attention. I didn't realise it at first, but he wanted the attention, craved it. From anyone, you know? He just couldn't survive without it."

Mac nodded, though she couldn't see the gesture. "I know the type. God, I shouldn't be having this conversation with you. I feel like I'm drunk."

"I am. A little anyway."

"You are?"

"Yes, Karen Martins showed up at my house. Gods, that's why I called you! I completely forgot. She said she'd been driving around all day and didn't want to go home. Realised she was nearby and thought she would see how I was getting on with the help I was giving you."

Mac sat up, staring at the phone intently.

"Go on."

"I couldn't very well tell my boss no, so I said she could come over for some takeout. She brought a couple of bottles of wine. She was...well, a bit weird, actually. Talked more tonight than in the entire time I've known her. Like suddenly there was no barrier between us. Almost as though we were real friends, if you know what I mean? I found the whole experience really sad."

"How so?"

"Because I think she was only doing it as she had nowhere else to go. She didn't want to go home."

Mac ran a hand across his forehead, trying to clear the fog of despair and desperation left from the interview with Ramsay Jones.

"I don't think her marriage is a happy one," he said.

"It isn't," Clio replied. "Not one bit. She told me she's afraid of him. That he's got anger problems. He's been violent in the past."

"To her?"

"Not directly, I don't think. More breaking stuff, glasses, plates, you know the sort of thing."

"In my experience, it's a progression. First shouting. Then breaking plates. Then faces," Mac said grimly.

"God, don't say that, Mac. I'm worried enough about her as it is. I offered her the sofa, but she said that he was already suspicious of her. If she stayed out all night, he'd think she was cheating again."

Mac's mind fastened on the last word. Something in his head clicked. Like a piece of a complicated puzzle suddenly shifting and sending the entire piece into a new configuration. A thrill of excitement burst through his fatigue.

"Did she mention anything about Alex's parentage?" he asked.

Clio was quiet for a moment. "How did you know she talked about that?"

"She obviously came to you for a heart-to-heart, Clio. It seems natural she'd get around to talking about it. Especially after a few glasses of wine. Karen Martins has cheated before; we both know that. Charles told Mel and me that Alex wasn't his. Their marriage is on the rocks and he's angry. Any man gets angry when a woman cheats on him, especially one with his ego. But if that cheating produced a child, a child that he'd paid for, fed, clothed..."

"Abused."

"Allegedly. But it fits, Clio. Alex was making serious accusations. Up to that point, Charles had got away with it, probably forced Alex to withdraw his original accusation and blame it on not taking his bi-polar medication, but what if that wasn't the end? What if Alex was telling more and more people, desperate for someone to listen and take him seriously? Ramsey obviously knows. How long before that would affect Charles' standing in the community? His reputation? His business?"

"You're not saying..."

"It all fits, Clio. It all fits."

CHAPTER THIRTY

THERE WASN'T YET any concrete evidence against Charles Martins. But Clio's words had triggered a gut reaction in Mac. Over the years, he had learned to trust those reactions. Every copper did. His first instinct after thanking Clio and promising to speak to her again the next day was to call Reid. Then he remembered AC. A call to Reid in the middle of the night would be questioned. No matter that it was legitimate police business. He stared at the phone for a long time, then put it down, let his head fall back. There was no use dragging his team out again to bring in Charles Martins. They needed to rest, and so did he. Martins wasn't going anywhere. If he decided to run, it would only confirm his guilt. First thing in the morning, Mac would call Reid and brief him. Then he would have Martins picked up. His movements needed to be established for the night of the two murders.

Martins had already stated that his wife was his alibi. Mac was pretty sure that was a lie. An abusive husband could easily demand his wife lie to provide him with an alibi. Karen Martins struck Mac as being too strong a woman to be coerced in that way. But you never could tell. And if Charles Martins was killing to cover up the truth, to stop those who Alex had told from talking about the abuse, then he was capable of anything. The Celtic symbols were a perplexing outlier, though. Contrary to what Clio believed, they became red herrings; there to make the police think there was something more to these murders, some purpose. Or to throw suspicion on his wife. After all, she'd found Alex's body and was one of the few people in the country who understood all that symbolism and mythological nonsense. That made more sense. For a long time, Mac thought about Karen and Charles Martins, their relationship, their history. He went to his laptop and looked up the firm Martins worked for, their buildings and his role in the firm. They were called Hitchcock, Merten, and Martins.

They appeared to specialise in commercial and industrial properties and Martins was a partner. So, on the surface, a man with plenty of money. Scrolling through the company website, he came across an anomaly that made him stop for a moment. In amongst the office buildings and factories, there was the image of a church. He clicked the link, bringing up information about the project, including dates and location, as well as information about the design and materials used. Charles Martins was listed as designer and chief architect on the project. The Church of Scotland was the customer, the work undertaken gratis by the company. Mac wondered if Martins had contributed to it personally, doing a pretty big favor for his friend Gordon Brunt. What did Charles Martins owe him when a brand new church was the payoff? Mac knew it was possible this was an entirely altruistic endeavor. But he didn't believe it for one minute. Rich people were rich because they didn't give away their money. Only the super-rich who had so much they could never spend it all did that.

Men like Charles Martins held onto their wealth, and a church just didn't look like a good investment. So why? Mac thought he knew, and it made him sick to his stomach, but there was no proof. That led to him looking up the minister. Gordon Brunt wasn't hard to find. Apart from his own social media presence, there was his role in the church. The police had nothing on him. No complaints or allegations. Not so much as a speeding ticket. Martins was almost as clean, apart from the accusation from his stepson and that was closed, complaint withdrawn. Notes from the investigating officer stated his belief that Alex was a mixed up adolescent who was venting his frustration and anger towards his step-father, a strict man with little tolerance. Mac opened up a file containing transcripts of the interviews conducted as part of the investigation. He stopped at the first line of the first transcript. The line detailed the time, date and location and stated who was present in the interview. Gordon Brunt was present, acting as solicitor to Charles Martins.

"Reid."

"I have a suspect in the McCullough and Black murders," Mac told him.

He was driving into Niddrie Mains Road station. Having sent texts to the team, ordering them into the office early for a briefing, he informed them they were bringing in a suspect. He was driving too fast, driven by the adrenaline rush that came with the imminence of an arrest. The more he thought about it, the more he was convinced that his instinct was correct. And Reid was an old school copper who understood gut instinct.

"Who?"

"His name is Charles Martins. His wife is an academic at the University of Edinburgh, an expert in Celtic mythology. He was accused of abusing his stepson, who later committed suicide. The circumstances of the suicide are similar to both killings. I think his son was talking to anyone who would listen about being abused. He'd been attending a support group organised by a journalist called Ramsay Jones. We brought him in yesterday and he revealed to us that Alex was opening up about what happened to him. Ramsay was convinced that Alex's step-father and others had abused the boy."

"But he's since been sectioned," Reid replied.

"You've checked the case file," Mac said, changing lanes without indicating and earning a blast of a horn from someone behind him.

"Yes, I'm keeping up. You're looking to make an arrest on the word of a nutter?"

"No, his wife has said that her husband has an anger problem. She's afraid of him. Through her work, he could have learned enough about Celtic symbolism to dress up the murder scenes, making us think there was some kind of ritual involved. He might even have got the idea from his son's band; they were into pagan images too. But I think this is all a cover up, possibly with the help of his friend, a Kirk minister who represented Martins when he was accused of child abuse."

"Christ, the press will love that one."

"I think he owed his friend a favor after he helped get him off. Martins' architect company built a church for him, for free. That's a project worth a few hundred thousand, surely."

"You think this priest is helping him now? I take it the second victim also knew about the abuse?"

"She may well have done. Evie ran her own label and Alex's band were signed to it. She'd been abused herself."

Mac thought of the crisscrossed white scars that Evie had worn proudly on her arms. She'd never been self-conscious of them or ashamed. It was a symbol that she was a survivor, not a victim. If she'd discovered that Alex was self-harming, she wouldn't have been able to stop herself from getting involved.

"OK, I think we've got enough to bring him in to answer some questions. I'm going to authorise a search of his home as well. You'll have the warrant by the time you get into the office. Good work on this one, Mac."

Mac hesitated. This was the moment he should tell Reid about the AC investigation. He didn't think they would inform Reid before they were ready to bring him in for questioning. And at that point, he'd be suspended from duty. Loyalty required him to tell his boss what was coming. But if there was any substance to it and Reid ran...

"Anything else, son?" Reid asked.

"You hear anything more about an AC investigation?" Mac asked, hedging.

"Nothing after the initial warning on the grapevine. I'm assuming they're watching me, listening to my phone calls. I haven't taken on any new officers, so I don't think there's any-one in the unit who's a mole."

That made Mac wince. AC wanted *him* to be the mole. Someone that Reid would never suspect.

"You hear anything?" Reid asked.

Mac swallowed. "No, nothing since the bungled surveil-lance. So either they've got someone better on the case or..."

"They don't give up, son," Reid said somberly. "You know that. If they think they have a case, they'll just wait in the shadows and bite when you least suspect. You remember how it goes."

"I do."

"Keep me posted."

Reid hung up. Mac looked ahead just in time to see the mass of red lights ahead of him. He stomped on the brakes and came to a halt just in time. The cars behind had seen the tailback coming, stopping in plenty of time. Mac swore, throwing the phone onto the seat beside him. He had to get his head straight. There was no way of knowing what Reid might have done to attract the interest of AC, and he didn't have time to be worrying about it now. He'd wanted to warn him. Wanted to ask him what he'd done and how he could help. Because he couldn't imagine Reid doing anything so bad that Mac wouldn't want to help. He might have bent some rules, even broken a few. But Reid was one of the good guys. He was no more a bent copper than Mac.

The search warrant had been delivered to Mac by email and he had Melissa print it out. A marked unit led them to the house in Ratho. Roof lit up but sirens kept off. Mac drove with Melissa at his side. Nari, fully recovered from her ordeal, drove Kai. A Scene-of-Crime van followed with another marked car bringing up the rear and ensuring the convoy wasn't separated. It was just after nine by the time they swung into the gravel driveway of the Martins' house. There were no cars in the drive, but the house had a garage which was closed. Mac remembered that Karen Martins would have left her car at Clio's house. Assuming she hadn't driven drunk. He strode to the front door and pressed the doorbell. There was no answer. He pressed again. Still no response except for the dog barking.

"Go round the back and see if the back door's open," he ordered.

Melissa led a uniform around the house at a brisk jog. The second marked car stopped at the entrance to the driveway, blocking it. Mac hammered on the door with the flat of his hand.

"Mr. Martins? Mrs. Martins? Karen? This is DCI McNeill, police. Could you open the door, please? This is important!"

Kai started to speak, and Mac quieted him with a chopping gesture. He thought he'd heard movement inside. Slow and soft.

"My husband is out," Karen Martin's voice came over the doorbell intercom.

"Then I need to speak to you, Karen," Mac replied.

"I've told you everything."

"I have some more questions. Open the door."

"No. Please just go. I can't help you."

Her words were faltering. He could hear the tears in that voice. The hitch in the throat, the thickness of the words themselves. He was about to more forcefully demand they be let in when it was opened from within. He saw Melissa standing there. Then, as the door opened further, he saw Karen Martins. Her left eye was swollen shut and that side of her face was battered, bruised and swollen. Her upper lip was cut as was the corner of her mouth. And her right cheek had three cuts and had bled. The dried blood was streaked down her face. Her hair was a tangled mess, and she hugged herself, standing back in the shadows.

"The back door was open," Melissa said. "You'd better come in."

A hulking uniform stood behind Karen as though to stop her from bolting. Mac gestured to the man.

"You're on sentry duty. No-one into the house without my say-so."

Karen shied away as the big man moved past her, seeming to collapse in on herself. Melissa went to her, trying to put an arm around her shoulders in comfort, but she winced as though in pain.

"Wait in the car," Mac whispered to Kai and Nari.

Then he stepped inside and closed the door.

CHAPTER THIRTY-ONE

MELISSA GUIDED KAREN to the living room. Although it was more an act of shepherding, as she did not want to be touched. As Melissa moved closer to Karen, the other woman moved away. Finally, Melissa sat on the sofa and Karen sat at the opposite end. Her hair hung over her face and Mac could smell the alcohol from the night before.

"What happened?" he asked, sitting down.

"I came home from Clio's house," she began in a monotone. "I'd had a few drinks there and was quite open with him about where I'd been, but he was suspicious. Kept asking and asking, making me go over and over it. I think he thought I'd been seeing another man. Except..."

She trailed off and Mac waited for her to speak, knowing that to press at this moment could send her into an uncommunicative state. She was in shock; he could see her hands trembling. It had happened a few hours ago, and she'd probably been getting herself together when the police had arrived.

Now she had to face the world knowing what she looked like. Knowing everyone was aware her husband had beaten her up. Having to relive the entire experience. Mac had seen it countless times before, the needless shame of a victim. She also knew the police wouldn't let it go, wouldn't just walk away and leave her. Something she'd said before Mel opened the door struck Mac at that moment. The first thing out of her mouth was the fact her husband wasn't home. She knew they were looking for him.

"I think he was more interested in what I'd said to you lot," she continued dully. "The police. He kept coming back to that. Then it was like he suddenly remembered he was supposed to be talking about me cheating on him. But, it's the police he was really worried about. I told him I hadn't spoken to anyone at the police other than the time he knew about. I said I'd been talking with Clio about the help she was giving, translating the inscriptions found at a crime scene. That's when he went crazy."

She was crying. Melissa produced a tissue from her pocket, and Karen buried her face in it.

"I was drunk, so I was just talking too much. And I was excited about what Clio was finding out for you. She was doing great work, using some of my previous studies, and it just seemed good that she could help you with something so important. But he didn't like it. He became furious and started breaking things. I tried to get out of his way, but he caught me across the face. It knocked me down, and he went upstairs. I heard him rummaging about and then when he came back down, he had a bag, a sports bag, over his shoulder. It looked full. I was angry and too drunk to be properly scared so I confronted him, grabbed at the bag and that's when he turned on me. Started hitting me and then when he'd knocked me down, kicking me. Stamping on me."

Again tears took over and this time her face was buried in her hands for a long time.

"Do you know where he's gone?" Mac asked.

"No. I only know one of his friends. The rest of our social circle are friends of mine. He never really mixed socially, not with anyone that I knew."

"What about Gordon Brunt?" Mac said.

Karen nodded. "Maybe. I never liked him. Charles spent a fortune of his own money building that bloody church for him and he's not set foot in a church since he was a child. God knows why he did it. It's creepy."

"In what way?" Mac asked.

"I thought maybe he was really gay and was trying to hide it. But, I don't know. Maybe that's what it is. Our marriage... the physical side, was a sham almost from the start. There's something between them that...I've never liked. When Alex said...what he said, Gordon never seemed to leave Charles's side. It was odd. And then suddenly Alex admitted he'd made it all up, and the investigation was dropped."

"It's important we find where your husband has gone, Mrs. Martins," Melissa said gently. "Can we have a look around the house? He might have left something behind that will tell us where he is."

Karen nodded silently, gulping. "Tear the bloody place apart for all I care. He's messed up and I'm starting to think he's the one...that he...Alex..."

Mac could hear the hysteria bubbling beneath the surface,

threatening to break through with every word. He leaned forward.

"Karen. This is also really important. Your husband told us you were with him between 8 and 9 the night before last. Do you remember if that was true?"

Karen looked up, frowning. "No. No, it's not true. I was here alone that night. Until, after midnight."

Mac drew Mel to one side and lowered his voice. "Stay with her until we can get a domestic abuse specialist out here to sit with her."

Melissa nodded curtly, turning her attention immediately back to Karen. Mac knew she would gently tell Karen what they needed from her in terms of evidence collection and what would happen next. He realised he hadn't seen or heard the dog, which had taken such an interest in him the last couple of times he'd been here. He went to the front door, opened it, and gestured to Kai and Nari.

"Martins has beaten up his wife badly and done a runner. Taken some stuff with him. Get the SOCO team in here. We'll start upstairs. Go through everything. When we get someone from the domestic abuse team over here to look after Karen, we can move downstairs. You know the drill. Anything that might tell us where he's gone. We treat him as a dangerous suspect."

He turned back into the house, hearing Kai whistle to the SOCO van. Mac made for the stairs to the mezzanine level he had seen the first time he'd been here. At the top, he saw something on the floor. It was a piece of paper about A4 size, but clearly antique. It was creased and stained. The image on it was faded but still recognisable as the east of Scotland, showing Edinburgh and its surroundings. Dark, straight lines covered it, all congregating in a small circle in the center of the page. Mac frowned, seeing marks along some of those lines in modern blue biro. There were four marks with no annotation to explain their significance. The sound of someone coming up the stairs distracted him. He turned and saw Nari, gloved and holding a pair of blue latex ones for him. He took them and handed the paper over to her.

"Bag it. Looks old, but it's been marked more recently."

Nari looked at it for a moment, then took a plastic bag from an inside pocket of her jacket. Before she slid it into the bag, Mac grabbed it. He was so hasty that the paper almost tore. Looking at the marks from the other side, with daylight shining through it from behind, Mac had suddenly understood the significance of the marks. Looking at the map head on was confusing because of the thick, black lines that obscured a lot of the image beneath. But, from the other side, he could see the modern marks and a rough outline of the city. It allowed him to place those marks geographically.

"That is where Craigmillar is now. That is not far from the Old Town, just off South Bridge," he said. "Our two murder sites, marked on a map."

"What are the other two?" Nari asked.

One was outside the city, to the west. It had been marked on a line that bisected Ratho. Another was approximately where Gorgie was now situated in Edinburgh. Mac frowned.

"Future murder sites?" Nari wondered.

"Possibly. Check out what is currently at those locations. Especially an address. Could be houses or…"

Mac went quiet, an address flashing into his mind. He'd seen it on a screen while reading a report. The coroner's report on the death of Alex Martins. The flat Alex had been found in was near Gorgie.

"That's where Alex killed himself," Mac said, pointing.

"Then what is this?" Nari asked, pointing to the mark that had been made to the west of Ratho.

Kai was coming up the stairs, followed by SOCO.

"Kai, job for you. Go to this location, as near as you can get to it. Tell us what's there now."

Kai frowned, taking out his phone. "Looks like an industrial estate."

He turned the phone around to show Mac a satellite view. Mac could see Ratho on the edge of the screen and a collection of buildings a few miles to the west.

"You and Nari get out there, take back up," Mac ordered.

"What are we looking for?" Nari asked.

"If we're already too late, a body," Mac said.

They left, taking one of the marked cars with them as backup. Mac hoped they wouldn't find anything. The site looked big, but at the same time there would be plenty of people working there. Plenty of eyes to notice a mutilated corpse. For the next hour, he and the SOCO team searched the Martins' house. Nari called. Nothing unusual at the industrial estate. A few tech companies, a few small manufacturing companies, a distillery. A lot of ground to cover with just four officers and no reports from anyone so far of unusual activity. He told them to keep looking, promised them extra manpower. He was about to call Reid to get the extra bodies authorised when one of the SOCO team called him. They were in one of the house's smaller bedrooms, examining the floor of a fitted wardrobe with a mirrored sliding door.

"Looks like a hidden panel in the floor here," the man said.

Mac peered in, looking down at what the man was shining a torch on. The carpet had been cut; beneath it was a panel of wood separate from the rest of the floorboards.

"Take it out," Mac ordered.

Within was a space three feet by three feet and approximately a foot deep. A thick, brown envelope lay on top, stuffed with paper. The SOCO handed it up to Mac. The papers held images printed from a computer. There were also photographs. All were children and all were explicit. Mac felt sick but forced himself to continue looking.

"There's more, sir."

A folder was lifted out. In it, held within clear plastic wallets, were more pictures. They showed an adult and a boy. The boy's face was clear, but the adult's wasn't. The pictures had been taken by a third party, positioned behind the man pictured. Mac couldn't see if that man was Charles Martins, but it resembled him in build and hair colour. The boy looked like Alex Martins.

"Christ," Mac whispered.

"Sir!" the SOCO exclaimed.

Mac looked. Beneath the folder lay a knife. It was long-bladed and wide with a black, rubber grip at one end. Beside it was a canvas bundle. When it was undone, it was found to contain other blades in a range of shapes and sizes. Perfect for cutting intricate and precise shapes into a human body.

"Bag it all. Then lock the place down. I need a full forensic sweep. This is a crime scene," Mac ordered, handing the pictures to another SOCO to be bagged. "And find their dog!"

He took out his phone and called Reid, a mixture of excitement and revulsion running through him. But Kenny Reid didn't answer his own phone. A woman did.

"DCI McNeill?" she said.

"Yes, who's this?" Mac replied, hurrying down the stairs and out the front door.

"DCS Dawlish, AC 7. DCS Reid has been suspended from duty pending an investigation. I believe one of my team made contact with you yesterday."

"They threatened me unless I co-operated," Mac replied, heading for his car.

"It shouldn't take a threat to get co-operation with Anti-Corruption, McNeill. It's in all our interests that corruption is routed out."

She sounded robotic, clinical, and cool. Mac knew Dawlish, disliked her intensely. He got into the car.

"I'm in the middle of a murder..."

"I'm taking over supervision of your case in DCS Reid's absence," Dawlish told him.

"What is he accused of?" Mac shot back.

"I'm not at liberty to say, but your close relationship with him is something I'm aware of. You will also be suspended from duty, effective immediately, until we can establish that you are not connected with our case."

"What!" Mac shouted. "You can't do that! I have a dangerous suspect on the loose and the possibility of a third murder either committed or about to be. I have a woman who's been beaten half to death and evidence that our suspect is also a paedophile and a predator. You can't just...!"

"I can, McNeill, and I will. Because until proved otherwise, I have to assume you're as crooked as your boss. DCI Lennox will take over from you. Inform your on-site team immediately about the change to the chain of command. Then I would like you to prepare a full report to hand over to Lennox to allow her to run the rest of the case. You will then be placed on suspension until further notice."

CHAPTER THIRTY-TWO

MAC STUMBLED THROUGH the rest of the day. He briefed Melissa and left her to contact Nari and Kai. Lennox was good. Mac had no concerns that she would allow Charles Martins to slip off the hook. With the evidence they had, he was going to prison. That would be used as leverage to get from him a confession to the two murders. They knew his motive and had caught him out in a lie. He had the opportunity to commit the second crime, according to his wife. The knives would be tested and forensically linked to both Martins and the victims. Case closed.

He didn't return home but stopped in an anonymous layby outside the city and smoked half a pack of cigarettes while composing a handover report on his phone and sending it to Lennox. He couldn't bring himself to call her. The need to ensure that Martins was nailed led him to co-operate in his own suspension, ensuring the case was properly handed off.

His throat felt raw after the cigarettes. He wasn't used to

smoking so many anymore. The maximum he'd smoked at any single time in the last few years had been two, chain-smoked at times of the highest stress. But it wasn't stress that drove him now. Knowing that he wouldn't be able to see the case through to its conclusion left a hole inside him. It was a feeling of emptiness that he could not bear. There was nothing for him to go home to except the void of his flat. Phone in hand, he felt an urge to call Siobhan that was almost impossible to resist. He compromised by opening a draft text message to her. But that didn't last. He had driven her away because he couldn't allow her to share him with his job. The job had always come first. Before her. Before Áine.

At the time, he'd been unable to understand how she couldn't see it. Did her job not consume her as well? Didn't she put it before herself on a daily basis? The answer was yes, but Siobhan's compassion as a mother and a nurse went to Áine first, then to her patients. She had told him that a partner could occupy the next place on the list after her child. A man she was in love with. With tears in her eyes, she'd told him how she'd begun to believe that he could be that man. But that was all over now. He'd blown it. Walked away after another row. Responded to the deep-seated need to get away, to escape the responsibility of the confrontation. Had stayed away, nursing his wounds, stoking his anger. Until she'd realised that she would never come first. By the time Mac had swallowed enough of his pride to contact her, she'd decided.

He threw the phone down, picked it up again, then threw it into the back of the car, out of reach. Out the way of temptation. He drove with no destination and no idea what he was going to do next. Suspension felt like a death sentence. He couldn't comprehend a day when there wasn't police work to be done, an office to go to, a crime under investigation. It was his reason for living. The idea of days, weeks, or months in limbo was torture. His travels eventually led him into the embrace of the city. Traffic and people enveloped him, but he was kept separate from them by the metal shell of the car. He watched them pass by, going about their day. Saw tourists gawping and pointing. Saw locals talking and laughing or just head down, intent on their own lives. Bars, cafes and shops flowed past as though he and the car were stationary and the city was moving, leaving him behind.

The streets of Gorgie were around him now. Not through any conscious decision of his. The streets were narrow canyons surrounded by terraces of brown stone. He passed a bar that he recognised. It was closed now; the windows boarded up and sprayed with graffiti. That told him where he was, though. The flat he had lived in when he first moved to Edinburgh was around the corner. The top floor of a run-down tenement. Plumbing barely functioned and there was damp in the living room. Callum McNeill, eighteen years old and with the few grand left from his father's estate, didn't care. That money would have got him a flat in a decent part of the city, for a while anyway. But that hadn't been Callum's priority. Oblivion had been. And he'd pursued that assiduously. Mac was driving on autopilot, passing the building he'd lived in and seeing the corner shop a few doors down. He pulled in on a double yellow across from it. The shop still bore the name Ansari.

The blood on the pavement outside was long since washed away. The blood from the skinheads he'd found vandalising

Rayan Ansari's shop one night. Callum had been a skinny nineteen-year-old, addicted to weed and on his way to something stronger. The Ansaris had been kind to him, though. The kindness had not been looked for or wanted. But they showed it anyway. Callum had taken on three men older and bigger than him. Bigger, but not as ferocious. Not as reckless. Their blood ended up on the pavement, and Callum had his first taste of justice. Now Mac watched the shop and wondered if he could make himself go in. Would the Ansaris still be running it or had they handed it over to one of their kids by now? Would they remember him? He got as far as opening the car door. Then he slammed it shut and started the engine. He pulled away from the kerb abruptly and got a beep from behind, which he ignored. He didn't look back as he pressed down on the accelerator, heading away from his past at speed.

There was no point looking back. Nothing to be gained. It was done. He couldn't take back not stopping Iona from going out on the night she'd been murdered. He couldn't take back beating Mark Souter almost to death. Couldn't take back not giving Siobhan the love and attention she deserved. Or following to the end the case that he'd solved. And that brought the biggest stab of pain. That made his jaw clench and his hands tighten on the wheel. That brought on the cavernous sense of loss. The case he'd been about to break wide open. The killer he'd been on the verge of catching. Justice. Gone. Someone else's glory now. He pulled in at the first bar he came across and walked inside.

Mac awoke to the touch of sunlight on his eyelids. The insistent touch of a female hand somewhere else. His eyes opened. He was in another unfamiliar bedroom. How many was that over the last month or so? Eight? Nine? He'd given up counting. Curtains hadn't been drawn. He glimpsed the city beyond the bay window. The room had a high moulded ceiling and a large bed. Glancing down, he saw dark, silky hair and felt the gentle stroke of a hand across his ribs and stomach. He felt a long leg draped over his. He was naked and so was she. Memory returned through the haze of an alcohol fueled night. Far from the first. Mac ran a hand through his hair, trying to dislodge the sleep that was clouding his mind. How many weeks since he had been suspended? Three? Four? Longer? Somewhere in the room came the sound of a phone buzzing.

"Your phone has been going off for the last hour," said a disgruntled female voice, muffled by his chest.

"Yeah," Mac said, unmoving.

"Could you get it, please?"

She lifted her head to look at him. She had blue eyes framed by raven hair. Mac remembered a slim body and a woman at least ten years his junior. Her name eluded him, as did most of what he had learned about her in the few hours they had spent in each other's company before going back to her place.

"I'm on crowd control at Tynecastle in three hours. I'd like to get a bit more sleep since you were so keen to keep me up all night...sir."

Mac suppressed a groan. He remembered now. She was a copper, five years on the job and in uniform. He'd picked her up at a popular coppers bar in the city. He sat up, dislodging her from her comfortable position. Still didn't remember her name. Getting out of bed naked, he walked across the room, sifting through discarded clothes for his phone.

"This is a nice flat for a PC's salary," he commented.

"I share it with two other girls," the woman said, moving into the warm space that Mac had just vacated. "You're welcome to come back once you've switched your phone off."

"Sir," Mac finished for her.

She giggled. "Sir."

Mac found the phone and turned it on. May 1st. Christ! What the hell happened to April? He groaned at the list of notifications. Texts, missed calls, voicemails. The bulk of them were from Clio. A handful from Melissa and one from DCI Lennox. He looked back at the girl in the bed. She was watching him from over her shoulder. The sheet had fallen away from her, revealing her back and the curve of her bum. She curled her leg up, dislodging it further and revealing more of a pert backside.

"Actually, who needs sleep?" she said.

Mac grinned. The rogue's smile. She had a smile just as roguish. He lifted the phone to his ear as he walked back to the bed and knelt beside her. She turned over, reaching out lazily to run her hand down his body, over tight pecs, and a flat stomach. The first voicemail was from Lennox.

"Just keeping you in the loop as a courtesy. We've found Martins. And his DNA is on the weapons as well as DNA belonging to both your victims. His DNA was also at both crime scenes. He denies everything, but we've got him on the pedo charges, so I'll break him for the rest. He doesn't have an alibi, and he drives a dark SUV, which was seen at both locations. Enough to pass the evidential threshold. CPS are proceeding. Sorry about how this played out. For what it's worth, you did a good job, Mac." There was a slight pause. "Oh, and DS Yun said you were asking about the dog. It's fine. Obviously escaped during the confusion. A neighbour has it and will look after it for the foreseeable."

Mac skipped to the next as the girl shifted over and then put her hand on his hip before running it around behind and pinching him. He seized her wrist and twisted it, holding her arm down beside her and then laying himself half over her. She lifted her head for a kiss, but Mac moved his own away, listening to the next message. Clio wanted to speak to him. Skip. Clio still wanted to speak to him. Skip. Melissa telling him that Clio had been to the station. Mac frowned as he felt a pair of hips push up against his own. A leg went around his, hooking around his calf. Last message.

"Mac, this is Clio again. You've ghosted me according to my daughter. I don't know why. Melissa says you can't be contacted but won't tell me anything more. No-one is interested in what I've got to say because Charles Martins has been arrested. For the murders? Well, it can't be him. I've finally translated the inscriptions and it just can't be him. You've got the wrong man, Mac. I'm giving you one more chance and then...I don't know if I should go to the press or...I don't know, but you've got the wrong man!"

Mac stared into the eyes of the woman beneath him. Saw desire and hunger there. He rolled away and stood up, grabbing at his clothes.

"Hey! Where are you going?"

"Work," Mac said.

CHAPTER THIRTY-THREE

MAC DROVE OUT to Clio's house, washing down paracetamol with a bottle of water he'd nicked from the girl's fridge before he left. Apparently, he'd taken her back to her flat in his car. Which meant he'd been over the limit the night before. He probably still was, but couldn't waste any more time. This was probably nothing. There was no way that Doctor Clio Wray could know that Charles Martins wasn't guilty. There was incontrovertible evidence placing him at both scenes. His car had been seen in both places. Except that he had driven away from the second scene before Mac arrived. Mac frowned. *Shit!* So it wasn't Charles Martins who had attacked him from the fire escape at Evie's flat. It couldn't have been. But if he wasn't involved, then why the hell was he there? He called Clio, but it went straight to voicemail. He told her tersely that he was on his way to see her. Then he called Melissa. She didn't answer. No surprise there. By now they'd have all been briefed by Lennox that they were not to communicate with their former DCI.

"Blood hell, guv, where have you been?" Kai said, the only one to pick up.

"Around." If he was honest with himself, Mac didn't know where he'd been. It was all a blur.

"I can't talk to you, and it's a holiday, anyway."

"I know, Kai, but I need your help. Did Melissa brief Lennox on the work Clio Wray was doing for us?"

"Yeah, guv. And Lennox dropped it. Said it wasn't relevant, just a smokescreen. It was all about Martins covering up what he'd been up to."

"On the CCTV footage, Martins' car was at Evie Black's flat, right?" Mac said urgently.

"Yeah."

"And it drove away before I got there."

"Yeah. Lennox thinks he doubled back and snuck in the front. That he might have taken Evie Black's keys after he'd killed her."

"Whoever attacked me was leaving the building, not going into it."

"But you don't remember too well, do you, guv?" Kai pointed out.

Mac had to admit defeat on that score. "If we assume he wasn't there to kill Evie Black, then why was he there?" Mac asked. "Think about it, Kai."

Kai sighed and was silent for a moment.

"He sat outside that building for a long time until you showed up," Kai said. "CCTV picked him up heading west out of the city. Presumably heading home."

"Not doubling back."

"But his DNA was there," Kai insisted. "And we found

online chats Evie Black had been involved in, where she hinted she knew the identity of a pedo. There were calls and messages between McCullough and her even after the band split up. He had a motive. To shut her up."

This was all news to Mac. They'd obviously been running the case pretty well without him. "Look, Kai, just think about this for a minute. Tell me why else Martins could have been there without wanting anyone to know."

"Because he was following someone," Kai said immediately. "He beat the crap out of his wife and she said it's because he thought she was cheating. So..."

His DC was on the same track as Mac now. "So, he followed his wife there and thought she was having an affair with someone who lived in the building," Mac finished.

"Not because he was going to kill Evie Black."

"Maybe not," Mac said.

"Jesus. But, it won't stand up, guv. The DNA and..."

"There's a doubt, and that's all the defence will need. Look, Kai, nothing would make me happier than for that utter shit Charles Martins to go away for a long time for this. And even if he's not guilty of these murders, he's still not innocent, so I'm happy for him to go down and rot in a cell for the rest of life. But, if that leaves the killer still out there..."

"What do you want me to do?" Kai asked, his voice suddenly crisp and alert.

"Get back to the CCTV footage. Trace it back to an earlier time on the day Evie Black was killed. See if there is any sign of Karen Martins going in or being anywhere in the area."

"There's no CCTV at the front of the building on High School Wynd," Kai said. "But there's a pub car park a few yards down the road I can take a look at. I stopped checking when we got Martins."

"Get started again, Kai. I can't come in or I'd do it myself."

"No worries, guv. I've got nothing better to do," Kai said. "And guv...we don't believe anything they tell us. You know... AC? Melissa and Nari are playing it by the book, but they don't like it. It's a stitch up."

"It's not about me. They're after Reid. And I can't say for sure he hasn't done something to deserve their scrutiny. But thank you, Kai. That means a lot."

He was heading west across the north of Edinburgh, taking the Ferry Road towards Pilton. He drove straight through a desert of waste ground and square blocks of flats. The dog walkers here had thickset animals on chains. Parks were heavy with vandalism and shops had metal grates over the windows. The car bumped over potholes that he was taking too fast; the concrete broken and patched. As he turned onto Cramond Road, the transformation was stark. Semi-detached houses and bungalows that were probably pre-war. Greenery lined the streets, trees, and hedges. The affluence of Cramond lived cheek by jowl with the poverty of Pilton and Muirhouse. He saw Clio's mini in the driveway of her house as he pulled up on the kerb. Only then did it occur to him to check the mirror.

Open-necked shirt, free of any stains. Jacket looked a little creased; it had been on the floor of a bedroom for a few hours. His hair was more ruffled than usual and he combed it hastily with his fingers. It felt like he was turning up for a first date and he tried to dispel the thought as he got out of the car and walked up to the house. Clio answered and for a moment stood there, mouth open.

"Can I come in?" Mac asked with the rogue's grin.

He saw she was holding a phone. "Mum, I'll have to call you back. I'll speak to Maia later."

Then she stood back, her eyes having never left Mac. He stepped into her house and she closed the door behind him. To his right was a living room dominated by a large bookcase. It was overflowing, books wedged into the shelves, others lying on top or stacked on the floor. A coffee table in the middle of the room was scattered with familiar paperwork; images of a murder scene and drawings of inscriptions. Mac's eyes were drawn to a picture that looked familiar and he entered the room.

"I've seen that picture before," he said, pointing to a map of Edinburgh, crisscrossed with thick black lines.

"It's a photocopy of a map I tried to get hold of but was beaten to it," Clio snapped.

"Showing ley lines," Mac finished with a nod, remembering her telling him about it.

"So, you're just going to show up after giving me the cold shoulder and chat about ley lines?" Clio said, coming fully into the room and standing in front of him, hands on hips.

He raised his hands placatingly. "I..." he began.

"You shut me out, Mac. Reject my help after I've put myself and my daughter at risk. She's staying with my mum right now because I couldn't sleep for fear that this psycho would come for us! You promised you would keep me and Maia safe! Where the hell have you been?"

Her eyes blazed. Mac looked right back at her. "I'm sorry. I was taken off the case," he said.

"What? And you couldn't have returned just one of my

calls to tell me that!" Clio retorted. "I've been trying to get hold of you every day for over a week."

"I...yeah, I could have done that. Should have. I'm sorry. No excuses. But right now I need to know what makes you think we got the wrong man."

Clio put her hands to her face and made an exasperated groan. "I swore I would put this to bed. Forget about it. Go and spend some time with Maia and my mum. But...you just turn up out of the blue after ignoring me for weeks, draw me back in and demand...Shit! You know what? Just sit down, Detective Inspector."

Mac didn't dare correct her as he sat on a sofa before the coffee table. She was clearly furious with him. Clio sat next to him and reached for the map.

"You've seen this somewhere, the original?" she asked.

"At the Martins' house. Charles Martins had marked on it the scenes of the murders."

"And another somewhere here," Clio indicated an area on the map close to where there had, in fact, been an unexplained mark.

"How do you know that?" Mac said.

"Because it's on a ley line. These other sites are all just off. She couldn't help where the first two victims were because they were killed at home. But the third victim had to be positioned in a place of power. Where ley lines converge. She could position them exactly where they needed to be."

"She?"

"It has to be Karen Martins," Clio said.

Mac could see that her hands were quaking. The paper she was holding was shaking from her trembling fingers. Gently,

247

Mac took her hands in his, clasping them together to still the tremors.

"Start from the beginning. Why her?" he said, looking into Clio's eyes.

She looked back, and for a moment, said nothing. Mac was aware of only her eyes and the feel of her soft skin. Then she blinked, as though startled.

"Because the inscriptions are an incantation, part of a ritual. It's a complex interweaving of ancient languages and even copying from his wife's work Charles Martins couldn't possibly have written them. It would be nonsense if someone were simply copying pictures. These crime scenes form a narrative. The killer was offering up a sacrifice and at the same time recalling past times. The drowning of the witch is a relic of Edinburgh's past four hundred years ago. The killing of Richard McCullough was a sacrifice and something of Alex's would have been present so that the gods of the underworld knew whose soul they were to release. There was a blood-soaked canvas, right? The third killing will be both sacrifice and another reaching back in time in order to recreate something from the past. I believe that must be the suicide of Alex Martins. The incantation, a spell if you will, is intended to release his soul. Bring him back. Who else would do it?"

Mac wanted to scoff. It was ludicrous and would get laughed out of court. But Clio was earnest, never breaking her eye contact with him. Her hands remained in his.

"I know what you're thinking, Mac. It sounds completely crazy. But while it's nonsense to us, it's not to her. She believes it. When she came to my house that night, she was talking about how Alex must be in torment. That he wasn't at rest.

That, as a mother, she would walk into hell to save him. Do you know that Karen Martins was in a psychiatric hospital?"

Mac nodded. "Mel has been trying to get a copy of her records but is being stonewalled. We don't have enough cause for them to be released because she's never been a viable suspect."

"But what if she never recovered, Mac? What if her psychosis just deepened?"

"She stepped into his world, a world of lost souls, hell and damnation. It became real for her and she formulated a plan, meticulously worked out, to free him from his torment," Mac mused, paraphrasing some of Omega's song lyrics.

"Well, that sounded really creepy," Clio said. "But, yes, that's what I think happened."

"And she's had plenty of time to resolve any issues and refine all details. Christ, I felt sure it couldn't be her. Every instinct I had said she was just a grieving mother. How could I have missed it? What did I miss? I must be losing my edge. Jesus, I've made some stupid errors on this case."

"Mac, for god's sake, stop feeling sorry for yourself and get a grip!" Mac blinked. "It's going to happen today. The third murder. It's Bealtaine. That's why I've been so frantic. I even called 999 and said I knew a murder was going to happen. The police officer I spoke to refused to take me seriously. Told me I would be reported if I made any more hoax calls."

Mac tried to let go of Clio's hands as he stood. But she stood with him and held on tight.

"I have to go. That location on the map is an industrial estate. It'll be closed for the holiday, there'll be no-one there. If you're right, I have to get there to stop it."

"I'm coming with you," Clio said.

"No, don't be stupid…"

"Oh, really, stupid am I? Don't you dare, Callum McNeill. Don't you bloody dare! We could have had a few more days' grace before this murder to plan properly if you hadn't gone off on a month long bender, trying to drown your own damn sorrows," Clio told him, poking him in the chest. "I can smell the booze, Detective Chief Inspector McNeill. I doubt you're even fit to drive."

CHAPTER THIRTY-FOUR

"It's an enormous site. Does that map give you any idea where we're supposed to be looking? I had officers down there when we went to arrest Charles Martins, but they couldn't see anything untoward."

"Because the time wasn't right. And I'm afraid not. It's very general. Nothing specific," Clio said as she powered the Audi south and west toward the industrial estate near Ratho.

"You know she was beaten pretty badly," Mac said. "No way she did that to herself."

"Maybe he did beat her up. Were there any marks on him?" Clio asked.

"I wasn't there when they arrested him," Mac admitted. "I don't even know where he was found. But it's obvious Karen Martins hated her husband enough to plant the murder weapons with his other...stuff, throwing us off her scent."

"I didn't know them very well as a couple, but...from what

I've heard, she could have provoked him into attacking her," Clio said.

"It doesn't matter. This theory is still so full of holes that that's the least of them," Mac said, looking at a map of the area they were heading into, looking for anything that might give a clue where Karen might be.

If she was the killer. If this wasn't more than a desperate fairy tale in defiance of all the evidence. He knew how ready he was to clutch at straws if it gave him purpose. Maybe Clio was too. But he was still struggling to make sense of it. Maybe this was a step too far. Surely his copper's instinct and intuition hadn't failed him that much? He stamped down on his doubts and concentrated on the digital map.

As he scrolled and zoomed, trying to identify each commercial property in the estate and make some kind of rational judgement as to the likelihood of Karen Martins being there, he saw that one lot was occupied by a building supply company. It was called Mertens. He stared through the screen. Coincidence? One of Martins' business partners was called Merten. What's the bet he owned a building supply company? Maybe that was what had secured this Merten, whoever he was, a partnership with the architectural firm in the first place. And what were the chances that Martins would have access to keys? Keys that his wife could steal.

"I think it might be here," he said. "Merten Building Supplies. I'll put it on the sat nav."

Clio was pushing the car harder than even Mac would have. He called Kai but didn't get an answer. For a moment, he considered calling 999 and claiming an officer was down at the Ratho Industrial Estate. But if this was a wild goose chase, then it would definitely be the end of his career, and he was on a slippery enough slope already. As it stood, only Clio would know if this all turned out to be bullshit, and they were making fools of themselves. If Charles Martins really was the killer and was already safely under lock and key.

He called Nari on the off chance and got her on the first ring.

"Jeez, Nari, I didn't think you'd pick up for me," Mac said.

"I spoke to Kai. He was very persuasive," Nari said. "Why do you think I'm here on holiday Monday?"

"Thank you Kai. Look, I barely believe this myself, but I'm on my way to an industrial estate outside of Ratho, the one you went to before. It's possible we're going to confront the real killer. I think it's Karen Martins, and I believe she's planning to kill her third and final victim. I can't explain why. Clio is with me. Don't get involved. I can't order it and I won't. You'd be mad to get involved, but…"

"We're on our way, guv!" he heard Kai's voice in the background. Obviously, Nari had put the call on speaker.

Nari hissed at him, then sighed audibly. "Guv, I hope you're not wrong about this, otherwise it's just a pointless excursion to the countryside and we'll all be in trouble. AC warned us all not to speak to you…"

"I know." Mac felt guilty about what he was asking for, but the more back up he brought with him, the better the chance of stopping the killer.

"We'll be there, guv," Nari finished.

"This is it," Clio said.

"I'm going to keep this call open, Nari," Mac told her as he slipped the phone into his pocket.

Clio dragged the Audi into a left turn and then over a speed bump that made Mac's teeth slam together. She slowed, looking from left to right as she followed the sat nav. They passed landscaped grounds around single-story buildings of plastic and red brick. Signage gave the name of the firms. Some had loading yards alongside and locked gates. One had mountains of barrels rising above it and a sign proclaiming its trade as distilling. Beyond the estate, there were wild trees and fields. Beyond that, to the north would be the M8 motorway mimicking the line of energy that ran through this place, if Clio was to be believed. Almost at the end of the estate was a brick building next to a yard stacked sky high with timber, bricks, blocks of concrete and other materials. The gates were open. A rented van, the name of the rental company emblazoned along its white sides, stood in the yard, back doors open and engine running.

"Stop the car," Mac ordered, senses immediately alert.

In a second he had gone from believing himself the biggest fool in Scotland to knowing with certainty that something was seriously wrong here. Clio stopped in the open gate and Mac got out. He walked towards the van, slowly and deliberately. A smell came to him on an errant breeze. An overpowering stench of petrol. He heard his car door open and close and turned, raising a hand.

"Stay there!" he hissed, pointing at Clio.

There was enough firmness in his voice that she remained where she was. He reached the van and glanced in the back. Blood was smeared against one side. It looked as though someone had been dragged out while bleeding, the claret fluid smearing the interior. He began walking towards the building attached to the yard. There was a closed door with a glass panel and windows to either side with their blinds pulled down. He reached the side of the door, back to the wall, and peered in. It looked like a reception area. More evidence of blood.

Mac's heart began to race as he caught a fleeting glimpse of a body being dragged through an interior door. Without hesitation, he lunged into the building, vaulting the reception desk, and charged through the door.

The overpowering stench of petrol hit him, making his eyes water and throat burn. Empty jerry cans lay scattered around, evidence of the volatile liquid that had been liberally splashed over the floor, the shelves, the walls, and the occupants. He quickly scanned the room, taking in the horrifying tableau.

A large storeroom, metal shelves lining the walls. A computer abandoned on a table. In the room's centre, a man tied to a chair, drenched in petrol, blood smeared across his face. Another man lay motionless on the floor, hands bound with wire that had cut deep into his flesh. Mac's gaze then locked onto the most chilling sight of all: Karen Martins.

Her eyes, wild and frenzied, bore into him. She held a blowtorch aloft, its blue flame hissing menacingly. The room seemed to shrink around Mac; the walls pressing in, the air thickening. Every instinct screamed at him to flee, but he couldn't. Not now.

"Leave, or you'll regret it," Karen's voice was a raspy whisper.

Mac swallowed hard, trying to keep his voice steady. "Karen, we can work this out. Let me help you."

The man in the chair whimpered, "Please, she's lost her mind!"

Recognition hit Mac like a punch. Gordon Brunt. And the man on the floor? Likely Jacek Andrysiak. The pieces fell into place, but the puzzle he was looking at was a complete nightmare.

Without warning, Karen struck Gordon with the heated blowtorch, setting his hair alight. Gordon's screams pierced the air, but Karen's manic laughter drowned them out as she beat the flames dead with a bare hand. Mac's stomach churned as the smell of burnt flesh assaulted his nostrils, but he forced himself to focus.

"Karen, hurting them won't bring Alex back," he pleaded, trying to reach whatever ounce of humanity remained inside.

"You're wrong! It will bring him back."

She ranted about sacrifices, ley lines, and ancient rituals. Her words were a jumbled mess of pain, anger, and desperation. Mac could see the precipice she was teetering on, and he knew he only had moments before she plunged into madness.

The room felt like a pressure cooker, the tension unbearable. Mac's mind raced, searching for a way out. He needed to keep her talking, to stall. But time was running out, and the hissing flame was a ticking bomb.

Then something Clio had said dropped into Mac's mind like a brick.

"The number three, Karen," he said. "Isn't that important? But you only killed two, Richard McCullough and Evie Black."

"Alex!" she screamed. "Alex was the first." Clio was right, Mac thought. Alex Martins' suicide was ground zero. He swallowed the rising panic. He'd made things worse.

Spittle flew from Karen's mouth as she spoke. She paced behind Brunt's chair like a caged animal. His eyes were wide with terror as he turned his head to follow the path of the hissing flame. He looked imploringly at Mac. All she had to do was drop the torch and the whole building would go up. With the wood in the yard outside, the entire site would be a blazing inferno in seconds. Mac glanced at Andrysiak. His bonds were thick plastic of some kind, zip ties possibly and therefore hard to cut through. He couldn't see a knot but doubted there would be enough time to untie him, even if there was one. Probably the same with Brunt. He looked at the priest with hatred and disgust. What a fucking cliché. But he was a copper, and he had to try to save him. Save them all.

Dismissing Brunt, he turned back to Karen. He needed to keep her talking, try to keep her calm. He could see she was unravelling, on the brink of insanity if she wasn't there already. It was only a matter of time before she fell into the abyss completely, but how long he had no idea. His neck and shoulders tensed and he could feel the cold sweat from his underarms pooling at the base of his spine.

"Let me take Jacek, Karen. He's innocent. He might have made mistakes in his life, but he didn't kill your son."

"No! There has to be three! Or it won't work!" Karen shouted.

"Let me take Jacek, get him out of here," he repeated. "Please. Then, I'll come back. I promise. I don't care about him," he lied, pointing at Brunt. "He deserves everything he's going to get. But Jacek has a mother as well. He's a son too, Karen."

"I just want my boy to have the life he should have had,"

Karen moaned, tears flowing freely. "I won't leave him in torment! I'm his mother and I will give me life for his!"

Mac felt a pang in his chest. Her grief was raw and overwhelming. He saw Iona's face. Her flowing dark hair and smile. Her life. Her energy. He missed her more with every passing day.

"It doesn't work like that, Karen," he said gently. "If I could give my life for my sister to live in my place, I would." His voice choked with unresolved grief. "But I can't. Revenge won't bring Alex back, Karen. He's gone."

"No!" Karen screeched, advancing towards Mac with the blow torch held in front of her.

He reacted with speed that surprised even him. Closing the gap, he seized the wrist that held the blowtorch. She fought, clawing at him with her free hand, dragging fingernails down his cheek, then going for his eyes. He butted his head forward and connected with hers. She stumbled back but clung tenaciously to the blowtorch. Mac went with her, still holding her wrist. But his hands were sweaty and her wrist was slipping. Then her eyes went beyond him. Mac didn't dare look away, so intent was he on their struggle. But he could hear Jacek being moved. Heard the dragging sound accompanied by low murmuring as he began to come around. If he looked, he knew he would see Clio hauling at the man's feet with all her strength.

Karen's eyes went as wide as they could go. Mac saw in them the knowledge of her own failure. Saw the grief take over, sweeping away her reason forever. In her mind, she had failed at the last hurdle to deliver her son from his torment. She screamed, and it was the soul-wrenching wail of a mother bereaved all over again. Then her body went limp. She fell to the floor and the dead weight was too much. Her arm slipped from Mac's grasp. He turned and managed two strides towards the doorway, where Jacek Andrysiak was halfway through, Clio red-faced and screaming with effort, tendons standing out on either side of her neck. Mac heard a soft whump and then felt the heat suddenly rising behind him. He stooped as low as he could get, put out his arms and got them under Jacek's shoulders, pushing with all his strength.

They got through the door as something hit Mac in the back, and he felt his hair burning. A tongue of fire surged overhead to lick the ceiling. Mac kicked out at the door, slamming it shut and felt Clio attacking him, battering at his burning back and hair. The pain hadn't reached him yet. His vision was narrowing into small points of light, consciousness slipping away. He knew that if he passed out, he would die. Jacek and Clio too. He still had his arms beneath Jacek's shoulders and he lifted, bellowing with the effort, forcing one step and then another. Together, they barely managed to get out of the building. Then something exploded. Mac threw himself over Jacek as the windows blew outward with questing spears of fire. The door sailed overhead to crash into the van. He heard sirens in the distance just before his world went black.

CHAPTER THIRTY-FIVE

MAC WORE JEANS AND A FLEECE over a t-shirt, and for the first time in weeks he felt relaxed. There was a chilly spring wind outside, blowing a blustery shower against the window. Inside was warm and noisy. Maia was chatting to him about a band he had introduced her to. The name alone horrified Clio, but Mac had assured her the guttural growls of the vocalist rendered lyrics utterly incomprehensible.

"Just don't buy her the vinyl or she'll be able to read the lyrics," Mac had said with a chuckle.

Maia, child of the earth, was well on her way to becoming a metal head and hopelessly besotted with her new uncle Callum.

"So, how are you keeping, Mac?" Clio asked from across the table.

"His name's Callum, mum," Maia put in, looking at her phone.

"Is it now Miss Smarty Pants?" Clio said with a smile.

"Actually, only my dad ever called me Callum," Mac said.

"And me," Maia said blithely.

Clio and Maia had matching beads in their hair. To Mac, they looked like hippies. But since almost being blown up, he'd found the calm chaos of Clio's life refreshing. He experienced it through regular phone calls, video calls and, recently, a weekly McDonalds' catch up.

"My back is still stiff," Mac said, flexing his shoulders. "From the burns."

"You kept your hair, though. I thought you'd be bald at the back," Clio said.

"No, just a little singed and shorter than I would like, but the fact I'm not bald is thanks to you. You didn't burn your hands?"

Clio held them up. "Nothing, just a little red. I'm thinking of walking over hot coals next week."

Mac laughed. "Or buy a lottery ticket. It's less risky."

"What do you think, Maia?" Mac asked, sipping his milkshake, knowing it left a foam mustache on the stubble of his lip.

Maia rolled her eyes, but he saw the grin she was trying to hide, which is why he did it. "You suit longer hair. Short hair makes you look boring," Maia commented.

"My thoughts exactly. Who wants to be normal, eh?" Mac said.

"Did you just roll your eyes at Mac, Maia Elizabeth Wray?" Clio said.

"No, I was just checking the back of my head."

Clio's mouth fell open, and Mac nearly choked on his drink.

"Now that's what I call an excellent answer," he said, still laughing.

Clio shook her head and grinned. She had to admit; it was pretty funny. "So, how long 'til you're back at work?" she asked Mac.

"Three more weeks."

She looked at him, head tilted and eyes narrowed.

"I swear," he said, raising his hands in mock surrender. "I swear. I'm in no rush. I almost died."

"We all did."

"Yeah, and Jacek would have died with me if it hadn't been for you," Mac said.

"My mum the hero. And I thought you were so conventional." Maia said, but Clio heard the pride in her daughter's voice.

"I didn't expect a medal though," Clio laughed.

"You must have loads, Callum," Maia said.

"Just the one, same as your mum. I feel like a bit of a fraud. I just happened to be stupid enough to walk into a room filled with petrol and a madwoman with..."

Maia's eyes went wide and not in horror. Mac shut his mouth and Clio glared at him.

"Enough said," she put in with finality.

Mac grimaced at Maia and mouthed, tell you later. She grinned. Mac felt his phone vibrating and fished it out. It was an email from Mel with an attachment. He clicked on it and began to read. When he finished, he looked at Clio, then briefly at Maia and back again.

"Maia, could you get us all another milkshake each?" Clio said, handing her a ten-pound note.

262

Maia looked at Mac's phone, then at her mother.

"You know, if you want a private conversation, all you had to do was ask," she grinned, taking the money and standing.

Clio nodded. "Yes, you're right. Off you go, you cheeky wee yin." Maia giggled and went to join the queue. Clio turned to Mac. "What is it?"

Mac handed her his phone. "Karen Martins' psychiatric report."

Clio swallowed and looked at the screen.

Patient: Karen Martins

Date of Admission: 6th November 2021

Date of Discharge: 10th December 2022

Diagnosis: Post-Traumatic Stress Disorder (PTSD) with co-morbid Major Depressive Disorder and Auditory Hallucinations and delusional beliefs.

Background: The patient was admitted on a voluntary basis following the traumatic discovery of her son's body. He committed suicide after alleged abuse by his step-father. The immediate aftermath of the discovery led to a severe psychological breakdown, prompting her to seek care at our facility.

Clinical Observations: Upon admission, the patient exhibited severe signs of trauma, including flashbacks, nightmares, and avoidance behaviors. She frequently reported both hearing her son's voice and seeing him, particularly in a state of torment, indicative of auditory and visual hallucinations. These experiences were intertwined with her delusional belief that her son's soul was not at peace, further exacerbating her distress. She had several episodes where she believed she was reliving the moment of discovery. Additionally, the patient displayed significant depressive symptoms, including profound sadness, feelings of guilt and worthlessness, and a preoccupation with death.

Treatment: A combination of cognitive-behavioral therapy (CBT), trauma-focused therapy, and group therapy sessions were employed. The patient was also prescribed a regimen of antidepressants and antipsychotic medications to manage her depressive and psychotic symptoms.

Throughout her stay, the patient showed a keen interest in her academic work, often using it as a coping mechanism. Her expertise in mythology, Celtic symbols, and the history thereof seemed to provide a grounding effect, allowing her moments of clarity and focus.

Progress and Recovery: Over the course of the year, the patient demonstrated significant improvement in managing her PTSD symptoms. The frequency and intensity of her flashbacks reduced, and she reported fewer auditory hallucinations. Her engagement in therapy, combined with her academic pursuits, seemed to provide a structured environment that facilitated her recovery.

Reasons for Discharge:

1. The patient showed consistent improvement in managing her symptoms.
2. She expressed a strong desire to return to her academic work and believed it would further aid her recovery.
3. Regular evaluations showed a reduction in depressive and psychotic symptoms.
4. The patient demonstrated an understanding of coping mechanisms and strategies to manage potential triggers in the future.

Recommendations: While the patient has been deemed fit for discharge, it is crucial for her to continue outpatient therapy and regular psychiatric evaluations. She should maintain her medication regimen and seek immediate help if she experiences a resurgence of symptoms. It is also recommended that she engage in a support group for individuals who have experienced traumatic loss.

Clio finished reading and looked up at Mac, tears in her eyes. "Oh my god, Mac, that poor woman. If only we'd had this sooner…"

"No. Don't go there, Clio. We couldn't have got it sooner, not legally. And it wouldn't have made any difference. McCullough was already dead, Jacek had disappeared and Evie…" Mac faltered. Clio wasn't aware of his history with Evie, but that wasn't the issue. Mac knew if he'd got there earlier, if he hadn't stopped and ate a bloody sandwich in his car at the petrol station, he could have saved her. He shook his head. It was another burden to carry. Just put it on the shelf with the rest of them.

"They never should have let her out," Clio said, handing Mac his phone.

"She was there voluntarily; she could walk out whenever she wanted."

"But she wasn't cured, Mac! Look what she did. How could she appear to be so normal on the outside?"

Mac scrolled through his phone and found the email Mel had forwarded. "Mel spoke to one of the doctors and asked the same question. She sent this reply." He handed the phone back to Clio.

To: DI Barland
From: Dr. E Whitfield
Subject: Re: Karen Martins

Dear DI Barland,

Following our telephone conversation, I understand the urgency and gravity of your inquiry regarding Karen Martins. Having been one of the primary psychiatrists overseeing her treatment during her stay at St. Ailred's Psychiatric Hospital, I can provide some insights into her condition.

Karen's case has always been a testament to the intricate nature of the human psyche. While her psychosis is profound, it manifested in a manner that allowed her to compartmentalise her symptoms, enabling her to function in daily life while still being deeply affected internally. Here's a breakdown:

1. **High Functioning:** Karen's intellectual and academic background in mythology and Celtic symbols meant she had a structured and analytical mindset. This allowed her to compartmentalise her delusional beliefs, keeping them separate from her professional life.

2. **Masking Symptoms:** Over time, Karen became skilled at concealing her symptoms. She developed coping mechanisms to hide her hallucinations and delusions, such as rationalising them or dismissing them as mere daydreams in public settings.

3. **Selective Disclosure:** She was very selective about whom she shared her beliefs and experiences with, avoiding discussions about her son or her beliefs about his afterlife in professional or casual settings.

4. **Environmental Triggers:** Certain environments or stressors might have intensified her symptoms. While she maintained composure in familiar settings, unfamiliar or stressful situations could exacerbate her delusions and hallucinations.

5. **Dissociation:** Karen might have experienced periods of dissociation, feeling detached from herself or her surroundings. These episodes were likely brief, allowing her to function normally most of the time.

6. **Treatment Effects:** The treatments Karen received during her hospital stay, including medications and therapy, might have provided temporary relief. However, if she discontinued treatment or if it wasn't tailored to her evolving condition, her symptoms could resurface.

7. **Rationalisation:** Her deep knowledge of mythology and symbols might have allowed her to intertwine her delusions with academic concepts, making them seem more logical to her.

In situations of extreme stress, such as the one you described, all these factors could converge, leading to a complete break from reality. The emotional weight of confronting those she believed harmed her son, combined with environmental triggers, likely pushed her past the point of rational thought.

I hope this provides some clarity on Karen's condition and her ability to function outwardly while grappling with her internal struggles. Please let me know if you need any further information or clarification.

Yours sincerely,

Dr. Eleanor Whitfield, MBChB, MRCPsych Consultant Psychiatrist St. Ailred's Psychiatric Hospital

—

"I suppose I can understand it now," Clio said. "But it doesn't make it any easier to bear. I knew her for a long time, considered us friends, but I had no idea who she really was or what she was going through."

"She didn't want you to, Clio. You read the Doctor's report. Selective Disclosure. However, it was only ever going to be a matter of time before her symptoms started to show. I doubt she was following any of the recommendations in the report you just read, and we found no drugs either at her home, her office, or the last crime scene."

"She didn't need them anymore, Mac. She was governed by the calendar. Her final act was always going to happen at Bealtaine."

Mac nodded. "Anyway, you'll be pleased to know that Jacek is doing well. He'll be released from the hospital next week and is going back to his parents. You saved his life, Clio, and mine. Hang on to that, eh?"

Clio gave a small smile and nodded. "How did Karen get Jacek to go with her? I thought he'd left the area from Melissa told me."

"He did. Kai found out he'd moved to Glasgow, but when he sent the local police in, they discovered he'd been missing for two weeks. Kai interviewed him at the hospital. Karen called him out of the blue and asked if they could meet in Edinburgh. She was the mother of one of his friends, so he didn't think it suspicious. Remember, he was the one who called Karen worried Alex was taking drugs?" Clio nodded. "Well, she'd kept the number. She apologised for being so angry with him, explaining it was worry for Alex. To cut a long story short, they met in a pub where Karen must have drugged him. She was driving, and he said he must have passed out in the car because the next thing he woke in a small concrete room and he was tied up."

"Oh, my god," Clio said. "Did he know where he was?"

"He'd no idea and neither have we, but considering Charles Martins' job, it was likely one of the building sites currently going up. Reid's got officers going through them all to try and find it."

"But why did she want to hurt him, Mac? He called her worried about Alex."

"Aye, but he also got Alex interested in all the pagan and devil worship stuff, according the texts we've found between McCullough and him. Besides, she needed three sacrifices for the ritual."

"So that's it then?"

"That's it," Mac said, just as Maia returned and his phone buzzed again.

Kenny Reid's name came up. He turned away from Clio and Maia, walking out of the restaurant.

"Sir."

"Mac, how you doing, son?"

"Surprised to be hearing from you, sir,"

"Don't be. DCS Dawlish has been reassigned. The case against me has been shelved. Translation is that there are more corrupt coppers than me out there and someone more senior than that cow Dawlish thought investigating me a waste of public money. Or they were persuaded of that, any-way. Pays to know people in high places. How's your recu-peration going, son?"

"Much needed. I still have three weeks," Mac said.

"Shame, there was a shooting this morning in Portobello. I need an experienced DCI. But Lennox is keen if you're not available."

Mac swore, and Reid laughed.

"Get the band back together, Mac, my boy. The likes of you and I don't need rest and recuperation. We stop swimming and we die. Barland has the details. Brief me when you know more."

He hung up. Mac stood for a moment, rain drizzling onto his shoulders.

"Duty calls?" Clio said.

She and Maia were leaving, carrying their milkshakes. Maia handed one to Mac.

"Yes, I'm afraid so."

"Three weeks?" Clio asked.

"Yeah, you know," Mac shrugged.

Melissa was calling just as Maia opened her mouth to say something. She closed it, looking disappointed as Mac turned away to take the call. He was dimly aware of the pair heading towards Clio's mini as he hurried to his own car. By the time he'd finished the call, Clio's car was gone. Mac swore and gunned the engine, tearing out of the car park and heading toward Clio's house. After a mile, he caught them up at traffic lights. He managed to get up alongside the mini and placed his hand flat on the horn. Maia saw him first and waved, a beaming grin breaking across her face. Clio looked. Mac saluted Maia with two fingers from his temple, then gave her a wink. She grinned harder, breathing on the window to write a message. Clio was attempting to look stern, but Mac saw the smile threatening to break through.

As the lights changed, she looked at him. Just a glance, but their eyes held. Clio smiled. Mac grinned. The rogue kind.

***

DCI McNeill will return soon in book 2

***

Want to be the first to know when 'Mac is back?'

Join the New Crime Club to get news, updates and more!

www.jacquelinenew.com

***

Enjoyed the book? It would be a great help if you could leave a brief review on Amazon. Thank you.

Printed in Great Britain
by Amazon